MW00780760

Bread and Roses

Book 1

Sweet Aspirations

REBECCAH WILSON

Sweet Aspirations

Copyright © 2023 by Rebeccah Wilson

All rights reserved.

No part of this publication may be reproduced, distributed, or transmitted in any form or by any means, including photocopying, recording, or other electronic or mechanical methods, without the prior written permission of the publisher, except as permitted by U.S. copyright law. For permission requests, contact Rebeccah Wilson at beccah.wilson.ma@gmail.com.

The story, all names, characters, and incidents portrayed in this production are fictitious. No identification with actual persons (living or deceased), places, buildings, and products is intended or should be inferred.

Book Cover Design and Interior Formatting by 100 Covers

To Rob, for your fathomless support, and muscly thighs.

Acknowledgements

I want to thank everyone who helped and supported me along this journey. First, my family, who endured the long nights, time taken away to attend meetings and workshops, and who did it all with enthusiastic support and heaps of praise. My editor, Eugenia, who helped shape this story into the finished product you have in your hands. And also the long list of friends and comrades in the writing trenches who gave so much of their time and guidance to help me to the finish line. I couldn't have done it without any of you.

Buckinghamshire, England 1893

The heat in the glittering ballroom was suffocating. The hundreds of guests seemed hardly to notice as they danced, chatted and sipped champagne. They seemed comfortable in their stifling finery, even the ladies weighed down by their jewels and elaborate hairstyles moved about with an easy elegance and grace.

Thalia Ward was an imposter among these elegant creatures. As a mere shopkeeper from the village, she was only in attendance as an emissary from the local orphanage where she spent much of her time volunteering. This event was a fundraiser for a new project she was pioneering on behalf of the orphanage, and so she was behooved to don an elaborate gown and smile her way through this long, painful evening.

Painful both metaphorically and literally. Her evening corset was laced much tighter than she normally wore, and it dug into her hips and constricted her breathing. How did fashionable women live this way? The only consolation was that Thalia had worn her everyday button-boots instead of a pinching pair of evening slippers…though only because she couldn't fit into a borrowed pair of those as well. After all, why should she purchase a fancy gown and shoes for one charity ball?

"Thalia, my dear, there you are!" an imperious voice called loudly, halting conversation around them with its natural authority.

Thalia turned to see the ball's distinguished hostess, the dowager countess of Berwick and generous benefactor of the local orphanage, fixing her with a stern look. Thalia knew hiding among the ferns was not why she had been asked to come tonight, but having never been to a grand ball before, she was feeling quite intimidated. This was not her world.

"Good evening, Lady Berwick, thank you again for inviting me tonight. This ball is splendid and very well attended," she managed after a perfunctory curtsy.

Lady Berwick tutted and tapped her shoulder with her fan imperiously. Her gray hair was artfully arranged in a stunning coiffure and topped with three large fluttering white ostrich feathers.

"This is a small country affair, dear, hardly anything to send you into hiding for. We shall have a short speech in a moment to announce the fundraising goal for the orphanage. I rather think you should explain in your own words for those gathered what they are paying for." At Thalia's terrified expression, she laughed. "Do not look at me like that, dear. It will come easily enough once you begin speaking. Only a few words are required, and I shall stay right by your side for support." She patted Thalia on the arm and offered a benevolent smile before gliding off to greet another guest.

Thalia nodded mutely, and tried to control her churning stomach. She really should not have eaten so many of those tarts while she was in hiding. Her heart hammered madly in her chest - which was itself quite constricted by her corset—and she felt a sudden urge to faint. She was not usually so timid, but the thought of having all those aristocratic eyes upon her, judging her, was not a comfortable one. Especially in this hideous dress. Perhaps she should sneak a glass of champagne to fortify herself.

She was thankful to have a gown to wear at all, but this particular one left something to be desired. It was several ghastly shades of pink and featured a plethora of bows and pleats. It also had a generous ring of lace dyed a garishly bright pink around the top of the bodice, which drew attention to the unfortunate amount of cleavage Thalia was showing off. It was hardly her fault that her good friend Mena was less endowed than she was, and the corset threatened to let her breasts fall out if she made a wrong move. Who had commissioned such an affront to fashion? It was no wonder Mena detested high society.

Lady Berwick called for attention, and all eyes swiveled towards the grand staircase where she had chosen to position herself. There appeared to be some genuine interest, but many people were already looking annoyed that the music had been interrupted. Thalia nervously smoothed her borrowed gown, and tried to marshal her courage as the countess began to speak.

"Thank you to all who have gathered this evening to hear about the important work being done at our local orphanage, St. James' Home for Children. A fine young woman has done me the honor of coming tonight to help explain her bold new vision for the young children in need. Please welcome Miss Ward." Lady Berwick's voice was practiced and authoritative. She swept an arm towards Thalia, indicating that she ought to come forward. The dowager's many large jewels twinkled in the lamplight.

Thalia forced herself to smile brightly, and nod to the crowd. She immediately felt the critical eyes of the guests picking apart her appearance, taking in her unsightly gown and lack of jewels. Thankfully her skirts were long enough to conceal her boots. She took a fortifying breath and began to speak in a clear, even voice.

"Good evening to you all. I am Thalia Ward." She was able to project a reasonably confident tone. "I am a local business owner, and have been volunteering my time to St. James' for three years now. The children there are being educated and are taught a trade and then are sent away when they come of age. While this is invaluable help for these children, and it provides them with a future, I have been wondering of late whether there might be more we can do for them."

Thalia paused, taking in the reaction of the crowd thus far. Several heads were tilted with open interest, and many others were covering their yawns and murmuring to their friends. The youngest ladies in attendance were clearly eager for the dancing to resume, and they furtively eyed the eligible men around them.

Thalia felt a stab of resentment that these entitled peacocks should lack an interest in lending their fellow man a helping hand, especially parentless children. She opened her mouth to explain her new plan, when her eyes met a pair of hard eyes set in a face chiseled from stone. The man was watching her closely, his mouth slightly turned to a frown. Beside him stood a woman with pinched lips and furrowed brow. Thalia could feel their disapproval despite the distance between them. She tore her gaze away, and forced herself to continue.

"I am hoping that each child at the orphanage will be afforded the opportunity to broaden their mind with entirely new experiences. Most of these children have never traveled outside the village, nor have they seen a work of art, and many have not heard professional music before. Imagine what a child might grow to accomplish given the proper nurturing and experience. And so

I ask everyone assembled here tonight to contribute to a supplemental education fund. With that fund, we at the orphanage plan to take the children to view art, listen to music, and bring in a few new instructors, such as a language tutor. We will be an example to all other orphanages in England, and produce the finest pupils who will have so many wonderful new opportunities for employment in the future. There are so many ways to be involved. Come visit the orphanage to see our work in action. Thank you for listening."

Thalia could tell that her ideas were only listened to by half the audience at most, and many who had appeared unimpressed. These children didn't stand a chance from these people. Most members of the aristocracy wouldn't understand why a child of no means would benefit from such exposure to the arts. Orphans were destined for menial and backbreaking labor, not linguistic careers and musicales.

At least the dowager gamely continued to support the idea, and thanked all for attending and considering a donation. Without her considerable financial support, the orphanage would be forced to close.

Thalia was disappointed, but not surprised in the least. She excused herself and retreated to the refreshment table. With a sigh she resolved to be less pessimistic about the fundraising goal. Maybe they would hit their financial target anyway. She decided to have a second champagne as a reward for her bravery, and slid out of hiding, clutching her prize. She could use some fresh air, and hopefully could manage to miss the remainder of the dancing.

After a quick look about, she settled on the best route to the terrace doors and quickly made her way to freedom. As a shop owner, she was comfortable addressing people, even crowds, but these snobs were a special bunch, and facing them down in a ridiculous frock was intimidating to say the least. A few minutes alone in the night air would be a relief.

"Miss Ward, dear!" the dowager called out, her hand raised and beckoning.

Thalia cursed and abandoned her escape plans. She waded back through the throngs of guests to the dowager's side. Lady Berwick was standing beside a man, her eyes dancing mischievously.

"Miss Ward, this is Sir Harley Marville, a local squire. He was quite moved by your words earlier, and asked for an introduction," she said.

Thalia dipped a curtsy. As she came up and met the gentleman's eyes, her heart thumped unpleasantly in her chest. He was tall and wiry, with a classically handsome face and ice-blue eyes. He smiled wolfishly, and insolently ran his gaze over her body, lingering on her breasts. There was something cruel about those eyes, they sent a shiver down her spine.

Sir Marville bowed over her hand, holding it for a fraction too long. "Pleased to make your acquaintance, Miss Ward." His voice sounded like wind rustling dried grass.

"Good evening, Sir Marville," Thalia replied.

"Would you deign to take a turn about the room with me? I would like to discuss your charity work, and how I might be of some use to these unfortunate children of yours," he asked, offering his arm.

Thalia did not want to go anywhere with this man, but couldn't think of a way to excuse herself. The dowager looked expectantly at her, knowing that gaining the interest of wealthy benefactors was entirely the point of this charity ball. Besides, if Sir Marville was truly interested in providing aid, she could hardly turn him down just because he gave her a bad feeling.

Perhaps she was being silly and misreading him entirely. It's not as though she needed to fear anyone in a crowded ballroom. She could always give him a kick in the shins and run. Disappointing, actually, that she couldn't just do that now.

She placed her hand on his proffered arm and went with him. Thalia carefully kept as physically distant as possible, though there was only so far she could retreat before it looked ridiculous with her arm stretched far out. She focused on maintaining a careful, neutral expression so as not to encourage any familiarity. She did not let so much as a fold of her skirts brush against his leg.

"It is wonderful to know there is some interest in the orphanage," she said, aiming for cordiality. But as she turned to look at him, she saw a peculiar glint in his eye that caused the hairs on the nape of her neck to rise. She quickly averted her gaze and steadied herself.

"You certainly aroused my interest, Miss Ward," he murmured. Thalia was sure she heard him place a special emphasis on the word aroused. Bild rose up in her throat.

She searched for a proper response. "I had thought it would be a difficult proposal for many to accept. It could be hard to see the point in opening up an orphan to artistic experiences, when they most likely will not grow up to become artists themselves. Though the purpose is, of course, to simply provide options and more freedom of thought. Perhaps one or two might have their entire life-course altered by this proposal."

Maybe if she talked a lot, he would get bored and leave. But he cut in.

"To be honest, it was your genuine compassion that garnered my interest. You clearly have such a soft heart." His gaze was on her breasts, which were unfortunately being squeezed upward by her tight dress. "I shall have to think on the particulars of how I would like to become involved. Perhaps we may meet again soon to discuss?"

Thalia felt her temper rising. She longed to slap this insolent cad, and leave this ball altogether. But she had to stay and endure his insults if she wanted his generosity for the children. He was quite obviously trying to get her to meet with him. Under the guise of charity work, no less. Frustrated, she turned to Sir Marville and smiled blandly.

"Of course, sir. Please feel welcome to come to the orphanage anytime you are able. We always appreciate the charity of such wonderful benefactors such as yourself."

This was clearly not what he had in mind as he pressed his lips into a thin line, though he didn't press her to meet elsewhere. For the moment. As they completed their walk, he faced her and expertly sketched a bow.

"I would be delighted to support your cause," he leaned close and murmured in her ear, causing an unpleasant reptilian shiver down Thalia's spine. *For a price*, she finished in her head. "Perhaps we could work closely together…to help those unfortunate children. Until we meet again, Miss Ward." His ice-cold eyes bored into Thalia's; a sly smile played at his handsome lips.

She did not need to guess what he would want in return for his generosity. She had been at the receiving end of many a come on over the past few years. Thalia maintained the bland smile on her face and pretended not to understand his meaning. Though she longed to do him violence.

"It would be much appreciated by the children, sir. Any assistance in bettering the lives of these young ones is a blessing. I thank you again for your interest in supporting the orphanage, Sir Marville." She dipped a perfunctory curtsy and fled.

Walking quickly, while still appearing calm and unhurried so as not to draw undue attention, Thalia slipped from the ballroom for some air. She fervently hoped that Sir Marville wouldn't dare try and follow.

Campbell Marlow leaned against a pillar as he observed the crowd swirling around him. He felt like the survivor of a shipwreck amidst a wild sea. He idly sipped from his glass of champagne–the only sign that he was a man of flesh and not in fact a statue. Every male guest was expected to spend his time dancing, but Cam preferred to avoid that particular activity, if he could help it.

He felt a familiar ambivalence about his fellow guests; he both despised them on principle as members of the wealthy elite, and also craved their acceptance. He wanted their lifestyle, but hated the ceremony of it as well. Would he never feel settled? He would not have come tonight except for the special request of the

Duke of Bedford, his close personal friend. Something about a fundraiser for some orphans or some such.

Apparently one important signal of wealth and power was the ability to give away one's hard-earned coin. Though obviously most of these aristocrats had never lifted so much as a finger to gain their riches. And the giving away of the funds showed everyone just how little they needed to concern themselves with such material concerns.

Cam was forever frustrated by the lack of self-awareness of the upper crust. There were thousands of orphans, downtrodden men and women, and elderly people who could use a helping hand, and yet they acted as though each new case before them was shocking in the extreme. Did they really not realize that the society of which they helped structure and maintain was the reason that so many were forced to go without? He suspected that they both knew and did not care that the circumstances of birth were like a lottery, and that it was most definitely not based on merit or moral fortitude.

Philanthropy based on individual whim would never be enough to solve, or even alleviate the real problem. Cam did not trouble himself much with politics though, as he knew the lengths to which these people would go to hold onto their power. It wasn't his duty to take them on – he was out for himself, and himself alone.

He drained his glass and made a decision to beat a hasty retreat to the garden before the speech could begin. He really could not stomach a charity ball at the moment. He itched to be alone at home with a good bottle of whiskey and some work, instead of attempting small talk with small-minded nobles.

Several important letters regarding various investments waited on his desk back at the estate, requiring his attention. Investments that were paving the way for Cam's ascension to the nobility, if he played his cards right.

Spying the terrace doors, Cam made his way there and resumed his nonchalant stance just outside them. He knew that running from this affair would not help his aim to move up in society. So he forced himself to stay within earshot of the goings on, in case there was anything he shouldn't miss. He wanted to maintain an eye on the crowd, but also be close enough to escape should he require some space from the gasps and false sympathy that followed a pitiful story of an orphanage in need of funds.

The ball's hostess, the Countess of Berwick, began to speak, drawing the attention of the crowd. Lady Berwick was quite a force in the village, always throwing her weight around to try and improve conditions for the working class. It was inspiring, but somehow also annoying. She was playing savior for people who just needed the boot off their necks long enough to save themselves. At least she was trying to help though, which is more than anyone else in attendance could boast.

A young woman from the orphanage began to speak next. She was the picture of confidence and looked like a classic English rose—all blonde hair piled up and creamy skin. Her rather unattractive bodice was blessedly low cut, displaying a bounty of bosom. This rose wore no jewels.

Cam felt a stab of disappointment. A woman without jewels at a ball was not a titled, pampered lady of the nobility, as any lady worth the title would never miss a chance to show off her finery. This Rose was not what he was looking for.

He turned away, ready to enjoy a cigar and, most importantly, evade the many females needing a dance partner. Something about the topic of poverty, especially viewed from the aristocracy's point of view, made him feel nauseous. He'd rather not think too much on that. He had worked hard since childhood to develop his rather acute ability to push away the bad thoughts.

Cam lit a cheroot and strolled across the terrace, which featured a staircase curving down into the elaborate gardens. Fat cherubic angels splashed about in the fountain at the center of the lawn. Several meandering gravel paths converged here before shooting off in all directions once again. Tall torches were placed about the grounds for illumination, thus allowing young ladies to enjoy a moment outside with a beau, without losing their good reputations.

At the back of the garden was a simple maze, nothing too elaborate. There was no torchlight there. Cam slid into the shadows and sighed in relief. The orchestra could be heard, but the sound was hushed, and crickets could be heard in the fields around the manor house. Cam would never cease to be enchanted by the country; it was far superior to the squalor of London where he spent too many years as a child.

As he was finishing his cheroot, the English Rose emerged from the terrace; her momentum made it look like she was running from someone. She even cast a furtive glance behind her as she sped past the fountain and into the maze. Cam instinctually leaned back into the shadows, unsure why he was hiding.

A few paces into the maze, she stopped and turned her face up to the sky, eyes fluttering closed. The moonlight caressed her face, causing her creamy skin to glow. Cam watched her pale shoulders as she breathed deeply of the night air, drawn to her for some mysterious reason he couldn't understand. Any sane person would have announced themselves. Or left. That's what he needed to do – leave. As he turned to make a hasty exit, a twig snapped loudly underfoot.

"Who's there?" she demanded, narrowing her eyes to peer into the darkness.

Cam swore softly and took a final draw on his cheroot before tossing it to the ground, stamping it out with his foot, and stepped out to reveal himself. She stiffened as he came into the light, and she crossed her arms over her chest in a protective gesture. Cam slid his hands into his pockets, doing his best to appear relaxed and non-threatening. Alone in the darkest reaches of the garden any woman would feel uneasy. He didn't want her to fear him.

"Why are you hiding in the bushes?" she asked. Her feet were planted apart. A confident woman.

"I was just out for a smoke," he said, shrugging his shoulders. "Balls can be rather tedious in my experience. I didn't mean to startle you."

Her shoulders relaxed a fraction, and she let her gaze travel over him. A graceful blush stained her cheeks.

"It's alright." She moved to sit on a nearby stone bench and sighed appreciatively. "I don't mind some company."

Cam glanced towards the house, reluctant to stay longer, but eventually his curiosity won out. There was something alluring about this woman, something unique he wanted to discover. Stepping closer, he leaned against the Roman style archway framing the entrance to the maze. From there they could see the house, and the light could touch them.

"Thalia Ward," she said suddenly.

He was momentarily confused before realizing that she was telling him her name. Cam looked her over again, from this closer vantage point. Her hair was obviously not put up by a lady's maid; at least not a qualified one. And her gown truly was hideous. Never before had a more frightening abomination been sewn onto a woman. He looked lower, and spied the tip of a sturdy brown boot, rather than a delicate slipper.

"I am Campbell Marlow. Lovely to meet you, Miss Ward," he said, his voice oddly husky. He swallowed hard.

"Are you afraid to dance, Mr. Marlow?" A coy smile tugged at her full lips.

Cam chuckled. "Not at all, Miss Ward. But it is rather suffocating in there." He nodded toward the house.

"Indeed it is. I am not one for attending balls, but alas here I am. Perhaps you heard my speech earlier?" she prompted, her head tilted to one side consideringly.

Cam nodded, but declined to speak. Too busy marveling at her beauty. He was surprised by how inexplicably nervous he felt in this woman's presence.

Miss Ward rushed to fill the silence. "I am not convinced that anyone would be willing to indulge my proposal and increase their financial support. The countess insisted that a charity ball would be just the idea to drum up support." Miss Ward sighed. "The Countess is quite a force to be reckoned with. What was your opinion of the idea, sir?" Her steady gaze made Cam feel much like an insect pinned under glass in a display.

He took a moment to respond, honestly struggling to deduce his own feelings on the subject. "It is admirable to support such a cause. Certainly there are many children who might benefit. However, I agree that it will be difficult to garner support, though it certainly does help to have the countess on your side," he finally replied. His words echoed hollowly in his head, sounding somehow fragile and false.

Cam knew how unappealing the idea of paying for such frivolous and unnecessary activities for an orphaned child would be. The wealthy considered the poor to be dirty and morally corrupt, and the unfortunate children thereof would be tainted beyond repair.

Such children would most likely end up working in the local mines, or various other unsavory jobs in town that involved fitting into tight spaces and getting filthy. They were both perceived to be unworthy and wholly incapable of appreciating anything such as art. The best Miss Ward could hope for would be a bit more coin donated to feed, clothe, and morally instruct—via a belt or switch—the urchins.

He would be lying though if he did not acknowledge how precious such pleasures would be to an impoverished, neglected child. Cam had a family, but he too had been deprived, growing up in miserable conditions. Living under the iron fist of his abusive father, he knew all too well the lack of hope and prospect these children had. A taste of beauty was often what gave a person the spirit to survive their miserable circumstances. It could even inspire the way out of poverty. People deserved both sustenance and pleasure in life, didn't they?

Truthfully, what Miss Ward had decided to pursue was a wondrous, life-altering mission. Cam felt his shriveled heart give a little lurch, as though awakening. He snorted; what a silly thought.

The rose was an idealist, though she looked old enough to have had that robbed of her by now, surely. She did not even possess a pair of decent evening footwear. She also lacked propriety by being out here with him. In the moonlight.

Cam suddenly was all too aware of how easy it would be to steal a kiss. He took a fortifying breath, and forced his gaze away from Miss Ward and her generous curves.

"Thank you for your honesty. I do hope that we might find some compassionate individuals from among the crowd tonight to make my appearance worth it." She gave a soft self-deprecating laugh. "I am eager to leave this awkward affair and get out of this ghastly dress."

Cam's gaze instantly shot back to Miss Ward. Her eyes had widened in surprise, a becoming blush staining her round cheeks. She pressed her lips together, as though forcing herself to stop making inappropriate statements.

Their gazes held, and he couldn't help but wonder if she was as conscious of their close proximity as he was. The increasing awareness between them set his every nerve on edge in anticipation. He opened his mouth to reassure her the gown was fetching—a lie, but decided against saying the words. This was not a woman who needed that sort of false flattery.

"Miss Ward, you seem to be a compelling and earnest woman. I do not doubt that you will rally many to your cause. Sheer tenacity is the way to victory." Cam's voice was thick with desire.

Miss Ward's jaw dropped open. She recovered quickly, snapping her mouth shut and looking away.

"You are the estate manager for the Duke of Bedford, are you not?" she asked, her voice slightly breathless.

"That's right." His mouth quirked up on one side. She knew about him? This was an intriguing development.

"Would you be shocked to discover that you are rather famous in the village?" she surprised him by saying.

Cam arched a brow at that. "I would, actually," he replied.

Miss Ward turned to him and unleashed the full power of her smile. It was bright as sunlight, and lit up her wide blue eyes. It almost burned with its luminance. Cam's heart sputtered in his chest at the sight, the world seeming to tilt on its axis for a brief moment.

"They say that you can drink any man under the table. And that you are something of a recluse." She wiggled her eyebrows in playful challenge. Her little smirk was entirely too adorable.

"Both are accurate," he allowed, maintaining an inscrutable expression as he struggled to control his physical response.

Miss Ward waited expectantly. But Cam wasn't going to give her any more information. She huffed a sigh that sounded a bit like a laugh. She stood to leave and shook out her skirts.

"Well sir, you make for stimulating conversation. But I think I had better get back inside and see if I am needed."

She offered him her hand. Cam bent over it, while marveling at the string of calluses along her palm. Who was this woman, he wondered.

Cam wanted her to stay. He enjoyed being with Miss Ward, who was both entertaining and beautiful. She also wasn't conniving. She simply enjoyed the night. It felt natural to talk with her, in a way that Cam had never felt before. His interactions with women were entirely transactional, for both work and pleasure. He did not have female friends. But he had no connection with this woman he had just met, and had to let her go despite the pull within urging him to find an excuse to keep her there.

"Have a lovely evening, Miss Ward," he said.

"You as well, Mr. Marlow," she replied.

She swept away toward the house. An enormous pink bow rested at the base of her bodice, and it flopped up and down as she walked. Cam wondered what she looked like in her usual clothes. Surely her entire wardrobe couldn't be this hideous.

Cam shook his head, attempting to clear the woman from his thoughts. Miss Ward had affected him far too much for his liking. Cam didn't need to be distracted by her right now, especially when he was finally ready to find a suitable bride. Everything he wanted was within his reach, everything he had worked so hard for, but only if he was focused. He resolved to wipe the captivating Miss Thalia Ward from his mind.

Three

ack at Mrs. Grantham's boardinghouse, where she had lived for the past ten years, Thalia trudged up the creaking main stairs eager for her bed. She had been able to leave the charity ball before dinner was served, but it had been a long evening. Most aristocrats would sleep late into the morning, whereas Thalia had to wake early for work.

She made her way down the hall to her door. Besides some soft chatter behind some of her neighbor's doors, it was quiet. Only a sliver of moonlight stretched across the floor illuminated her path. The gas lamps lining the long hall were turned down, and at the end a window was open to let in the cool night air. Thalia couldn't wait to collapse onto her small bed. Who knew balls were so exhausting?

As her hand reached for the brass knob to her own room, the door suddenly flew open to reveal two women. The taller, raven-haired woman laughed at Thalia's yelp of surprise, and turned to jump onto the small bed, which protested but held strong despite the onslaught.

Thalia's heart continued to try and leap from her chest, and she gripped the doorframe. "Don't do that!" she chided, even though she was always pleased to see her friends.

Clementine, the raven-haired woman, lay on her stomach, chin propped in her hands. She grinned expectantly. The other woman, Mena, took the worn wingback chair in the corner for herself. Mena was a quiet brunette who often went unnoticed, but her friends knew her sharp intellect and quick wit.

"Tell us everything!" Clementine demanded cheerfully. Her bright green eyes flashed like gemstones in her excitement.

"We've been waiting for ages for you to return. Your landlady was getting tired of us hanging about the kitchen and sent us up here instead. You must be exhausted," Mena said. After bringing over the hideous gown earlier, Mena and Clem had waited around for Thalia to tell them all about the ball. And worn out their welcome with Mrs. Grantham apparently.

"I'll gladly relay everything, but you must release me from this prison of a gown first," Thalia replied, closing the door behind her. She was resolved never to wear a ball gown again. Or attend a ball.

Thalia went to sit on the bed, giving Clementine access to the many buttons and laces along the back of the gown. Clementine set to work at once, with only a few muttered curses and huffs of annoyance as she struggled to free her friend. Once Thalia had it removed, she stood to put on the worn blue dressing gown that had been thrown over the end of the bed, leaving the offending pink gown crumpled on the floor.

"I happened to meet the duke's estate manager," Thalia said teasingly. She flashed her friends a mischievous smile before bending to begin the process of removing her boots.

"Is that so?" Clementine asked; her lips curving into a knowing smile. "Everyone says he is handsome as sin."

"Sadly it was in the garden that we met, so I did not get a proper look at the man. But I will confess that there was something about him that I found instinctually attractive," Thalia shrugged. She was still puzzling over their interaction, particularly the fluttery feeling in her belly when she remembered the timber of Mr. Marlow's velvety voice.

"Animal attraction," Mena said with gravity, causing the other two to burst into laughter. Mena scowled. "I am serious!"

"Don't fret, Mena," Thalia said, still breathless with mirth. "We are not laughing at you…at least I'm not." She shot a warning look at Clementine. "I just found that statement rather scandalous. Though I did feel quite feral in the man's presence," she added, narrowing her eyes in mock seriousness.

"Poor man isn't ready for the likes of you," Clem said approvingly.

"What did you two discuss?" Mena asked.

"Oh just about the ball and the charity. Nothing salacious." Thalia gestured at her torso. "Doubtless he found me unappealing for the obvious reasons."

Hers was not the ideal female form, with her far too generous curves. More than one man had informed Thalia of the fact she was too large to be beautiful.

"Please, you think far too little of yourself. Men drool over you; I've seen it myself many times," Clementine said firmly. Mena zealously nodded her agreement.

Thalia's friends were always trying to build up her confidence. Mena, who was content with her own quiet life, was always sharing the wisdom learned in her own finishing school upbringing with Thalia. Mena had learned perfectly well what it took to be a confident young woman, even though she had vowed to never again bow to the rules of society that her draconian mother had forced on her before her passing. She would rather remain in the country, a spinster, than marry some toff and play hostess for the sake of fitting in with high society.

Clementine was one who had no problems dealing with men and was quite self-assured in that arena. Why she remained unmarried was truly a mystery. With glossy curls and eyes like clear emeralds framed by thick lashes, Clem drew attention everywhere she went. She had full, naturally red lips, and the tall slim ideal body every woman desired to have. It would be easy to dislike her out of petty jealousy, but she had a character of pure gold.

Thalia stood and crossed to the tall mirror that stood in the corner. She pulled the dressing gown aside and considered herself in the chipped glass, her eyes snagging on the extra bits of flesh she carried on her hips and thighs. Self-loathing bubbled up, burning her throat. Why couldn't she control herself? Other women had no trouble keeping their figures trim, why did she struggle so?

"Why are you so hard on yourself?" Clem asked, irritated. "You have the body of a Greek statue."

With a harsh exhale, Thalia pressed a hand to her stomach, turning to the side to see the effect. A corset could only do so much to hold her in, and it was uncomfortable - not to mention unhealthy to lace too tightly. It hindered her work. But that was the crux of the issue...her work consisted of making sweets. Naturally she had to test each batch, and the caramel and chocolate clung to her frame like a wet gown. Who could look at her with lust when she looked like this? No wonder no man had ever wanted a second go after unwrapping her for a tumble.

Disgusted, Thalia belted her wrap with fierce tugs, tossing her head to flip the loose strands of hair from her eyes, and chewed her lip. Even covered she was an enormous monstrosity. She turned sharply away from her reflection. Returning to the bed, she lay back across the mattress by Clementine's feet.

"I hardly believe that I'm leaving men swooning in my wake, but you are sweet to say so, Clem. I must remind you both that I don't need some man sniffing around. I have a shop to run, and I do not intend to marry just so a man can assume control over what's mine."

Clementine scoffed. "Who said anything about marriage? I'm merely suggesting using this man for your pleasure."

Thalia and Mena both practically choked on their surprise; Mena's freckled cheeks turned bright pink at the notion. Thalia suppressed the rising discomfort within her, knowing her secret—that she had already indulged in liaisons with men, several times, but it had only ended in crushing disappointment. She was loath to confide such truth with anyone, not even her closest friends, due to the shame and embarrassment.

The idea that she could have Campbell Marlow for her lover was simply too ridiculous. He did not seem the type of man one toyed with. And he did not seem the type of man one married either. He was firmly in a third category: men to avoid.

Clem scowled at her friends. "I fail to see what is so funny, ladies." She sniffed. "Men take their pleasure where they please, and why shouldn't we do the same?"

Mena spoke up, her cheeks still suffering from her private discomfort. "Men have the upper hand. They cannot bear children, and so they have no consequence from such interactions."

Clem seized on that idea. "A good man should be as interested in keeping their private liaisons from producing children as their female partner. Besides, there are ways to be almost entirely assured of no such result," she said with a self-assured nod.

"Like what?" Mena asked earnestly, her natural scientific curiosity far outweighing her shyness about this subject.

Clem shrugged mysteriously and smiled. "I listen and ask questions," she said simply.

Clem's father was a physician. Thalia was not shocked to learn that Dr. Blakely dealt with such things as contraceptives, since the many factories and other employment for women would require some form of family planning so one could be a reliable laborer. The notion that Dr. Blakely allowed his precious only daughter to be privy to such information, however, was anathema to what Thalia knew about him. Apparently Clem was an even better snoop than Thalia had realized.

"My goodness, your father would drop dead if he knew you had heard about such things," Mena said, her voice tinged with awe.

Clem preened under their attention. "He would survive the ordeal, I'm sure. Anyways, I refused to stay in ignorance of something so important to my life and wellbeing. Knowledge is power, is it not?"

Mena and Thalia both firmly agreed.

"Well...shall I describe the toffs at the ball for you ladies?" Thalia asked, eager to change the subject.

She arranged herself against the footboard of the bed, crossing her legs.

"Well, Lady Berwick had her hair arranged like she was Marie Antoinette with diamonds the size of eggs hanging off her ears," she began. It felt cathartic to poke some fun at the upper crust.

Then her mind snagged on a different memory. Thalia swallowed, nervous. She loathed to speak about the wretched Sir Marville and the uneasy feeling he gave her. But she wanted her friend's support. And also to know if her instinctive fears were unfounded.

"There was a man there -"

"A handsome man?" Clem asked, cutting in with excitement.

"No...well, that is not to say that he was unattractive," Thalia said, haltingly.

"Did he behave badly?" Mena asked, concerned and looking ready to sweep Thalia into her nurturing embrace.

Thalia shook her head, warmed by the show of support. "No I cannot say that either. He just gave me an odd feeling...there was something about him that was unsettling," she replied.

"Who was he?" Clem asked. She knew everyone in town, and was ready to unveil their backstories if needed.

"Sir Marville."

"Bloody hell," Clem cursed, eyes wide.

"Do you know of him?" Mena asked Clem.

"Yes, unfortunately," Clem replied, curling her lip. "Sir Harley Marville is known to be highly unscrupulous in his business, which is shipping, and has made himself the enemy of all reformers. But he is considered untouchable."

"Why?" Thalia asked, her belly full of ice.

Clem tilted her head, thinking. "Family connection," she said with a shrug. "Same old story. There was talk about his misuse of a maid at the family estate years ago. Cost them a small fortune to bury the gossip, but it was done. And ever since no one has dared cross him."

"What did he say to you, Thalia?" Mena asked, brow furrowed.

Thalia's fingers dug into the slippery fabric of her robe. "He made an offer."

Clem's brows crashed down in fury. "What? That's disgusting. As if you would ever have anything to do with the awful man. Stay clear of him."

"I know, I know," Thalia said, fisting the fabric until her knuckles turned white. "I just have a hard time...if someone is gentry...what could I have said?"

Mena patted her knee, eyes warm. "You are not to blame at all."

"Exactly. It is Marville's fault for being a disgusting ass," Clem added with a firm nod.

Thalia was relieved to hear her friend's words, even though she logically knew she was not to blame, it was incredibly difficult to keep a firm grasp on that concept when society was busy undermining every woman's self-confidence.

"Thank you both. I am so grateful to have you in my life," Thalia said, her throat constricted from burgeoning tears.

"You have us forever and ever. Now, tell us about the rest of the peacocks you danced with," Clem said.

Thalia blew out a breath, and then described the various aristocrats in all their finery, entertaining her friends with the various details of the charity ball until they were all yawning. It was a wonderful distraction, and soon she had forgotten all about Sir Marville. When they finally bid each other good night, Thalia finally got some sleep.

Sadly, it felt like she had barely nodded off before a firm knock at her door woke her again. The morning wakeup call came just after dawn. Thalia wanted to cry from exhaustion, but she forced herself to get up and dress. There was always work to be done.

* * *

Whimpering in the darkness of his room, gripped by sheer terror, Cam was curled into a protective ball. His muscles were tense, waiting for the pain to come.

"Love is a useless emotion. Don't ever let a woman make a fool of you, son." His father's words sounded from the darkness.

"Dad please, it's not ma's fault!" Cam's voice was high and thin with terror.

No amount of begging would stop the painful blows from raining down. Again and again the lash slapped against Cam's bare skin, each time causing an eruption of white sparks behind his eyes from the all-encompassing pain.

It was always the same. First Cam would taste his father's wrath, and then it was his mother's turn. Every week when Elias Marlow picked up his wages, the man immediately went to the gin house to nurse his bruised ego. Then he came home to take out his frustrations on his family with a belt.

This time Cam had attempted to lock his father out of the apartment. He had pushed a heavy chest of drawers in front of the door. But the flimsy wood framing in their tenement building shattered under the force of his father's shoulder. The older, stronger man had easily gained entry.

"That useless woman got herself tossed out of a job."

Cam cowered, instinctually knowing that resistance would only make the beating worse. Later he would remember how to clean and cover his wounds. His mother would have to clean her own blood off the floor.

Suddenly Cam's father grabbed him by the collar and lifted him several inches off the floor.

"And now she thinks to earn coin by lying on her back!" he spat.

Cam whimpered pitifully.

"Are you as worthless as your mother, boy?" his father demanded.

Then he suddenly let go, and Cam slammed to the floor.

Rather than feel the pain of hitting the floor however, Cam startled awake. It was dark in his bedroom, with a gentle summer breeze coming through the window. Cam lay in his bed, sheets tangled around his legs. Sweat had beaded along his forehead.

He still felt the gripping terror of the nightmare but reassured himself that his father no longer had any control over him. The man was long dead. Cam took several deep breaths and forced himself to relax.

Outside his window the first streaks of sunlight were creeping over the horizon. It had been a long time since he had been visited by this particular nightmare.

Throwing aside the sheets, Cam sat up and swung his legs over the side of the bed. He rubbed both hands over his face and through his hair, making it stand up. He would never fall back asleep now.

The fact that his degenerate father could still make him afraid infuriated Cam. He wanted to scream from the lack of power he felt. Perhaps a vigorous ride would ease the tension he carried.

Four

After a hard morning ride about the estate fields, Cam left his horse at the stables, and made his way to the main house. He didn't bother to change first, driven by a fierce hunger that refused delay. The last vestiges of his bad dream had been wiped away by the calming ache of his muscles, leaving him feeling rather buoyant…for him anyway.

The breakfast room at the Duke of Bedford's estate was garishly bright in the morning sun. The light poured in from windows on three sides of the room and bounced off the silver buffet service lining the sideboard. Cam had to squint as he loaded his plate with the delicious offerings, but it felt like attempting to stare directly into the sun.

Garrett, the duke, was sitting at his usual place at the breakfast table. He eyed his friend casually as Cam filled his plate. The two had been friends since they were schoolboys together, despite their differences in social standing.

When the duke had offered Cam the opportunity to work for him and manage his properties more than a decade earlier, Cam had recognized it for what it was—the chance to escape his future toiling for a pittance as a clerk and instead get his foot in the door of high society.

The chance to guarantee safety from poverty was too good to pass up, even if he had no idea how to run a large estate. Thankfully, Cam found most answers in the library, where the late duke kept an impressive collection of farming related books. Accounts were simple, and far more interesting than the copying he had been doing at the clerk's office. Everything else he learned on the go, and had enjoyed every moment of it.

Their friendship was strong and Garrett's trust in Cam was stronger. He had wanted to give complete control of his holdings over to Cam so he could be free to live the life of leisure and entertainment he was used to. With that kind of support, Campbell would be able to use Garrett's financial backing and aristocratic connections to make a name for himself, find a suitable bride for himself, and establish himself as the man of wealth and power that he had always longed to be. Thus proving his father wrong, and finally exorcizing the power he held over Cam since childhood.

"Bloody hell," Cam said, struggling to keep from being blinded by the sun. He tried to blink away the burning of his retinas. He never cooked food like this for himself and was thus forced to come to the main house if he wanted to eat. He started to wonder if it was worth it, as his eyes didn't deserve this assault.

Cam topped off his plate, then took a seat facing away from the blistering sight of the buffet table. He buttered a slice of bread absently.

"What do you know of a Miss Ward," he asked causally, his voice breaking the amiable silence.

Cam strove to keep his tone nonchalant, though his curiosity was overwhelming. He reminded himself that he was not considering a liaison with the woman. Not even one tiny bit. So why did he feel a bit like an eager schoolboy? Probably because he knew better than to be lusting after a local proprietress.

Garrett for his part didn't even bat an eyelash as he continued to peruse the newspaper he was reading over breakfast. He took a bite of his toast and spoke while chewing. "I don't know everything about everyone in town, you know Campbell."

Cam rolled his eyes in irritation. Garrett knew a lot more than he would readily admit. Though he was still a bit of a reprobate and a wastrel, he had become quite a knowledgeable landholder. Not to mention that the Bedford title trumped all others in the vicinity. Garrett was a powerful man.

Cam had chafed at first when his friend began to show more interest in his holdings, but over time they found that they worked very well together and shared the same goals – namely wealth and power. They did have some differences however, which meshed usefully.

Garrett was a people lover, who could converse with everyone comfortably for hours, and was well thought of because of his humor and humility. He was also very handsome, and the ladies flocked to him. But neither did he alienate the men, who looked to him as someone they could trust and confide in. Cam had none of this easy charm, but he did have a ruthless business sense and a strong sense of loyalty that others admired. He was often sought out for advice, and of course his close connection to the duke was a huge benefit.

"Stop being so modest, your grace," Cam admonished, with a lopsided grin.

Garrett set aside his newspaper and sat back in his chair. "Alright, I do know something about Miss Ward. She owns a confectionary in town. Though knowing this fact has absolutely nothing to do with my love of sweets and chocolates. Obviously." He gestured at his athletic physique with a neatly manicured hand.

"Naturally," Cam agreed dryly. He could just picture Garrett sitting in the privacy of his rooms eating an entire box of chocolates; wrappers strewn everywhere. Probably in a velvet robe. The hedonist.

"Both of her parents have passed on. She has been living at Mrs. Grantham's Boarding House ever since. She opened the confectionery two years ago, and from what I gather is a bit of a success." Garrett picked up his newspaper again, and turned to the next page, which required a lot of crinkling and folding. Once satisfied, he took another bite of toast.

Garrett knew a lot for all his pretending disinterest in, well, everything. He played at being a gentleman, but he had become quite a skilled farmer and businessman over the past decade. Because it appeared important to Garrett that he be seen as a lazeabout, Cam didn't let the pretense drop. For all of Garrett's pretense otherwise, he was a downright gossip.

Campbell considered this news and couldn't help a growing feeling of admiration and sympathy for Miss Ward. He knew what it was to make your own way, though Lord knew it was much harder for a young woman than for a man. Miss Ward must have a keen business sense to have accomplished so much on her own. He suddenly frowned into his breakfast plate, a hot stab of some alien feeling at a new idea: perhaps Miss Ward had someone helping her. This odd sensation was certainly not jealousy, something Campbell was very proud to have never experienced. And he never would. Perhaps Garrett would know if Miss Ward had a business partner, but how to ask without sounding ridiculously obvious?

"I assume Miss Ward has a brother, otherwise she could never have secured the bank loan nor the lease for this enterprise." Cam busied himself with sawing a sausage into pieces, keeping his expression inscrutable.

Garrett shrugged one elegantly aristocratic shoulder, and did that slight head shake of his to flip his golden hair back into place. God he was annoying sometimes with his foppishness.

"As far as I know, Miss Ward is entirely on her own, ever since her parents died in a carriage accident when she was all of seventeen. It's a tragic story. She has friends of course, but no men around that I'm aware of. Which is exceedingly odd given what a delectable treat she is." He slid a glance over at Cam, a knowing glint in his eyes.

Cam met the look with a sarcastic eyebrow lift of his own, even as his heart clenched at the thought of Miss Ward at the mercy of the cruel world at such a young age. As he had been. Then he snorted with false humor, shoving away those thoughts. "Trust me, I am not interested in some shopkeeper."

His tone was one of derision and condescension, though his pulse hammered erratically and his mind conjured up all sorts of delicious images. Garrett had long known of, and supported, Cam's marital aspirations. Aspirations that Cam wished to preserve and therefore did not want to give his friend a reason to suspect that he was currently growing an infatuation.

"Say what you will, Campbell, but a man would have to be blind to not notice that woman's allure. I would have already made her mine if she were at all interested." A wistful sigh. "Unfortunately, she appears to be immune to my charm." Garrett lamented with a sad shake of his head, as though this were the greatest tragedy of his life.

"I was unaware that there were any women on this earth who were immune to your looks and, more importantly, your money."

Garrett put a hand to his chest. "You wound me, Campbell. Women enjoy me for myself, and not for my wealth. At least I think they do," Garrett pretended to ponder this, as he took a sip of tea. He tapped his chin, drawing attention to the strong line of his jaw.

"Garrett, I don't even enjoy you for yourself. Our relationship is entirely about the money." This caused Garett to burst into genuine laughter, which elicited another little smile from Cam.

Garrett swiped at his eyes with his exorbitantly expensive coat sleeve. "If only you could be humorous with others, Campbell, you would have even more friends to insult. Now, I'll tell you something else about Miss Ward." Garrett leaned in closer, his green eyes honest and serious for once. "Thalia Ward is a genuinely good person. She is generous with her time in support of local charities. She is well thought of."

Cam watched his friend steadily, then forced himself to take a bite of his eggs and chew. The meaning was clear: don't chase Miss Ward only to walk away after.

"Thanks for that pointed bit of information. You are a very benevolent overlord, your grace," he deflected with an exaggerated bow of his head.

"I do what I can for the people," Garrett said simply, and returned his attention to his breakfast. He set about shoveling the food in as quickly as possible before he needed to leave for London. "Campbell, I need you to do me a favor while I am away."

Cam continued to chew his food. He was very good at waiting people out.

Garrett speared him with a stern look—rather out of character for him. "You need to make plans for this weekend party you want me to host. I refuse to do all of the legwork for you. Decide which women you want to consider trapping into marriage. You also need to speak with the cook about the menus, and the housekeeper and butler about other arrangements."

"So, what exactly will you be doing to help out then?" Campbell was amused despite his trepidation about putting on such a fancy affair. He spread apricot jam across a piece of toasted bread.

His friend snorted in derision. "I am lending you my home as well as my support. That should be sufficient for your needs." With that Garrett took a last swig of tea and stood. He brushed his clothing free from crumbs. "I shall see you in a few days. There's some business I need to see to in London. I expect to see this all settled when I am back."

"Have an excellent trip, Garrett. And say hello to Maggie for me," Cam smiled slyly, his allusion to Garrett's mistress one of their running jokes. Garrett pretended to lunge in for a quick jab, which Cam easily blocked. Then Garrett left, footsteps eagerly heading out to his awaiting carriage.

Once the duke was gone, Cam rose from his seat and walked to the windows overlooking the vast gardens and released a long sigh. He already knew that despite his own internal warnings against doing so, he would visit Miss Ward—Thalia—at her shop. Some invisible thread pulled him to her, and he wasn't sure that he could fight its power. He simply wanted to see her again, and with Garrett gone Campbell was especially susceptible. He rubbed his hands over his face and groaned, leaving his hair disheveled. Surely, he would regret this impulse.

* * *

In the late afternoon, Thalia went around to the orphanage to speak with the headmistress. Mrs. Farningham was in her cluttered office. The poor woman was forever buried under paperwork and lists.

Thalia knocked on the glass window of the door. Mrs. Farningham looked up, her thick brows drawn together. She looked rather intimidating with her fiercely tight chignon at the back of her head, and a plain black dress buttoned up to her chin. She was a spare woman of sixty, though she moved about like a man in his twenties.

"Come," the older woman barked out.

Thalia entered the room and took a small package from her pocket.

"I brought you something new I have been working on. It's a sort of bonbon with a cherry at the center." She handed the headmistress the wax paper package tied with butcher's twine.

"Thank you, dear," Mrs. Farningham took the package and placed it on her desk before standing. "We received a good sum from the charity ball. It was a great success actually, so well done."

"Oh yes? That is good to hear," Thalia exclaimed, clapping her hands together.

The older woman went to the shelves across the room and shuffled through some baskets filled with loose scraps of paper. She finally found what she was looking for, and nodded in satisfaction.

"There it is. Oh, and you received a rather large bouquet as well, my dear." She raised a questioning brow. "It is over there by the window."

She jerked a thumb behind her where several potted plants graced the windowsill. A tall lush display of hothouse flowers was awkwardly shoved in the center of this jungle.

Thalia's mouth opened and then closed again. She had no idea who would have sent her flowers. Unconsciously she put a hand up to check her hair. Mrs. Farningham handed over the paper she held; it was a card made of thick cream paper. Expensive paper. Thalia unfolded it and read the words.

Miss Ward, it was a delight to meet you last evening. When I took a morning walk I saw these lovely blooms, and thought of you. Sir Marville.

Thalia's breath sucked in. Her shoulders instinctually curved inwards as her stomach plummeted to the floor.

"Not a suitor then?" Mrs. Farningham asked. Her thin lips were pinched together, emphasizing the lines around them.

Thalia looked over at the headmistress. She shook her head and crumpled the note in her hand. A shakiness settled into her muscles as she pressed a hand to her chest and struggled for calm. There was no need to panic. Yet.

"Someone I'd rather avoid actually," she answered uncomfortably. "Sir Marville. Do you know him?"

"Oh I certainly do," Mrs. Farningham said, mouth pinched and brows furrowed. "Best to steer clear of the man entirely. There are some dreadful stories."

With ice in her stomach, Thalia forced herself to ask, "What stories?"

Mrs. Farningham sighed, her eyes darting to the door and back to Thalia. She lowered her voice before replying, "He never was a respectful man. He goes about doing as he pleases and suffers no consequences. There was a maid who was forced out after she could no longer hide the child he carried. His child. The girl was all of sixteen. That is not even the worst of the rumors."

Bile rose up in Thalia's throat, along with rage. "And nothing could be done?" Impotent rage burned in her chest.

Mrs. Farningham shook her head, eyes sad and intense. "No. There are no consequences for men like Sir Marville. And you are vulnerable, as an unmarried, unprotected woman. The board will continue to take his money, of course. Nothing I say will sway their opinion. Not when he gives as generously as he does. Promise you will avoid him."

"I will, yes, I promise."

The older woman looked relieved, and patted Thalia's shoulder. "Good. You have always been a smart girl. Now, let's change the subject. Would you like to see the list of donors? We should keep them in mind for future fundraisers. Perhaps send a note of thanks." She picked up a paper off her desk and held it out.

Thalia took it, forcing away the terrible thoughts about Sir Marville, and quickly scanned the names. Many of them were familiar ones; people tended to favor one charity over another and continue to support it for years. Most were eager to build some monument to their supposed selflessness, and a pet project was an excellent avenue.

One name caused her heart to skip a beat: Mr. Campbell Marlow. He had donated fifty pounds, an enormous sum. A small fortune really. Her traitorous mind immediately conjured Mr. Marlow's broad shoulders, and the deep voice that had sent delicious shivers down her spine.

Thalia had wanted to throw herself at him in the garden and feel his strength surrounding her. It was not often that she felt that kind of comfort. Actually, she never felt the comfort of a larger, stronger person holding her. Thalia curled one arm around herself, stricken with an urgent, piercing need. Pathetic.

"Mr. Marlow gave a generous donation. Has he donated before?" she asked.

Mrs. Farningham looked over her shoulder. "Not that I am aware. The duke's estate man?" She asked.

"Yes. I spoke with him last night," Thalia said thoughtfully.

The headmistress gave her a searching look. "Did you now?"

Thalia raised her brows, wary of the older woman's tone. "Yes. But he did not indicate that he meant to donate at all, let alone such a large sum."

"Well, perhaps something enticed him to do so," Mrs. Farningham retorted with a chuckle. She crossed her arms over her boney chest, grinning.

Thalia scowled at her. "I'm sorry to disappoint you, but I did not flirt for coin. Not even for the children."

"Oh tosh, I am teasing you, dear," said Mrs. Faringham. She reached out to pat Thalia's shoulder. "Mr. Marlow is not known to donate to any charity." She tapped her chin in thought. "I honestly did not think him the sort to attend local events. He is not often seen in the village."

"That's what Mena told me."

"So, you were discussing Mr. Marlow with your friends?" The older woman asked gleefully.

Thalia grimaced. "I was simply relaying the details of the ball, not swooning over Mr. Marlow." She rolled her eyes, even as she was currently doing exactly that.

Mrs. Farningham grunted and left the topic alone, though she looked like she did not believe Thalia's defense. Then she was back to shuffling through the papers that littered her desk. It was the headmistress' signal that time for chit chat had ended.

"Thank you, Mrs. Farningham. I will see you at the next board meeting. Good afternoon," Thalia said, heading for the door.

The older woman waved a hand in acknowledgement but kept her spectacled eyes on her papers.

Everyone knew not to cause a delay in Mrs. Farningham's work. The woman was on duty round the clock, tirelessly devoting herself to the children who lived at the orphanage. Though she appeared rather gruff and serious, Mrs. Farningham was a loyal and tender-hearted woman.

Mrs. Farningham had succeeded in running a charity unlike any other in the country. Namely, keeping the church out of the orphanage's affairs. The Anglican church held a lot of power in the country, and she was unique in her preference to align herself with neither branch.

She despised the judgmental preaching, and the depressing quality of the charities they ran. Most served the poorest meals to the children, gave them rags to wear, and struck them—or worse—if they stepped ever so slightly out of line. Other orphanages were gray, lifeless institutions where joy was a sign of sin run rampant.

Children should be silent, still, and serious. Education should be strictly religious, with a heavy emphasis on propriety and shame. And then the children would age out and end up in depressing manual labor jobs that barely kept them off the streets. Many died on those streets mere months later. It was a grim business, being poor.

Instead, Mrs. Farningham had procured funding via selective targeting of fashionable women in the area, women who spent much of their time in London and abroad yet were reliable with their coin. Over time she had freed the orphanage from the control of the Ragged School founders, who had very different ideas about education, and made her own decisions, though still hampered by a board that controlled the bank account. All men, of course.

Leaving the headmistress to her work, Thalia made her way down the hallway, her boot heels clicking on the floor as she headed back to her shop. The late afternoon was their busiest time, and she had several chocolates to set up before closing tonight.

She felt unsettled, both by the strange donation by Mr. Marlow, and by the offensive gift from Sir Marville. Hopefully by simply ignoring the man, he would leave off bothering her and attach himself to someone else. And Mr. Marlow should definitely be ignored as well. Though Thalia wasn't sure what she would do if their paths crossed once again.

A part of her longed to see him again, to have a second chance with his attention on her. At the very least, she wanted to see the man in better lighting, to confirm what she already suspected–that Campbell Marlow was the most handsome man she had ever laid eyes on.

Five

The morning had seemed to drag on as the heat had steadily built. Thalia had spent the earliest hours in the back room, boiling sugar down and then rolling out the candies as they cooled. It was always more difficult in the summer season, because the sweets stayed sticky and hot far longer than it did in the cooler seasons. Thalia had been forced to use extra fine corn flour to keep the finished pieces from clumping back together.

The back door of the shop was open to the alley behind and offered little in the way of a breeze. But the fresh air was still pleasant. Thalia heard the distant church bells calling out the noon hour. She stood and stretched her back, arching until she felt a deep crack in her spine. It was time to take a quick lunch break.

Most days Thalia ran out and grabbed a quick pie from a street vendor. With the current temperature outside, she couldn't quite stomach the idea of a hot meal today though, so she decided to get a cold sandwich from the shop around the corner. If she were really lucky, they might have a watercress and cheese; her personal favorite.

Thalia hung up her work apron, and told Abigail, her shop assistant, that she was ducking out for a bite. Then she went out the back door, as it was a faster walk through the alley. She jumped over an oily puddle and rounded the corner onto the main street. Throngs of people trudged along both sides of the street, and Thalia had to simply jam herself into the crowd. Most of the factories let out their workers at noon for their break, and most people desperately wanted a cold beer.

The sandwich shop was on the next corner. It was a quick in and out, and then she had her sandwich in hand. Sadly, not the watercress, but a cucumber one instead, which was good too.

Thalia stepped down from the shop's door and threaded back into the crowd of people. It took a moment to get through to the alley once she reached it. A procession of school children blocked the way.

Suddenly someone bumped into her with enough force for Thalia to be knocked into the alley and against one of the brick walls. She grunted, but managed to stay upright and keep a hold of her lunch. She looked up, prepared to yell at the offender, but no one was there.

She frowned. How infuriating. She wanted to yell at the person. Huffing, Thalia shook herself off and turned to continue on her way. But a shadow blurred the dim alleyway, and she stopped short. A man became visible. He flashed a smile, before disappearing down the alley in the opposite direction.

Thalia squinted. She was almost sure that it was Sir Marville. A streak of ice-cold terror sliced down her spine, raising the hairs on her neck. She scrambled backwards, fingers dragging along the wall to her right. Once safely at the main street again, she stopped, heart pounding. She looked around, searching for him in the crowd. There was no sight of Sir Marville.

Thalia released the breath she had been holding and tried to calm her racing heart. Surely that hadn't really been Sir Marville. Why on earth would he be hiding in her alleyway?

Thalia forced herself to laugh, though it sounded false to her own ears. Then she went the longer way around to the front door of her shop. She forced a smile to her face, nodding to Abigail, and ate her sandwich sitting at the little table in the back storeroom, after locking the door to the alley. Each bite took an eternity to chew and swallow. Her mouth felt dry, and she was jittery. She got up to double check the lock was secure.

That evening, Thalia closed the front door of the shop with a soft snick. She dropped the brass key into her pocket before turning to the street. At the usual time she closed up, the streets teemed with people heading home from work at the mills and railway yard. She was leaving work far later than she had intended, and was unused to the silence that greeted her.

The full moon offered some assistance as she walked, her pace quick. She was just coming to believe her own assurances that there was nothing to fear when she froze, sensing danger. Heavy footsteps were coming up behind her. A bright knife of fear sliced through her as her heart pounded in her chest.

She spun around to see who it was, her hand raised defensively, gripping the handle of her umbrella. Not a standard weapon, but useful just the same.

"Calm yourself, Miss Ward. You look as though you're fending off rabid wolves," came a deep, velvety voice that she recognized instantly. Ever fiber of her being instantly relaxed, understanding she was safe now. Safe with him.

It was then Thalia realized how utterly ridiculous she looked, her raised arms out in front of her, wielding an umbrella of all things. Fending off wolves indeed. Perhaps it was just one wolf who was prowling tonight, she thought. Lowering the weapon, she eyed the large man standing nearby. They were alone in the shadows once again, her inner desire come to life.

"Good evening, Mr. Marlow. I was startled to see anyone on the street. It was certainly nothing personal, I assure you," she said, cheeks warming beneath his perceptive gaze.

"Are you only just leaving work at this hour?" He frowned, looking concerned.

"Yes, I am. Unfortunately, it took much longer than expected to complete my work. I don't make it a habit to stay out so late. I like my sleep, and know I'll be sorry for this in the morning." She smiled, struggling to control her joy at seeing him again.

She wondered what Mr. Marlow would think of an independent woman running her business her own way, beholden to no one. She could see a gleam in his eyes, though whether it was due to approval or laughter she couldn't say. She hoped it was approval, but she had been disappointed time and time again.

Most men thought of her shop as an adorable child's game she played, and they enjoyed her concoctions, but didn't take her seriously. And then there were the others. The men who viewed her as a threat; an unhealthy example for other women and girls who might dare to dream of a life of their own. These men were dangerous and she had learned to be careful.

"It is rather late to be out walking alone. It is hardly appropriate," Mr. Marlow chided, the playful arch of his eyebrow threatening to buckle her knees.

Thalia took a steadying breath, determined not to be a ninny. She raised a brow and couldn't help but laugh at that. "You are welcome to walk me home if you are so concerned, sir." She strove to not appear over-eager.

Daring to hold his gaze, Thalia watched as a lop-sided grin appeared on his face. The effect was alarming in its seductive power. The man didn't seem the sort to waste his displays of emotion, and he had chosen to give her one of his few smiles. Her entire body was warm and tingling, threatening to melt into a puddle right there on the street.

"I would be happy to escort you, though only if you would tell me more about your business, Miss Ward," he said.

He stepped closer, offering his arm. Thalia entwined her arm, battling the blush burning her cheeks. Would he notice? His arm was hard and muscled beneath his coat, and she could smell his spiced cologne, along with the faint scent of gin. She wanted to know everything about the man, but he had asked about her work.

Focus, Thalia, she chided herself.

"I shall be happy to indulge your curiosity," she said. "I was making a special chocolate for Lady Whitehall's upcoming garden party. She desired something unique that would be something of a signature delight. I had to rework the recipe several times before I got it right. And now the chocolates must set for some hours before they will be ready to box—otherwise we would be risking a large and unappetizing mess."

They walked along and had made several turns before Thalia realized that Mr. Marlow was leading her home. She hadn't told him where she lived, had she? Her mind felt fuzzy with exhaustion, and her feet throbbed with each step. Why must the boarding house be so bloody far away? Thalia had to work against Mr. Marlow's natural gravitational pull. He was strong and warm, and she longed to lean into him. Damn the man for being so alluring.

"May I ask what the final result tastes like?" he asked.

Thalia was confused, having completely forgotten what they had been talking about. She looked up at him, questioning. Mr. Marlow raised his brows, his eyes looked her over, taking in the dark circles under her eyes. He frowned again.

"You need to rest, Miss Ward," he said, his voice soft but with an edge of concern.

Thalia laughed, exhaustion making her feel a bit mad. "I intend to fall into bed immediately upon entry of my home," she assured him, lifting her free hand to pat his arm mockingly.

Their gazes held, and Thalia felt momentarily dazed by the sight of Mr. Marlow as a streetlamp illuminated his face. Her breath caught as she took in the sharp lines and angles of his nose and jaw, the cheeks covered in dark stubble. His warm, honey-colored eyes were framed by thick, black lashes. No man had a right to eyes like that. Nor should a man have such full lips.

Why was she thinking about Mr. Marlow's lips? Thalia shook herself, realizing they had stopped walking and were standing still together in the street. She looked away, and saw that the boarding house was within sight.

"Almost there," she said brightly, and began walking again, pulling him along as she still clutched his arm, reluctant to let go.

They made their way to the front door. The hall light still burned, which meant that she could still get something to eat from the kitchen. Thalia glanced up at her window reflexively, and then back at Mr. Marlow. Suddenly feeling a bit awkward, she smiled and released him, clasping her hands in front of her. If she invited him in, how would he respond?

Stop it, you ninny.

"Thank you so much for the escort home, Mr. Marlow," she said brightly.

He looked at her with an inscrutable expression, but those eyes held such an intensity that it nearly took Thalia's breath away. He looked as though he might consume her body and soul.

Then he leaned closer until his body was mere inches from hers. "Good evening, Miss Ward." His breath fanned her ear, sending goosebumps spreading across her skin.

"It was lovely to see you again," she heard herself say; her breathless voice betrayed her reaction to him. There was something primal about her body's reaction to this man. And he likely wouldn't give her a second thought the moment this interaction was over. How utterly embarrassing.

* * *

Campbell watched Miss Ward shut the door behind her, pierced by a deep regret that he had to let her go. She was a beautiful woman and she positively lit up when she spoke of her work. He would bet his entire bank account that she was passionate in all activities she pursued. Unfortunately, he did not consider it wise to seduce a local shop owner, no matter how much he wanted to. He would simply have to be satisfied to have had a chance to see her again.

Walking past her shop on his way back to the estate had not been entirely intentional, his feet had seemed to carry him here of their own accord. And he certainly hadn't expected Miss Ward to still be at work. It had been enough to imagine peering into the darkened window, to see a little slice of her world. But stealing a moment alone with her again was a pleasant surprise, and he was thankful he had been called to the village on estate business when he had.

"Sleep well, Miss Ward," he said softly to the closed door. Regret tore at him, urging him to find an excuse to see her again, to give in to whatever it was that drew him to her. It was an irresistible pull he didn't understand, and was afraid to ponder too deeply.

The sight of Miss Ward in her prim, striped work dress was far more seductive than her ball gown had been. The row of tiny buttons that went up to the base of her throat had sent his mind reeling with images of slowly undoing each clasp, revealing her smooth creamy skin as he went. Something about a sensible dress made him wild. Cam wondered how her golden hair would look spread across his pillows.

He definitely had to be careful about Miss Ward. If only he could convince himself to forget her. Shaking his head ruefully, Campbell continued to walk on to the nearby inn, where his horse awaited him.

Six

This was not forgetting Miss Ward. This was the exact opposite of that. Campbell inwardly kicked himself, but did not break stride as he approached the small confectionary.

He had laid in bed without sleeping all night and was feeling disoriented. He was a person who liked a strict schedule, thriving on routine. And now his routine was thrown off by a woman who worked for a living. Had the world turned upside down?

The tidy little shop was located on the main street that cut through the center of the village. Most nearby buildings were Tudor style and had maintained their classic brown and white face through the centuries. But the confectionery was in the middle of a modern brick row with a wide glass window for display. A jaunty wooden sign hung above the door.

Last night he hadn't been able to properly see it, but the large front window featured an array of cavorting animals in a lush green field of spun sugar. Had Miss Ward done it all herself? It was impressive, showing off her skill and artistry.

Cam paused, feeling oddly nervous, and peered into the window before pushing open the door. A little bell rang, signaling his entry. The shop was empty, save for Miss Ward who stood behind a gleaming counter.

She was wiping her hands on a cloth, humming softly to herself, and assessing a tray of misshapen brown lumps. At the sounds of the bell she looked up. Her brows raised slightly, her lips parted in surprise, but she quickly recovered and smiled.

Cam let the door shut behind him and stood there uncertainly. He wasn't even sure why he had come, when all logic demanded he stay away. But when she saw him and smiled broadly, he felt it–the pull of her. Miss Ward was pure sunshine, and it called to his dark and cynical soul. He wanted to bask in her warmth, even if it could only be for a fleeting moment.

He drank in the sight of Miss Ward in her plain dark blue skirt and a crisp white blouse, covered with a clean white apron. Her hair was pulled back into a simple twisted arrangement. She looked much like any other working woman, and yet something about her was special. Different. In her wide blue eyes, there was genuine warmth as she regarded him.

"Good morning, Miss Ward." His deep voice sounded too loud in a space that was filled from floor to ceiling with fragile glass jars. A figurative bull in a china shop.

"Good morning, Mr. Marlow." Miss Ward's smile grew, revealing twin dimples in her rounded cheeks. "I was wondering when you might come in for a visit."

Was she flirting with him, Cam wondered. Her eyes danced with mischief as he cautiously approached.

She looked delightful with her cheeks pink from exertion, tendrils of hair flying free from her tight chignon. As she wiped her hands on the apron, chocolate smeared across the white cloth. She was more alive here at work than she had been at a fancy ball. What a curious woman.

Along the wall behind the counter were mirrored shelves. With white paint and a large front window, the shop was bright and almost clinical. The air smelled sugary with a hint of lemon.

"Would you believe it if I said that I was here to buy my favorite sweet?" he asked with a friendly smile, as he leaned against the counter on his elbow.

Cam hoped that she couldn't guess the indecent direction of his thoughts. People generally accused him of being hard to read, so at least there was some comfort in that.

Miss Ward narrowed her eyes and shook her head in mock severity.

"Somehow I do doubt that," she said tartly, but the color creeping onto her cheeks belied her tone.

Then she pulled a covered dish from beneath the counter. "But I did make these first thing this morning. It was a guess." She removed the cloth cover, revealing a wealth of small round yellow disks. Butterscotch sweets.

Cam was speechless, blindsided by her uncanny ability to guess correctly. He had long ago lost his taste for sweets and desserts, but there was one boyhood favorite that he occasionally savored. No one else knew about this practice.

Cam realized that he was staring. He wasn't at all sure what to make of this.

She smiled uncertainly at him. "This is rather embarrassing, but I figured it was just a matter of time before I bumped into you again. And these came to mind." She gestured at the sweets.

He reached for one of the small candies and popped it into his mouth. Smooth sweet lusciousness filled his senses, and he closed his eyes briefly against the pleasant assault.

The taste brought back memories of a warm kitchen. His mother, smiling and doting upon him and his brother, insisting they have an extra sweet. For being such good and lovely boys, she had said. Then reality would hit when his father returned home, enraged at the waste of money on luxuries.

The sugar turned bitter on his tongue at the memory of the smack of heavy fists against his fragile mother's body, her struggling to constrain her cries of pain. Intense emotion threatened to swamp him, and he almost choked on the lump in his throat.

All at once, through some strange mix of emotion and physical need for connection, he felt a need to kiss Miss Ward. Cam closed the distance between them and placed one hand on the counter behind Miss Ward's back. His thumb brushed against her trim waist. Her gaze was fixed on his mouth, her chin angled up in invitation.

"You guessed correctly," he said softly.

Her eyes had darkened with desire. Slowly he lowered his head, and brushed his lips against hers, just barely touching. Then again, before settling more firmly, giving her plenty of time to decide if she wanted it too. Miss Ward brought her hands up to settle on his shoulders with a sigh and leaned into him, pressing her lush body against his. With incredible control, he forced himself to keep his hands on the counter and off of Miss Ward.

He wanted to haul her body against his and show her his rampant desire. His mind conjured an image of Thalia seated upon her clean countertop, skirts up at her thighs, spread before him, begging him to fill her. He wanted that dream to be real, and knew he needed to stop this insanity now or else he would lose control.

Cam never lost control. He prided himself on that. What about this woman affected him so?

Cam broke the kiss and stepped back to put distance between them. Miss Ward's expression was a bit dazed, her red swollen lips were parted slightly. Her tongue darted out to wet them. Cam very nearly kissed her again. The sound of their breathing filled the electric silence.

Cam attempted to affect a relaxed posture, causally sliding his hands into his trouser pockets—mostly to keep them where they belonged.

"My apologies, Miss Ward," he said carefully, retreating to the safety of formality. "I should not have assaulted you so."

She choked out a laugh, pressing a hand to her chest. "Calm yourself, Mr. Marlow, I am hardly going to demand you marry me," she reassured him, eyes fairly twinkling in mischievous delight.

Cam felt an absurd stab of regret. "I have no intention of doing so, Miss Ward. We haven't come even close to necessitating such an act." *Yet*, he had almost added.

She seemed to share his inner dialogue for a moment, as her gaze grew heated. Slowly her eyes traveled over his form, her lips curving up in open appreciation. Perhaps he had misjudged Miss Ward; she could play the seductress well enough. Maybe she had in the past. For some reason that thought bothered him, though he knew it was a ridiculously hypocritical idea. It was not as though he had lived the life of a monk.

"I see. Well, I am perfectly content as I am, and do not desire a husband in the slightest," she replied airily.

Miss Ward smiled confidently, but no humor lit her eyes. She turned and walked around the counter to busy herself with some task, effectively dismissing him.

Cam looked at her with growing frustration. She behaved as though the kiss hadn't affected her at all. He found that he actually wanted her to care, but knew that it was unfair of him to feel that way. He couldn't and wouldn't marry her; therefore he should leave her be and stop acting like an idiot. So why couldn't he bring himself to take his leave?

"You don't require a man at all?" He smirked, fully aware that he was trying to goad her.

"Not at all," she replied, affixing him with a look that defied him to prove her wrong.

Lord, how he wanted to show her what men were most useful for, but he held himself in control. He settled for a lazy smile that caused the heat in her cheeks to bloom larger and spread to her ears. Her gaze traveled down to his lips, lingering there.

"Perhaps when you grow tired of living in a boarding house, and working on your feet all day, you may regret your choice not to settle down," he returned, thinking of how he would resent living so simply. But he quickly realized his mistake.

Miss Ward's mouth tightened, and her eyes grew cold.

"I assure you, sir, that I can provide myself anything I require," she clipped, fiddling with the tray of butterscotches.

Cam frowned, struggling with a perverse urge to argue with her. "You could buy a house, but you prefer to live in a boarding house?" He raised a brow skeptically.

What was he doing? It was past time to leave.

Miss Ward looked up, her nostrils flared in warning. "Yes, I do. I live as I wish, Mr. Marlow."

He had made a real mess of things.

"Indeed." Cam shoved his hands into his pockets. "Well, I won't keep you any longer, Miss Ward. Enjoy your afternoon." He donned his hat and strolled out of the shop without looking back.

His stomach churned with frustration. Like Icarus, he had flown too close to the sun and was suffering the consequences of his arrogance. Hopefully this incident would cure him of his bizarre fixation. It was certainly a reminder to listen to his logical mind rather than another organ, no matter how insistent it was.

* * *

Rain pattered on the window glass, but the night air was still warm and the added humidity was stifling. The window was stuck closed, as it always was during a storm. The wood swelled and any effort to force it open could damage the old casings.

Clementine had unbuttoned the top of her bodice and hiked up her skirts to her knees for relief. She sat on Thalia's bed, leaning back on the headboard with her legs splayed out like a rag-doll. It had been a long day of organizing for her; it was campaign season and the local elections were set for two weeks hence. Clem would not have a good night's sleep until after the vote counts.

Mena sat in the spare chair and read aloud from a book about dog breeding—her favorite topic—which her friends endeavored to suffer through because they appreciated her, and because her voice was very soothing. It was relaxing to listen to Mena wax poetic about the virtues of the Labrador and Scottish terrier.

Laying back on across the foot of the bed, Thalia stared blindly at the ceiling. She was bone weary, but had to get up and do yet more work again soon. It never ended. She needed to remember to wash her stockings later. Just one more task on a long, never-ending list, which included finding a venue to host the musicale she was planning for the orphanage.

The friends gathered together in Thalia's room at the boarding house most evenings, as it was the only space where they were free from fatherly oversight. Both Clem and Mena lived at home with their fathers, Mena's a minister, and Clem's a doctor. While they often hosted dinners, the friends all agreed that the privacy of Thalia's rooms made for a better regular meeting spot.

They each had busy lives, and as they grew older they had made this a regular appointment. As a fierce Suffragette and activist, Clementine often brought work with her and would practice speeches with her friends. It was highly unlike her to be doing something as mundane as embroidery, but she was deftly stabbing her way through an elaborate anatomical design, claiming it helped her think. Thalia often brought home sweets, but today her pockets had been empty. Mena, ever calm and contained, had brought thick slices of a homemade cake and a book on dogs.

"You seem distracted," Clem observed, interrupting Mena mid-sentence.

Clementine stabbed at the embroidery project she held. She was making some unsightly orange and blue flowers on a handkerchief as a gift for her father. Her winged black eyebrows were furrowed in concentration, and she growled periodically as she worked.

"Hmm?" Thalia murmured dreamily.

She was lost in the memory of her delicious kiss with Mr. Marlow, Campbell. The idea of using his first name caused a stir of excitement throughout her body. She couldn't stop thinking about that kiss and felt positively effervescent with delight. The way his lips had felt on hers, the warmth of his skin, it was impossible not to be distracted by the memory. He had kissed her!

Clem laid her embroidery on her lap and considered her friend with narrow-eyed suspicion. A slow grin spread across her heart-shaped face, a wicked gleam in her eyes. "You are thinking about a man!" She crowed triumphantly.

Thalia startled, her eyes darting back and forth between her friends to gauge their expressions. "I am not." She tried to laugh derisively, but had a sinking feeling that no one was convinced.

"Who is he?" Clem demanded. Once her full attention was targeted on something she would never let it go without ferreting out the truth. She had the focus and tenacity of a rat terrier.

Thalia groaned, and buried her face in her hands. "Mr. Marlow," she mumbled through her fingers.

"Why do I remember that name?" Clem asked.

"He's the duke's estate manager, right?" Mena asked, her soft voice belied her enthusiastic curiosity.

"Yes, that's the one," Thalia said. She lowered her hands and felt a fierce blush creeping up to flame her cheeks.

"Don't be embarrassed, love!" Clem exclaimed. "Though I demand to know every detail of what occurred that is causing you to blush so fiercely."

Mena nodded vigorously in agreement and leaned forward eagerly in order to catch every word.

Thalia sighed. "Very well…I met him while walking home the other night, and I suggested that he visit the shop. And he did. The very next morning."

"He must have been unable to stop thinking about you, Thalia," Mena said. Her normally plain countenance was lit with excitement and humor, transforming her entirely. She was truly beautiful in these moments when she was not hiding her thoughts. A thick braid of chestnut hair lay over her shoulder and down almost to her waist.

"He's certainly not playing hard-to-get," Clem agreed, her eyebrows raised in surprise.

"Well, I'm not sure that I'm driving him wild, but he did kiss me," Thalia admitted. Her cheeks burned more fiercely. Clem and Mena fairly screamed in delight.

"Was it good?" That was Clem's foremost concern, of course. She was always one to get right to the point.

Sighing in resignation, Thalia raised her eyes to the ceiling. "I enjoyed it, yes," she replied, "But it was very brief—not a grand, passionate kiss. I suspect that Mr. Marlow did not intend at all to do it, and he rushed to apologize afterwards."

She worried her lower lip with her teeth, thinking over the event with fresh perspective. Perhaps he had made an impulsive mistake, and she was a complete fool for mooning over him. He had probably forgotten all about it by now.

"Animal attraction," Mena reminded them, nodding her head resolutely.

"If he acted on such impulse, then I would say you are driving him wild," Clem agreed.

"If you say so," Thalia said with a soft chuckle. She still could not imagine why a glorious specimen of a man like Mr. Marlow would possibly be interested in her. "I don't think it would be wise to pursue this particular animal though. It would be so incredibly awkward afterwards if it did not work out."

"Why?" Clem asked, characteristically unwilling to concede defeat in any form. The woman was the very definition of the word stubborn. "You would be able to avoid ever seeing him again quite easily. He rarely comes into town, and you don't visit the pub."

This was true, Thalia admitted to herself. It gave her mind all the encouragement it needed to start daydreaming. Just as long as she kept her heart strictly under lock and key, perhaps she could indulge in a little mischief with a tall, dark almost-stranger. Bless her friends for being such bad influences. She resolved to neither pursue nor avoid Mr. Marlow in the future, and simply see where this led. She could use a little fun, after all. Life was short.

"Well...perhaps it might not be such a terrible indulgence after all," she ventured with a little smile.

$\mathcal{O}\!eff\!even$

wo weeks later, it was Thalia's turn to lead the children's Tuesday calisthenics exercises at St. James' Orphanage. She shared the duty with a rotating staff of other volunteers, and usually took the final Tuesday of the month. The summer was coming to a close, but the heat hadn't yet dissipated. It lingered, weighing everything down and slowing life to a sluggish crawl.

The children were laughing as they went through the motions of their morning exercises. They loved these mornings spent moving their bodies in the fresh air, excising their typically bottled-up energies. They grew frustrated and fidgety as they sat for long hours in their schoolroom memorizing numbers and bible passages.

It was not at all uncommon for a child to be punished when they could not contain their natural urge to move about, when their instructor insisted that they sit still and silent. The weather never seemed to slow them down, and they especially loved their visits from Miss Ward, with her covertly distributed sweets.

Thalia was also feeling freer now, both due to the movement and the company of the smiling children. After waiting in vain for another visit from Mr. Marlow that hadn't come, disappointment had settled in, dampening her spirit. She had really wanted a different outcome, one without this stinging embarrassment at being tossed aside yet again. But who could be sad when surrounded by delightful children?

When they had finished the exercise routine, Thalia wiped her forehead on the loose sleeve of her muslin dress. She was thirsty and called the children to form a line and follow her into the coolness of the brick building of the orphanage for a much-needed drink. She led them down the long dark entrance hall and into the cafeteria.

Thankfully, Clem and Mena were both there helping to put out a luncheon for the children. They laughed when they saw the bright pink cheeks and damp hair of the children as they filed in, led by an equally pink and damp Thalia. Mena handed her a glass of water, which she took gratefully and drank down in three long gulps.

Thalia waved goodbye to the children and headed up to the main staircase, toward the offices. She wanted to check in with Mrs. Farningham and discuss her latest idea for a musical event. She was eager to begin the first implementation of her project to expose the children to new artistic experiences and had found a way to combine them with a fundraiser for the orphanage. They could sell tickets to people in town and invite them to listen along with the children. The event could raise a lot of funds for future musical experiences, as well as provide the money needed to pay an art instructor.

As she rounded the corner on the third floor where the offices were, she ran—quite literally—into Sir Marville. He held a sheaf of papers under his right arm and was using an ornate walking stick in his left. Thalia bumped into his tall frame, ending up squashing her breasts against his firm chest. She immediately recoiled, embarrassed and horrified.

"Oh, I am so sorry!" She yelped, jumping back away from him.

Her hands went to her face, burning hot with a fierce blush. A satisfied smile slowly grew on his face, doing little to bring warmth to his cold, yet handsome features. He did not seem apologetic in the least. Thalia fought back a rising nausea, still unconvinced that she hadn't seen him in the alley. Was he following her about?

"No apology necessary, Miss Ward. I cannot bring myself to regret running into you like this," he said. Thalia heard the not-so-subtle innuendo in his words. "I hope you weren't injured."

His hand stretched toward her, and Thalia jerked herself back another step to avoid his touch. She smiled thinly.

"I am perfectly hale and hearty. Not to worry," she said firmly, and quickly sidestepped him to continue down the hall. "Good day, Sir Marville," she called, moving quickly.

Thankfully he let her pass without attempting to stop her, though he called after her. "Until we meet again, Miss Ward."

Thalia suppressed a shudder. She wished that she could avoid this man forever, though somehow she knew he would be back.

When she reached the Mrs. Farningham's office door, she knocked while entering. There was no time for formalities when avoiding unsettling men. The office smelled like soup and old books. There was something oddly comforting about that, though Thalia didn't particularly like soup or old books. Maybe it was because the homey scent brought to mind rainy days spent in the library with family.

Thalia's childhood home had not had a library, but a girl could use her imagination, nonetheless. Her father had been an avid collector of Greek history texts, which he had kept in stacks around the family sitting room. A familiar ache bloomed in her chest at the memory, and she quickly pushed it aside.

The headmistress sat behind her desk, eating lunch with one hand while scribbling in a ledger with the other. Never a spare moment. Her lunch looked rather paltry: a plate of fruit and a hunk of bread to accompany a small bowl of soup.

"Good morning, ma'am. You are looking ravishing, as usual," Thalia said brightly. Her blood still rushed loudly in her ears from the encounter in the hallway but she was genuinely comforted to see the older woman.

"Good morning, dear," Mrs. Farningham responded without bothering to look up, her tone warm but distracted.

"What's troubling you today?" Thalia approached the desk and cocked her head to try and see the ledger.

The older woman huffed out a breath, stirring the loose hairs framing her face. "Debts to the grocer and butcher. Unfortunately, we are running up quite a tally. However, we are saving on coal as this weather has been unusually warm. The children have not complained about being cold at night, which is a relief after that damp spring we had."

Mrs. Farningham closed the ledger with a firm snap and laid it aside. She interlaced her fingers and placed them on the desk before her. Her bright gray eyes peered at Thalia over her spectacles, narrowed and waiting. Thalia clearly wanted something.

"Well, I'm quite sure we will settle those debts soon, because I have an idea!" Thalia announced, deciding not to draw it out this time.

"I'm sure you do," came the tart reply, a thin smile playing at the corners of Mrs. Farningham's mouth.

It was not surprising why many people found the headmistress intimidating, but Thalia knew how tender she was beneath the tough exterior. It was Mrs. Farningham who had taken Thalia under her wing after her parents' death, helping her find a path out of the all consuming grief. The older woman was like a surrogate mother to her now.

Thalia smiled cheerfully. "You love my ideas, admit it."

Mrs. Farningham lowered her chin, clearly trying to hide her growing smile.

"Often I do, that is true, dear," she allowed. "Go on and tell me about this new one of yours then."

"Well, I was thinking about hosting a musicale here at the orphanage. We could invite people from the village to purchase the tickets and come hear an evening of wonderful music. The children would attend, of course, and would be enriched by the experience. After the ball at Lady Berwick's, this would be the best place to begin our plan to introduce the children to these new ideas and opportunities."

Mrs. Farningham absorbed this without comment. She was silent for a moment, and then nodded firmly. "Yes, I do like this idea, Thalia. Very good. Let's move forward with a plan to host this event at the end of the month. Would a Thursday or a Friday evening be best, do you think?"

Thalia smiled, relieved. "A Thursday early evening would be an excellent time to hold the event. We should also serve refreshments. Perhaps we could get some of our benefactors to supply those for us as a donation. Those individuals could donate in lieu of purchasing a ticket, and then come with their families. We could even put their names on a sign to thank them and spread word of their generosity. People do love to have their name on philanthropic endeavors," she finished dryly.

Mrs. Farningham snorted in response, but she was still nodding thoughtfully. "Yes, this is an excellent idea, Thalia. I heartily approve. Would Lady Berwick be interested in donating something, do you suppose?"

"I'm sure she could be persuaded. She does love to advertise her good deeds, and being the center of attention as well. And she has a French chef," Thalia responded. She made a mental note to pay Lady Berwick a visit in the near future.

"Who else could we bring in on this" Mrs. Farningham tapped her chin in thought. "Sir Marville would be likely interested. He seems very ambitious to make some waves in local society. I don't know if there's any stopping him from offering, should he hear of this." She speared Thalia with a bleak look.

Thalia suppressed a shudder at the mention of that name. "Yes, he did seem eager to be of support to the orphanage when we spoke at Lady Berwick's ball."

She swiftly changed the subject. Who else did she know who could be tapped for support? Thalia didn't exactly move in big circles in town and knew almost no one with such extra income. A face flashed in her mind, and she immediately seized on the idea.

"I was considering asking the Duke of Bedford," Thalia blurted out. She swallowed, and forced herself to continue. "His grace has visited my shop before, though I wouldn't dare assume he would remember me. Oh, but since I had the pleasure of meeting Mr. Marlow, his grace's estate manager at the ball, we could lean on that acquaintance. He seemed very interested."

She tucked an errant curl behind her ear, averting her eyes from the headmistress's critical gaze. She felt exposed, and worried that her fixation with Mr. Marlow was somehow transparent to Mrs. Farningham.

"It would be most wonderful to have a duke involved! Think of how much good publicity it would be to have a duke here supporting our cause." Mrs. Farningham was almost bouncing in her seat with excitement. "We should invite the press, Get photographs."

The older woman never got so animated, and Thalia felt proud to have been the cause. It was a good idea, and it could pay off the debts as well. It was wonderful to be a part of this admirable establishment, which was so unlike other public institutions throughout the country. And it would put to rest the idea of drawing on Sir Marville's support.

Most orphans could only expect to receive a cursory handout from the parish. They would be forced to wear rags and eat less than starvation portions while being beaten and worked to exhaustion. And then one day they were kicked out onto the streets.

Life at St. James' Orphanage was a bit more progressive. The children wore better clothes, though still a uniform of dreary gray, and ate far better than at other institutions. They also each had their own beds, which not all orphanages could boast. They had their weekly exercise class outside and did not have to perform dull tasks all day to turn a profit for their bread.

'Knowledge is power' was Mrs. Farningham's favorite saying. In many ways she dared not be too outspoken in her progressivism, or she could easily incur the wrath of the church or worse, the gentry. After all, the orphanage was under the control of a board of directors, all of whom were local aristocracy.

With the increasing number of factories springing up, more people were moving in and having children. Inevitably there was a rise in children given over to the care of the parish. Mrs. Farningham struggled to cover all the costs as the number of mouths increased. The pressure to give up her independence, and conform to the standard set by the other children's homes and workhouses, grew stronger by the month, as sure as the vendor's bills.

Thalia glanced at the pocket watch she carried and was surprised to see that it had gotten so late.

"I'd best be off, ma'am," she said. "Enjoy your lunch."

Mrs. Farningham waved her off and turned back to her ledger.

As Thalia walked down the hall, she thought about how she was going to gain the duke's assistance with the musicale. The only way forward was to prevail upon her acquaintance with Mr. Marlow, which would be awkward, although the excuse to see him again was too good to pass up. Little butterflies flew around her stomach when she thought of it.

Now she just had to decide how to hunt the man down.

Eight

Campbell and Garrett sat in their usual comfortable chairs in the estate library, relaxing after a long day of labor; for one of them anyways. Cam had been busy visiting the tract of land currently being converted over to the new drainage system, and then had to go to the chalk mine, which was having problems with flooding. It seemed that most of his time was spent diverting water around the property to more advantageous locations.

He had worked his body to exhaustion in an attempt to get his mind off of that kiss. His thoughts had returned again and again to Miss Ward. Thalia. Her lush curves and soft, sweet lips were driving him mad. He found himself growing distracted and unfocused, and it was starting to affect his work. Most of last night was spent rewriting ledgers that he had added wrongly.

Campbell had never found himself in such a state before. Maybe he had gone too long without female companionship. Yes, surely that was the problem. When was the last time he had gone to London? He could surely excise this obsession with a dalliance with an experienced courtesan. Miss Ward was just an artless country lass, after all.

He was determined to not think of Miss Ward again. He would put her out of mind. Starting now.

The problem was that he burned with an intense lust he'd never experienced before. It was a little worrying to be honest, how much he wanted her. He was tempted to give into his urges but knew that he would be filled with self-loathing for fucking her and then leaving to pursue another. Besides, a small part of him was concerned that he wouldn't be satisfied with one taste of Miss Ward.

"Ducks," Garrett's voice cut through Cam's brain fog, startling him out of his musings.

"What about them?" Cam asked, confused.

Garrett raised a brow and sipped his whiskey.

"You haven't been listening, clearly," he said, using his Duke voice; the deep and authoritative one. It typically cowed the listener, but Cam wasn't falling for it.

"No, your grace, I have rather a lot on my mind," Cam responded sardonically.

"We need to think about new ventures for the tenants, and everyone in London was talking of ducks. And butter. Apparently, some of our neighbors are making money hand over fist," Garrett said, sounding a little sullen.

Cam's mouth quirked, which was the equivalent of an eye roll, coming from him.

"Yes, well, we can tackle that idea once we are done with the irrigation problem. We should consider digging a third canal along the western edge of the field, in order to divert the coming spring rains. It would hopefully increase the harvest from that particular parcel tenfold, and barley prices are still holding firm for now," Campbell said flatly.

He considered the paper he held; a list of farming projects that needed doing this year in order to head off trouble. Everything had changed since the expansion of the railroads. And then the Americans had invented the refrigerated railcar, which gave them the ability to ship their meat across the world for very little cost. New Zealand was sending in cheap lamb, undercutting local wool prices as well. Russia was supplying wheat and other grains. Gone were the advantages of the local farmers, and they were now having to consider big changes. Or give up and go into manufacturing, as so many people were.

"My God, I am sick to death of discussing drainage!" Garrett declared, throwing himself dramatically back into his chair. "Couldn't we discuss the ducks instead? They are infinitely more interesting. Or even cows. I would love to discuss them!"

Cam snorted and laid his list aside. "I have nothing to say on either of those two topics. If you are seriously interested in ducks, I'll look into it."

"Well then, cottage repairs?" Garrett asked hopefully.

"I have a meeting with the tenants coming up this week to discuss the rents and any necessary repairs." Cam refilled his glass with the expensive amber liquid.

Garrett sighed, disappointed. He sat back up and took a long drink, emptying his glass. "Estate business is dreadfully boring, Campbell. We could talk about London instead. You should have come with me!"

Cam took a long swallow of whiskey and relished the burn as it slid down his throat. He tried to force his mind to stay on topic, but at the mention of London he felt the irresistible pull of

Miss Ward. He definitely should have gone with Garrett to London rather than kissing local shopkeepers.

With a low growl, he reminded himself to stay focused on his goals. Dalliances with local shopkeepers might be fun, they weren't going to help him get any nearer to his goal of securing a titled bride.

Garrett looked over the rim of his glass at his friend, an assessing look in his eyes. He rested his glass on his knee, with a knowing smirk.

"How was your visit with Miss Ward?" he asked casually.

"What makes you think I paid her a visit?" Cam asked, striving for a bored tone, and hoping that his friend couldn't see right through him.

Unfortunately, it appeared that Garret could, for he chuckled to himself, clearly disbelieving, and took a long drink from his expensive crystal glass.

Cam shifted uncomfortably in his chair. "I am not trying to get her into my bed, Garrett," he snapped.

The duke raised his hands defensively. "Of course not, you are simply becoming a connoisseur of chocolates all of a sudden and want me to share in your hedonistic tendencies. It really is unbecoming of you, my friend. Now, tell me all about this woman and her obviously ample charms." He grinned widely and crossed his arms.

Cam knew it was no use denying his attraction to the woman, and there was no way out of this conversation now. Sighing, he rested his head back against his chair, and closed his eyes in resignation.

"Miss Ward is very pretty. She is also most likely an innocent, and is beyond my reach."

Garrett snorted, "Please, no woman is beyond your reach. It is quite annoying being your friend, you know. Women only come to me when you are otherwise engaged. It is most annoying."

Cam knew Garrett was mostly whining for effect, as he always seemed to attract his fair share of attention.

"I meant that she is not someone to dally with. She is the marrying type."

Garrett mock shuddered at that. He often waxed poetic about his complete abhorrence of the idea of marriage. He intended to leave his money and property to his second cousin, and never produce his own heirs. Cam had never discovered why this was so, but he respected his friend's privacy. After all, Cam wasn't exactly forthcoming about his own upbringing. He rubbed his chin, distracted by memories calling from the shadows of his mind. Skin prickling, Cam forced his hand away, battling the sudden urge to run.

"I might change my mind on the whole 'not marrying thing' if Miss Ward were to be the bride though," Garrett mused.

There was a devilish glint in his eye as he waited for Cam's reaction.

Cam shot his friend a sharp warning look, which made Garrett burst out laughing.

"My God, you do like her, don't you!"

"It's not like that," Cam protested, taking a drink.

"The hell it's not."

"Forget I ever mentioned her."

"Fine," Garret relented, pouring another round of drinks. "Now tell me, when shall we begin drawing up the marriage contracts?"

Cam glowered into his glass. He knew Garrett would never leave off teasing him about this now.

"I am not pursuing Miss Ward," Cam slammed his glass down rather loudly on the small table between their chairs. He rolled his shoulders to ease the tension building up there. "Let's finalize plans for the party you are hosting." He grinned at Garrett's unhappy frown.

"Very well, but if one of those husband hunters tries to corner me, you must promise to intervene. I'll not end up with a duchess by the end of the weekend," Garrett demanded.

"I thought that perhaps your sister could be prevailed upon to play hostess. It would be a nice buffer between you and those marriage-minded mamas," Cam suggested reasonably.

His aim was to trap a wife himself, so he could hardly fault women for having the same plans. Garrett was a catch - wealthy, titled, handsome, and in possession of all his teeth and limbs; not an easy find these days. But he would feel guilty for causing Garrett unhappiness, and so he would help ensure some protection.

Garrett was already shaking his head at the idea, however.

"No way in hell am I inviting Claire here. The woman is a sharp-tongued harpy. It would hardly help you gain a bride with her flying around insulting everyone," Garrett said flatly.

"She is not," Cam protested. The duke could be a perfect jackass when he wanted to be. Then an idea struck. "It is important to have a hostess...I suppose we could ask your mother. Shall I write to her?" he asked innocently.

Garrett practically fell out of his chair. "Don't you dare! I'll write to Claire," he scrambled to say, spilling whiskey in the process.

Cam wasn't sure what Garrett's relationship with his sister was like these days, despite having seen the two siblings together on several occasions over the years. Lady Claire Sumner was certainly willful, but she was lovely and fun. Surely, she would be a wonderful hostess, as she was trained to be from birth. Perhaps she was in league with Garrett's mother to leg shackle her brother; that would certainly explain his hostility.

Either way, it was hardly Cam's concern. Garrett could be as dramatic as he liked, but Cam needed a bride and he needed Lady Claire's help to gain one. So he wouldn't feel badly at all about his manipulation. Every ambitious man had to use manipulation from time to time. Morality was a relative concept, after all.

Nine

am should have been helping dig the new drainage trench, but instead he had been given a new directive. At Garrett's behest, several tenants had professed interest in raising ducks. And now Cam was forced on a long duck-related quest. First, he'd been to see the tenants, then to a neighboring estate to see their flock, and now finally to the grocer to talk pricing and supply.

Bloody water fowl, he thought, shaking his head.

Cam scowled in frustration as he stalked across the street to the grocer's shop. It had a green and white striped awning under which was a row of wooden cradles filled with fruit. Being summer, it was mostly a selection of last year's apples, brought up from storage and looking rather shriveled. But there were some fresh fruits on display as well, a cradle filled with peaches and one of plums.

The front door to the shop was held open with a large wooden wedge, letting in what little breeze could be had. Cam saw the crush of people inside and decided to wait out front. He waved to signal the grocer, Mr. Thomas, who nodded but gestured helplessly to the line of customers.

Cam was fine to wait a few minutes, but it had been a long day and he was in desperate need of a bath and a drink. He shoved his hands into his pockets and leaned against the brick wall. He squinted up at the sky.

The sun was starting its slow descent behind the buildings. Throngs of factory employees were leaving work, purchasing something for dinner along the way. Many men chose to duck into the pubs and gin houses for a drink before heading home to their wives.

How many of those men would drink themselves into a stupor, and then go home and inflict terror and pain upon their families tonight? It wasn't payday, but many men didn't wait until the end of the work week to take their frustrations and personal disappointments out on their loved ones. An oily fear slid down into the pit of his stomach as his mind started to probe the shadows he struggled to hold back.

Cam had worked hard to escape the future that had awaited him: becoming like his father. When one changes from a victim into the victimizer, the cycle is complete. Inescapable as an infinity loop. All roads lead to the same destination. But Cam had managed to get himself away from the drudgery of factory labor and squalid flats. Sheer dumb luck and force of will had brought him this far.

The next step away from the muck of poverty was an advantageous marriage. One that was handled like any other business transaction. Coldly, unemotionally, strategically. Agreed upon terms – a mutually beneficial arrangement. The unemotional part was very important. Emotions led to those heavy feelings; the ones that led to violent behavior. He must keep that under strict lock and key.

Mr. Thomas came out just then, interrupting the dark turn of Cam's thoughts.

"Sorry for the delay, Mr. Marlow. Now what can I be helping you with today?" the grocer asked cheerfully, wiping his hands on his apron.

"I came to ask about ducks," Cam responded, forcing a laugh to shove the darkness down, back to where it belonged.

* * *

On Wednesdays Thalia went to the grocer and the baker. It was a weekly tradition to have dinner at Mena's house on Wednesday evenings, and she liked to bring something for her hosts. Mena's father was a rather prominent vicar; he had the wealthiest families in his church pews every Sunday.

The Harvey-Morton's lived in a large white house beside the village green, complete with a spire and ridiculously ornate carvings. It was a bit like a castle made of wooden lace. As girls they had all gushed about wanting a house just like it, once they had each found their literal prince to marry. Oh, how wrong they had turned out to be regarding their futures.

It was also a tradition for Thalia to bring something sweet for Mena's father. The man was a bit of a curmudgeon about most things, but he liked his sweets and was very supportive of Thalia's business.

It was nice to have a family to eat with. Living at the boarding house had its drawbacks, not the least of which being that she had no kitchen of her own. She also had to share the bathroom, but that was another matter. She should count herself lucky that she had a place to live at all. And friends.

As she turned onto the market street, she was surprised to see Mr. Marlow standing out in front of the grocer's. Well, hunting him down was certainly going to be a lot easier than she'd expected. What luck!

Mr. Marlow certainly seemed to turn up in town quite a bit for someone who was supposedly not often seen here. He was listening, his face serious and intent, as Mr. Thomas, the grocer, talked with wildly gesticulating hands.

After a moment Mr. Marlow nodded and clapped him on the shoulder. His mouth moved as he imparted some wisdom, which Mr. Thomas seemed to accept happily. The grocer nodded vigorously, and then the men shook hands.

Thalia watched, hesitating on the street corner, until Mr. Thomas had gone back inside, and Mr. Marlow checked his pocket watch. He placed it back into his pocket and turned toward where Thalia stood. He stilled as he recognized her, and she immediately went to him, as though pulled by an invisible thread.

"Mr. Marlow, good afternoon." Thalia averted her eyes while she spoke, unsure why she was suddenly feeling so shy. She was here on important business, and had completely put aside the fact of their earlier kiss. The mistake, as she had come to think of it.

Not knowing what to do with her hands, she found herself twisting them into her skirts. She forced them to still, and did her best to channel serenity. Nothing would rattle her, not even the most handsome man she had ever been kissed by. *Blast.* There she went again, thinking about the mistake.

Mr. Marlow looked at her with an intensity in his eyes that curled her toes. "Good afternoon, Miss Ward," he said.

His deep voice sent little shivers down her spine. She felt the hairs on her nape stand to attention. Thalia had the urge to giggle madly.

Don't be an idiot, she scolded herself. "I confess that I was hoping to run into you, Mr. Marlow," Thalia admitted sheepishly.

He raised his brow, but did not comment. She felt a blush creeping up her neck.

"It is actually in regards to the orphanage," she explained.

"I am at your service, Miss Ward," Mr. Marlow replied.

Thalia's mind immediately went to work and she felt a deep stirring as she thought of the many ways that he could service her.

Stop that, she commanded herself.

Instead, she forced herself to smile politely and say, "We are planning to host a musicale in the coming weeks, and I am looking for donors for the event. Do you think His Grace would be interested in assisting us? He would be invited to attend, of course, and he would have his name displayed for all to see his generosity."

Mr. Marlow was silent for a moment. Thalia grew nervous that perhaps she had overestimated their acquaintance. Was she being too forward? Maybe Mr. Marlow was resentful that she sought to use him for his connection to the duke. Her heart beat frantically as she waited for his response.

"You are very generous with your time. I don't expect you have much of it to give, what with running a business. That is no small feat." He finally said, his voice warm with praise.

Heat bloomed in her chest at the compliment. Did this mean that he was not offended by her request?

"Oh, it isn't easy to find the time, but I make the effort regardless. I am an orphan myself, and so I feel a kinship with these children. It means a lot to me to be able to help them in any way that I can," Thalia said simply.

"I can understand that. I too am without parents." His voice was strangely hard and unemotional.

There was something forbidding in his expression, something that sent goosebumps down her arms as a muscle in his jaw twitched.

"It is hard for children to make their way without strong family support. Perhaps though it teaches us to be more empathetic to the less fortunate. So many people look down on the poor, as if they are immoral in some way."

"Immorality and poverty are two entirely different things."

"Agreed," she fiercely replied. "So do you think the duke might be interested in being a part of this event?" she asked hopefully.

"Bedford would be glad to be of any assistance, Miss Ward, I assure you." He watched her intently, as if he longed to possess her.

Despite the assurance he gave her, it was his gaze that disarmed her. Her smile slowly dissipated as those little flutters returned to her lower belly and a tantalizing heat began to pool. They stood like that for a moment, neither willing to break the spell.

Finally, Mr. Marlow cleared his throat and tore his gaze away. "Come to tea with His Grace when you are available to discuss the particulars. Just send a note ahead of time, and the arrangements will be made. The duke is a proper gentleman; doesn't do much of anything except lie about his mansion," he teased.

Thalia swallowed, forcing herself to breathe normally and not throw herself at this man before her.

"Will you be there?" she heard herself ask.

So much for not throwing herself at him. She could kick herself.

Mr. Marlow's gaze returned to hers, and his hungry look practically singed her with its heat.

"I will be, if you desire it." His eyes flashed with intensity as he spoke, unleashing a fresh wave of flutter that made her shiver with the anticipation of pleasure.

Thalia wished they weren't on a public street. She wanted to kiss him again, but forced herself to settle for reaching out and gently placing her hand on his arm. She smiled tentatively as she gazed up at him, feeling the heat of him burning through his sleeve.

"I would like it very much, Mr. Marlow. Dukes can be awfully intimidating." When he barked a laugh at that, she smiled coyly. "I believe I can come by on Friday after my meeting at the orphanage."

"I look forward to it, Miss Ward. Until then."

He smoothly took her hand from his sleeve and brought it up to brush a kiss across her knuckles. Thalia shivered in response.

"Goodbye, Mr. Marlow," she replied, her voice breathless.

She quickly turned to continue along the street before she did something to humiliate herself. Daring a glance back to catch a last look at him, she was delighted to find him doing the same. Smiling, she gave him a little wave and then hurried onward.

She wanted to skip, but kept it contained. She was going to end up grinning and blushing her way through dinner because of this chance encounter. The joy bubbling up inside her was difficult to contain. In just two days, a mere matter of hours, she would be having tea with Mr. Marlow and the Duke of Bedford.

Suddenly she realized the problem: she didn't have anything decent to wear. Groaning, Thalia realized that she was going to be raiding someone's closet, and the results probably wouldn't be very encouraging. Hopefully it would be better than that pink monstrosity.

Ten

With snarling gargoyles and pointed spires, St. Jame's Orphanage was an intimidating piece of architecture. The massive front entrance was arched, with a large round window above. Campbell stood in the afternoon sunshine, staring up at the gothic façade.

There was a dull twisting in his gut. Cam knew what sort of horrors such institutions contained. Workhouses for the indigent poor; places where people howled in pain and eventually lost their minds. Whole seas of gray, ragged, starving souls crammed into aging buildings. In the name of helping, the parish used the poor as slave labor and kept them in deplorable conditions. Why punish poverty, when the source was not the individual, but rather the whole of society working in concert?

Taking a deep breath, Cam pushed away those thoughts and firmly resolved himself to focus on his objective—to see Miss Ward and offer her a ride out to the estate in the ducal carriage. He hadn't liked the idea of Miss Ward walking all the way to the estate, after a full day of work no less. He was just being considerate, Cam told himself. Though if he were being honest, he would also have to admit that he wanted to be alone with her.

He propelled himself up the wide stone steps to one of the wooden doors and let himself in. His shoes clicked on the tiled floor of the grand entrance. With graceful, vaulted ceilings, it had a spaciousness that seemed out of place in a parish charity home. This place evoked a monastic atmosphere. There were even stained glass windows depicting bucolic scenes. A singular pale bust sat tucked into an alcove, but there was no other adornment.

Cam wasn't quite sure where to go from there. Two hallways went off on opposite sides, and a staircase went up the middle. It was almost silent, and not a single person could be seen. He hesitated, debating which direction to turn.

Thankfully he heard echoing footsteps approaching from down the long corridor to the right of him. The footsteps grew closer and closer, and a tall, dark haired woman appeared carrying a small wooden crate. She jerked slightly at the sight of him and narrowed her eyes.

"Can I help you?" she demanded with no pretense of politeness.

So much for a welcoming atmosphere.

Cam nodded to the woman and quickly said, "Sorry for the intrusion. I am Campbell Marlow. I came to escort Miss Ward to tea with the Duke of Bedford."

The woman's eyebrows shot up nearly into her hairline, and her mouth fell open. Her eyes ran over him again, this time with new interest.

"Oh, I see! Let me…let me…I'll just go find her for you. Hang on," she stammered, and turned around to race back down the hall.

Cam watched her go. He was bemused by her odd response to him. There was nothing like mentioning a duke to get a woman excited. He tried not to feel annoyed at the reminder that Garrett was considered so much more important than Cam ever would be—it was hardly his fault for being born to his status after all. But it was annoying anyway.

Cam shoved his hands into his pockets and shifted his weight back and forth as he waited. He didn't have to wait long however, before he heard two pairs of footsteps approaching.

Miss Ward and the dark-haired woman came into view, whispering animatedly, but they stopped abruptly once they saw him.

Miss Ward smiled warmly and called out, "Hello there, Mr. Marlow! It's so good to see you again."

"Miss Ward, good afternoon." He nodded to her, and was gratified to see a rosy blush coloring her dimpled cheeks. "I came to escort you to the estate. It is too far of a walk."

Miss Ward's eyes widened slightly, her lips curving.

"That is so kind of you, Mr. Marlow. Thank you," she said. Her eyes turned mischievous, and she added "I assume the offer includes a ride home as well?"

Campbell smiled, surprised by her cheek. "Of course, Miss Ward. What kind of gentleman would I be if I did not return you safely home?"

He surprised himself by winking. When had he ever winked before, for God's sake?

The dark-haired woman had been entirely forgotten, and she cleared her throat meaningfully. She was looking pointedly at Miss Ward.

"Oh dear, how rude of me. Mr. Marlow, this is my good friend Miss Clementine Blakely. Clem, this is Mr. Marlow," she said, gesturing between them as a warm blush spread across her cheeks.

Campbell sketched a bow to Miss Blakely, who raised an elegant brow and smiled like she knew a good secret that she wasn't planning to share.

"It is good to meet you, Mr. Marlow," she said evenly. There was certainly an air of boldness about the woman, made all the more notable by her stunning beauty. No doubt she intimidated many, and left a string of broken hearts in her wake.

"You as well, Miss Blakely. Are you by any chance related to Dr. Howard Blakely?" Cam asked.

Miss Blakely suddenly became quite alert, and speared him with a fierce look.

"Yes, he is my father," she said in a clipped staccato as she tipped her chin up defiantly.

Cam suddenly felt like he had stepped into a pit of vipers.

"He is a greatly respected doctor. You should be proud of him," Cam said, hoping to set the young woman at ease.

He had heard the rumors about Dr. Blakely; that he was too radical and progressive, and that he didn't give enough deference to the elders of his profession. Cam thought that was all horseshit. He respected a man who knew when he was right and acted on it, and Dr. Blakely was known to be on the forefront of many medical breakthroughs. How interesting that Miss Ward was close friends with the good doctor's daughter.

"Thank you, Mr. Marlow," Miss Blakely replied, her guard coming down instantly. She considered him with new eyes, and nodded finally to herself, as though satisfied with what she had found. He had passed some kind of test, it seemed. "I apologize, but I must be going. I need to bring this to the schoolroom."

She picked up the crate she had set aside earlier and excused herself. Once Miss Blakely was gone, Cam looked to Miss Ward. Her eyes shone with admiration as she met his gaze. The way she looked at him made Cam crave more of her attention, more of her praise. He was growing addicted to her approval. Lord help him.

"Are you able to leave now, or is there something you must see to first?" he asked.

Miss Ward looked apologetic. "Unfortunately I am not finished just yet. I cannot leave without having a word with the headmistress. If you wouldn't mind waiting, I would really appreciate the lift to the estate," she said.

"It is no trouble at all. I can wait," Cam replied smoothly.

He looked around, uninspired by the lack of seating available to him. Miss Ward followed his gaze, and grimaced.

"This is a rather uncomfortable place to be left waiting. You are welcome to sit in the garden, it is beautiful this time of year," she offered.

"Wonderful, I shall wait for you there. Take all the time you need," Cam smiled.

Miss Ward pointed the way before excusing herself, and Cam made his way outside.

The garden was larger than he had expected and boasted a good-sized lawn for games and several wooden benches strategically placed around the perimeter. He saw no children about, but suspected that they might be shut away in a schoolroom somewhere, or being fed some sort of lumpy gruel at the moment.

Cam claimed one of the benches and watched a small bird hopping about hunting worms. Beside each bench was a large pot full of flowers or herbs. There were several recently planted fruit trees as well. It was a charming space, and it complimented the decadent style of the building itself. It was nothing like the orphanages he had seen before. This place was lovely and calm. The children here were very lucky. An absurd stab of envy hit him, but Cam shoved that away. He was a grown man, for God's sake.

After what felt like an eternity, Cam checked his pocket watch and saw that it had been only a half hour since he had sat down. He disliked this kind of useless inactivity. He tried not to think about the numerous tasks that he could be doing right now.

After another ten minutes went by, Cam needed to stretch his legs. He walked the gravel path that meandered about the garden back to the door that led back inside. Cam decided to escape the sun and wait in the foyer.

As the door shut behind him, he noticed voices coming from the main hall. He recognized one as Miss Ward, sounding distressed. The other voice belonged to a man. Cam picked up his pace, and rounded the corner, just in time to see a tall man standing far too close to Miss Ward, trapping her against the wall. Her eyes darted around nervously. Cam felt his control snap as he rushed towards them.

"What is going on here?" He demanded as he completed the distance between himself and Miss Ward, unable to slow his response to the perceived threat to her safety.

Cam's full attention was on the man before him, a tall angular dandy, with slicked back white-blonde hair. His blue eyes were pale and sharp. The man recovered his shock from the intrusion and drew himself up to his full height so he was peering down his nose at Cam.

"Excuse me, sir. The lady and I were having a private conversation," he sneered.

Cam shifted his stance to take up more space, keeping Miss Ward behind him, and placed his hands calmly into his pockets.

"Unfortunately for you, the lady and I are leaving for tea with the duke of Bedford presently," he said with a false calmness that did little to hide the challenge in his tone.

Mentioning Garrett had the desired effect. Honestly, when didn't it? The man sucked in his cheeks and glared as he looked back over his shoulder to Miss Ward.

"We will have to continue this conversation another time, Miss Ward. Enjoy your tea," he said.

Miss Ward did not respond. She stood there woodenly and watched the man leave with a pale, tight expression. Cam stared after the man as he left, making sure he was gone before turning to Miss Ward. She seemed quite relieved.

"Is everything alright, Miss Ward?" Cam asked.

"He would not let me pass," she replied. Her voice practically dripped with venom and he could see that her shoulders were shaking. She met Cam's eyes and he saw a depth of anger in them that made him want to wrap her in his arms and protect her.

"Who was he?" Cam asked.

"Sir Marville." She spat his name like a curse. "I met him at Lady Berwick's charity ball and seem to keep running into him." She frowned dubiously.

Cam absorbed this. He didn't know Sir Marville, but he knew how certain men behaved. Entitled men. Sometimes such men required a lesson or two in how to treat a woman. Cam would be quite happy to oblige.

Cam escorted Miss Ward to the stables, where the carriage awaited them. He handed Miss Ward into the carriage and followed her in after she had settled her skirts. As he closed the door, he rapped on the ceiling to tell the driver to head out. It would have been more exciting to have used the open carriage, but Cam wouldn't complain about the privacy afforded by the walls around them.

The carriage immediately set off, the wheels bouncing over the paving stones, and the horses' hooves clip-clopping jauntily onward. Cam sat across from Miss Ward. She peered out the window with fascination, though she was well acquainted with the scenery. Cam enjoyed watching her; she seemed to be truly relaxed and enjoying herself. Her carefree freedom was intoxicating. But he also couldn't help but want her to focus her attentions on him rather than the world passing by outside the carriage.

He broke the silence and said, "I have been meaning to ask you, Miss Ward, about the idea of apprenticing an orphan boy."

The idea had sprung into his mind, and he had blurted it out without thought. Cam was never impulsive. He cleared his throat awkwardly.

Miss Ward sat back from the window and considered him. Cam sat still as stone, his expression blank, but inside he was a wreck of nervousness and his heart was pounding. He hoped that she couldn't see how she affected him. Most people found him intimidating, but Miss Ward didn't seem to think so.

A slow smile spread over her face as she looked at Cam, sending a jolt of heat through him. She looked as though she knew that he was flesh and blood, and wanted to prove it. God how he wanted her to. Cam shifted uncomfortably in his seat. There it was again–her approval making him want to preen. It was dangerous.

Miss Ward cocked her head to the side flirtatiously. Cam had to clench his hands into fists to keep from reaching for her. He wanted to haul her against him and kiss her.

He forced himself to speak. "Miss Ward," he began.

"Thalia," she interrupted.

Her gaze was fixed on his mouth.

"Thalia," Cam repeated, enjoying the feeling of her name on his lips. "Campbell."

And he offered his hand to shake. Thalia laughed softly, and put her hand in his. They shook, as though meeting for the first time. Cam felt the loss when she withdrew her hand and re-settled it in her lap.

With effort, Cam refocused his mind to the conversation. Keeping his hands off Miss Ward—Thalia—was proving much harder than he had anticipated. He was slowly losing his mind. And his patience. He was supposed to be finding a suitable bride. But all he could think about was this woman before him.

Thankfully, Thalia spoke first.

"For you to take in a boy would be so wonderful, Campbell," she said. "Most of the boys end up in domestic service, and are very lucky to have those jobs. It is not unusual for orphans to be given over to chimney sweeps or some other horrible occupation. We do our best to give our children better opportunities, but it is still difficult to find a place for every child that comes our way."

Her expression grew troubled, and she looked out the window again.

"I understand," he replied quietly. "As the town grows in number, the number of orphans grows as well, I assume?"

Thalia looked at him with cynicism in her eyes.

"That is very true," she agreed.

They locked eyes, and they shared a silent moment of un-derstanding. Not everyone had a safe, privileged upbringing.

"I have the means to send a boy on to higher education, and can teach him as he works alongside me here as well. When grown, he would do quite well for himself." He paused, a muscle in his jaw twitched. "It would feel good to be able to give that to a young boy who has nothing."

Thalia's eyebrows rose in surprise.

"I admire your generosity, Mr. Marlow. It would be such a wonderful change in circumstance for the boy you apprentice," she said warmly.

"Do you have an apprentice, Miss Ward?" Cam asked.

He vaguely remembered a second woman at the confectionery when he visited. He wondered if she had seen them kiss.

Thalia smiled and replied, "I do. Her name is Abigail, and she is a lovely, energetic young woman. A quick study too, and most helpful. I am so happy to have her. If you are serious about this interest, please do come to the orphanage and speak with Mrs. Farningham. She will get the process started. Unfortunately, there are some legal considerations, as both you and the child will be entering into a contractual relationship."

She grimaced at that, clearly doubting the consensual nature of such a contract involving children.

Cam nodded sympathetically and said, "I will return within the week to begin the process."

Thalia smiled and looked at him like he had put the sun in the sky. "I hope to run into you when you visit," she said shyly.

Cam managed a nod, but held himself very still. He didn't trust himself not to touch her, if given half a chance. Thankfully they were almost at the estate. He looked out the window and recognized the symmetrical poplars lining the road, which had become very smooth as they approached Berkham Manor.

Cam was torn between relief that he was saved from this torture, and remorse that his privacy with Thalia was ending.

The carriage rolled down the long tree-lined drive, its pace slowing as it neared the estate. Thalia looked out the window, her mouth falling open at the sight of Berkham Manor.

Lord Garrett Sumner, 10th Duke of Bedford, resided in Berkham Manor, located just outside of the village, along the river. The land was a soft rolling ocean of vibrant green, with elegant willows trailing their fronds in the lazy water. The occasional swan family serenely waded by. This was the quintessential English countryside.

Like all other members of the Ton, His Grace lived in London while Parliament was in session in a spacious mansion in the most fashionable part of the city, Mayfair. He also owned several other properties, one of the perks of being a duke, including one remote castle in northern Scotland. Berkham Manor was the duke's main home, and he lived alone, according to Clem who had done research into his background. Fortunately, Clem hadn't turned up anything nefarious.

Manor implied a modest house, which this was most certainly not. Instead, Berkham Manor was a vast sprawling palace of glowing light-colored stone. The front was Roman style, with a long line of graceful columns along the front, and arched windows above. The many small shrubs decorating the terrace were perfectly manicured into cones and rectangles.

Thalia was quite literally breathless at the sight of the romantic vining roses creeping over the portico. This house looked like it had been plucked from a children's book of fanciful tales.

"Oh my," was the best she could muster as the carriage rolled to a stop.

She glanced at Mr. Marlow. Campbell, she corrected herself while heat pooled low in her belly. Her body vibrated with awareness of the man enclosed in the carriage alone with her.

He watched her intently, as though fascinated by her.

Thalia had longed to be bold and sit beside him, perhaps even kiss him again, but the nagging self-doubt in the corner of her mind had held her back. Maybe Campbell preferred a demure woman who let him take the reins. The indecision had lingered and now they were out of time.

The carriage stopped, and within seconds the door was wrenched open by a footman in sparkling clean livery, and the moment was gone, evaporated. Campbell jumped out with athletic agility and held out his hand to help her down. Thalia placed her hand in his and attempted to exit the contraption with some modicum of poise. Unfortunately, she stepped on her own hem, and almost fell over.

It seemed she was never going to escape the problem of borrowed dresses. This black and white striped visiting dress was in desperate need of hemming, and dragged a bit along the ground when she walked. Mena had proudly held this one up as a triumph of elegance, yet she overlooked the critical detail of length. At least it was quite flattering to Thalia's figure.

She clutched Campbell's hand like her life depended on it, before hastily righting herself and relaxing her grip. How embarrassing. Thankfully Campbell merely helped steady her without even seeming to notice. He placed her hand into the crook of his arm and led her to the entrance of the manor.

The massive front door swung open to reveal a severe looking butler, who looked down his long nose as they approached. He bobbed a perfunctory bow and gestured them in.

"His Grace is in the Egyptian room, Mr. Marlow, Miss Ward," he intoned in a deep baritone.

"Thank you, Graves," Campbell said, and swept past, pulling Thalia along with him.

They turned right and walked along a wide hallway lined with portraits in heavy gilt frames. Thalia couldn't help but gawk at the priceless art on the beautifully papered walls, the gold everything, the fragile ancient vases and busts, the luxuriously thick carpets underfoot.

She experienced a sudden attack of nerves, and almost spun around to leave. Thalia wasn't sure what made her more nervous, the fact that Bedford was a duke, or that he was Campbell's friend.

If she were being entirely honest, she would admit to herself that she wanted the duke to like her. Because she wanted Campbell to like her. Because she liked him.

"This is truly amazing, Mr. Marlow. I've never seen such a place," she confided, keeping her voice low.

His arm shook with quiet laughter. "I felt the same as you when I first saw it. Honestly, I still feel out of place here." He admitted, endearing him even more to her.

Thalia was glad that he was not a snobby aristocrat, but someone like herself. Someone who understood how most people lived their lives. It certainly wasn't anything approximating this.

They reached the open door of the parlor, and she took a fortifying breath before stepping inside to meet the duke. The room itself was far cozier than she had expected, for a wealthy duke. Why it was called the Egyptian room was beyond her understanding, as nothing about the room looked remotely Egyptian.

Thalia turned to Campbell, forming the question when she noticed an outrageously handsome man strolling across the room. She stopped, staring as this man with an angel's face came to stand before her, his smile revealing a perfect row of blinding white teeth. It almost hurt to look right at him, and Thalia had to force herself not to squint.

"Good afternoon, Miss Ward, and welcome to my home," he said warmly, bowing low; the epitome of relaxed aristocratic charm.

"Miss Ward, I believe you have already met the Duke of Bedford. Garrett, here is the famous Sugar Queen of our humble village," Mr. Marlow said.

A startled laugh escaped her at the moniker. She rather liked the idea of being Sugar Queen. Especially spoken in Mr. Marlow's deep, velvety voice.

"Sugar Queen? Surely no one calls me that," she protested weakly.

It was hardly her fault she was tongue tied. Somehow Thalia kept forgetting how obscenely handsome the duke of Bedford was from his brief visit to her shop, once upon a time. It was a wonder

REBECCAH WILSON

there weren't scores of women lining up out the door to be ruined by him. The man looked like a golden angel.

Thalia struggled to make her brain and mouth operate appropriately before she ruined this advantageous meeting.

"It is a sobriquet to be proud of, Miss Ward," the duke said, his brown eyes fairly twinkling in amusement. "I am pleased to meet you once again, and here in my home no less. Please be seated and have a cup of tea."

His Grace was smooth and charming, because of course he was, and his every movement was refined. Thalia sat in a lovely velvet chair and pasted a polite expression on her face.

She was astonished when Bedford began to serve the tea himself. Surely important men would employ a servant to such a task when they lacked a hostess. There was something slightly off about this situation, and Thalia was sure that she liked it. Rules and protocol didn't appear to be so important here. She relaxed; the tension eased from her shoulders.

"First order of business, Garrett," Mr. Marlow began, "Miss Ward needs your money. You should give her lots of it."

He sipped his tea innocently after delivering such a shocking statement. Thalia burst out laughing, and almost dropped her tea. Horrified, she clapped a hand to her mouth, and turned her wide eyes to the duke.

"I assure you, Miss Ward, I am not offended by Campbell's utter lack of decorum," the duke said sardonically, and rolled his eyes. "When Campbell suggested this meeting, I had already planned to pledge an exorbitant amount of money to the orphanage for whatever purpose you require." He waved a hand indicating his lack of concern for such worldly things.

Thalia met Mr. Marlow's eyes, and he had the audacity to wink. The cheeky man! She ruthlessly smothered the laughter that threatened to erupt again.

94

"That is wonderful news, your grace. Thank you so much for your generosity," she replied with sincerity.

Bedford sat back in a relaxed manner, smiling happily. He looked at Campbell, and his smile grew a mischievous edge.

"Now, let's get right to the details. What do you have in mind with my money, and how much fawning will I receive for it?" His Grace remanded suddenly.

Thalia was startled, her eyes snapping up to gauge the duke's mood. He looked like a child who had done something naughty, and expected to get away with it too. But of course he did. Dukes could be as outrageous as they liked, and still people would gather to fawn over them.

Thalia found that she rather liked the duke. There was something wicked about him, and it only added to his charm, damn him.

"You will receive heaps of praise, your grace, as is your due. Also, you will have the satisfaction of knowing you are providing an indispensable education for some very deserving local children," she replied tartly, having decided to affect a bored demeanor.

Thalia sipped the obviously expensive tea from a delicate cup rimmed with gold. It was very good. It made her wonder if she had ever actually tasted real tea before.

The duke nodded, his expression grave. "Very good, Miss Ward. I approve of your efforts. I am yours to be used," he said, with a flourishing sweep of his arms and a bow of his head.

Campbell cleared his throat in what sounded more like a growl. The duke slid a sly glance his way and clarified, "I am at your service to provide financial support, Miss Ward." He raised both hands, one still holding his teacup.

Campbell scowled, and said "Don't let Garrett fool you, he is quite the secret philanthropist. He doesn't like to take credit for all of his good deeds, or he could be branded a socialist and cut off from some very good connections."

The duke rolled his eyes, but a hint of color had crept over his exquisitely chiseled cheekbones. He shrugged and took a deep drink from his cup. Thalia considered the duke, who was quickly becoming a very interesting aristocrat indeed.

Along with the tea, a platter of cakes and biscuits had been served. It had been several hours since breakfast, and Thalia had missed luncheon. Her stomach growled audibly, and she chewed her lip.

It was awkward to eat in front of other people, and she didn't want to look unsightly, shoveling down cakes. Like she needed to get any bigger. She had resolved to not eat, when Mr. Marlow leaned forward, and began assembling a small plate with several selections. He handed it to her without comment, and then sat back to observe her.

Thalia hesitated for a moment, but her stomach quickly won out, and she eagerly bit into one of the little sugared cakes.

"Mmmm," she sighed appreciatively, letting her eyes close for a moment as she savored the flavor.

Mr. Marlow cleared his throat again as he shifted uncomfortably in his chair and looked away.

"I wish I could say that I bake them myself," The duke lamented, taking a cake for himself. "My chef was trained in France and makes some truly inspired concoctions. Though she refuses to attempt chocolates, which is the real reason why I've asked to meet you, Miss Ward."

Thalia swallowed the last of her cake and took another sip of tea. "Oh. This is a surprise, your grace. What are you interested in?"

The duke smiled wolfishly.

"Well," he began, "I am hosting a weekend party next month, and was hoping to be able to offer some assorted chocolates. During the parlor games and such." He gestured vaguely, seeming somewhat confused about the idea.

"If you don't mind my asking, how many ladies are expected to attend?" she asked.

Bedford looked a bit panicked and swallowed. "I believe it will be about twelve, including my sister."

Thalia smiled. "You have a sister? That is wonderful. You must be looking forward to her visit."

The duke grimaced and busied himself refilling his teacup. Perhaps he was not pleased to see his sister. That or it was the eleven other women that he was concerned with. It sounded suspiciously like a marriage plot to Thalia.

"Garrett's sister, Lady Claire, is very gracious to come host a party. She is an avid traveler and is on her way home from Russia," Mr. Marlow offered.

He was tapping his left foot on the carpet in a nervous tick. His expression was hard, but Thalia was learning to see what others would perhaps miss—his guarded eyes held sympathy for his friend.

She nodded thoughtfully. An idea was forming in her mind.

"What about a welcome gift awaiting each lady in her chamber? A box of assorted chocolates for her to enjoy at her leisure. In private. It would be quite decadent and a touch scandalous," she suggested, practically bouncing in her seat with excitement.

Both men stared at her.

"I may not be the best source on such things, but is that appropriate?" The duke asked.

Thalia laughed in delight. "It would be a gift from the hostess and given to every guest. There's nothing technically improper about it, but it is skirting the edge just a bit. If you want to make an impression, this would certainly do it," she said with a shrug.

The duke slapped his knee with a laugh, and said "I knew I would like you, Miss Ward. Yes, let's do it! Let us be scandalous. It will drive my sister wild."

He smiled with glee, like a boy putting a frog in his sister's apron pocket. Yes, that was the word for it; the duke was boyish. Whereas Campbell was...hard.

Thalia looked over at him. He looked like he had sprung from the womb fully formed, and already cynical. There was something tragically vulnerable in that. He sat there drinking tea with all the enthusiasm of a man headed to the gallows.

Thalia wanted to kick herself. Here she went again, getting lost in her own imagination. When it came to men, she was overly romantic, and wound up disappointed every single time. She should know better than to start writing backstory for men she barely knew.

She forced her attention back to the duke and took a small notebook and pencil from her reticule and started jotting down notes.

"Would you want the boxes to be filled the same, or would each one be unique or personalized in some way?" she asked.

"I hadn't considered that actually," the duke said thoughtfully. He sat back and rubbed his chin. "I suppose they had better be uniform, or else I run the risk of insulting someone unintentionally, or worse yet – accidentally implying favoritism to a young lady."

He made a face. So he was averse to being pursued, then why invite a contingent of ladies to his home for a party? Surely the idea was to select one as a bride. Thalia wanted to puzzle that out but decided against comment.

She made another note: all boxes filled the same.

"I have several chocolates that could make a nice array, and you might like to include a caramel or two," she said, still writing.

She wanted to get this right and impress the duke. He could provide her with so much free marketing. Each lady guest could be a potential customer, and they might tell others as well.

"I should like the boxes to be fairly plain. Absolutely nothing romantic about them at all, The duke demanded.

The man was very serious about avoiding the accidental innuendo about romance, it seemed.

"Understood. I can have them done up in some very attractive, but entirely unromantic packaging and tissue. There will be no hearts or anything else that could possibly imply the idea of courting or marriage," she assured him, smothering a smile.

"Good. Very good," he said, and took a long sip from his cup, seeming to relax again.

"So that leaves just the date to settle on, and the number of boxes you need," Thalia said, looking up hopefully.

"Oh what did we decide, Campbell?" Bedford asked casually, but his eyes looked wicked again.

"I believe you settled on exactly one month from tomorrow," Campbell replied, his teeth bared in something other than a smile.

Thalia was mystified by their behavior. The duke did not seem happy about selecting a bride, and Campbell was uncomfortable discussing the topic at all. It made no sense. But then, men were rarely sensible creatures when it came to marriage.

The duke practically dragged a hand over his face in dismay. "Ugh, yes that sounds right. Good God I wish we had a bit more time." He seemed very put out about hosting his party.

"Have no fear, I can get it done in time gentlemen," Thalia smiled reassuringly, as she tucked her pencil and notebook away.

It wasn't anything too complicated. She just needed to source the boxes, but she knew just where to get them. Several months earlier she had discovered the local stationer offered boxes in a variety of sizes made of colored paper. They would be perfect paired with a bit of ribbon.

What she couldn't figure out is why the duke was hosting a house full of ladies if he was determined to avoid marriage. It could be that his mother was alive and insisting on grandchildren. Lord knew that quality men took their time settling down, but The duke looked young. It was also possible that he was merely pretending to be put out, in order to keep up his image as a rakehell.

Twelve

"Bloody hell," Thalia cursed.

Her voice bounced off the walls of the empty shop, amplifying the words. Outside the dying sunlight was leaving a purple sky behind. Gaslights were turned up, shining like fireflies in the growing dark.

Thalia didn't want to stay out late, but she was working on the duke's chocolate arrangements. She was making the list of choices to include in the assortment, such as a lovely smooth coconut filling she had developed recently, and those cherry ones with the liquid center.

It was important to be both sophisticated and attractive, while also not appearing like a romantic gift. She decided to mimic the color scheme of the estate itself, but not the lovely roses which would surely imply passion and seduction. A cream and blue color scheme would do nicely, and she would use a gold threaded ribbon as well.

Very good, she nodded to herself, feeling immensely satisfied.

And tired. She was more than ready to head to her bed for a rest.

It had been a few days since Thalia had been able to meet for her usual evening chat with Clem and Mena, mostly due to Clem's newest project keeping her at the office late into the night. But tomorrow the three of them were going to meet for a picnic by the river in the afternoon. Thalia was excited to tell them about her meeting with the duke.

Just then, the shop bell rang, announcing someone. Footsteps tapped their way in, heavy and slow. A man.

Thalia looked up from the counter, hope and anticipation blossoming in her chest. She smiled, but once her eyes landed on the man who had entered, the smile quickly died. Ice cold fear slashed through her, causing an instant jump in her heart rate. Sir Marville, with his tall, lithe frame, moved toward her with the grace of a panther. He stalked his prey—in this case, her—with the slow purpose of a practiced hunter.

Her gaze flicked to the window, hoping to find the street still well populated. But it was empty; the sky was getting darker by the moment. She was very much alone.

As Sir Marville drew close, Thalia saw the mischievous gleam in his eye. He was practically licking his lips in anticipation.

Thalia felt an impotent terror building inside her, and she struggled to keep a cool head. She needed to stay calm and maintain control. She willed her legs to move and began to ease backward toward the back door.

"My dear, I've come to see for myself your lovely little shop. You make such delightful-looking trifles. I long for a taste," Sir Marville said, his raspy voice heavy with innuendo as he advanced on her.

Thalia refused to let her eyes off him for even a moment, nor would she turn her back to flee. She tried to think through the fear rioting through her. If she could think clearly, then surely there would be a way out. She backed up, keeping her eyes trained on the threat before her.

"You should come back when the shop is open, my Lord," she managed, "I am closed for business now."

She strove for a firm tone and lifted her chin to punctuate her words. Surely, he would back off. He couldn't possibly mean to press on when she was quite clear.

Sir Marville came around the counter, his lips twisting in a sly grin. Thalia bumped into the wall at the end of the counter, wincing at the resulting pain in her hip. She had to make a gamble on whether to try to get out the back or make a run for the front door. She felt frozen to the spot with indecision, her fingers gripping the counter behind her.

She scarcely drew breath as he stopped before her. He lifted a hand and reached for her hair, touching her so lightly, a strange look of wonder in his eyes.

"How lovely," he said softly, his hot breath fanning her cheek.

Thalia cringed under his touch and scuttled to the left to put more distance between them. Sir Marville was quick though, and he followed her dodge easily. He caught her, and braced his hands on the counter on either side of her body, and laughed. The sound was mirthless and chilling.

Sir Marville set a single long finger under her chin, and lifted her face up to meet his frigid blue eyes.

"I will have you, little bird, if it's the last thing I do. You are too lovely a specimen to allow to sit on a shelf, or—God forbid—to let another man possess you."

His crude intimation turned Thalia's stomach.

She abruptly moved to push him away, feeling a fierce blast of outrage at his behavior. But as her hands shoved at his thin chest, she was surprised by the resistance. He didn't even budge.

Marville chuckled wickedly, and grabbed her right wrist, spinning her around and twisting her arm sharply up behind her back. With the barest effort, she knew he could snap her wrist or worse if he was so inclined. Thalia's breaths turned to pants as she struggled to hold herself still enough to keep her wrist from hurting more.

She was hauled up against Marville's sinewy body. He leaned to speak close to her ear.

"I don't mind a little spirit in my bedpartners," he said, before abruptly releasing her.

Thalia scrambled away, turning to keep him in her sights as she fled to the front door. Marville flashed his gleaming teeth menacingly. He might be handsome, but his eyes had no soul.

Just then the front door banged open, rattling the glass window so hard Thalia thought it broke. As though summoned by the intensity of her need, Mr. Marlow stepped into the shop, looking like an avenging angel – tall, broad and very angry.

Thalia could feel the energy radiating from him as he advanced. He looked ready to do violence, and she felt a shiver of anticipation run down her spine.

"What's going on in here?"

Thalia felt empowered by the deceptive calm she heard in his voice. His breathing was calm, his voice didn't waver, yet his fists were clenched and ready to do bodily harm to someone.

Her knees threatened to collapse in relief. How had he known that she needed him?

"You are interrupting a private moment, Marlow," Sir Marville sneered. "This little bird and I were getting better acquainted."

* * *

Cam looked into Thalia's frightened eyes, and his temper flared even hotter. His fists ached to do damage to Sir Marville.

"Get out," he said slowly and clearly.

The sinewy lecher eyed Cam's large fists with a sneer.

"I shall see you again soon, my little bird," Marville promised as he slunk toward the door.

Cam remained planted in the doorway, and Marville was obliged to turn as he tried to pass. Cam stared him down, itching to punch him in the face. Finally, Marville was out the door, and the cad had the bollocks to whistle a jaunty tune as he strolled away, hands in his pockets.

Cam watched him go, making sure Marville was truly gone before locking the door and coming to Thalia's side. She was quivering and fighting off tears. Cam put an arm around her shoulders, gently guiding her to the back room where she could sit down.

He helped her into a chair, and then checked the lock on the back door, before closing the curtain that separated the back room from the shop space.

Thalia spoke to herself, "I am a strong independent woman. I am a business owner. I am not afraid of anyone and I know my own mind."

Her voice shook.

"Yes, you are," Cam agreed.

He fumbled around to find a carafe of water and poured Thalia a glass. She took it without meeting his eyes. Her shoulders were folded in protectively as she sipped.

"I can't believe that I just stood there while he…I just…I couldn't move, couldn't scream…" she said finally, her fine brows knit together.

"When faced with a threat people have two choices, to run or to fight. Your response was perfectly normal," Cam reassured her.

He reached for hands, holding them within his own to help still them. The fierceness of her frown softened a bit, and she finally looked up and met his eyes.

"You were afraid," Cam said softly, his voice purred in his chest.

"Yes I was. I still am. He may return," Thalia said, chewing her lower lip nervously.

"I will keep you safe," he pledged.

Thalia looked at Cam, her eyes wide and trusting. Cam willed her to see the genuine warmth and kindness in his eyes. He wanted her to know she could trust him.

Thalia slowly leaned closer, over the table, and pressed a chaste kiss to his lips. Cam stilled, instinctually wanting to make her feel safe, though his body burned to deepen the kiss. Her lips moved shyly over his, with the teasing lightness of a feather. He was dying of frustration, but held himself still for this sweet torment.

Thalia furthered her explorations, creeping her fingers up to stroke along Cam's jaw, and then plunged into his hair. Her other hand was still caught in his grasp. She brushed over his lips again and again, taking what she wanted from him as she let out a contented sigh.

Cam's cock strained against his trousers, and he prayed she didn't notice. He would put an end to this dalliance...soon. Perhaps just another moment of sweet pleasure, and then he would stop.

But when he heard Thalia's whimper of need, Cam felt his resolve breaking. He was, after all, only a man.

Cam released her hand, and reached instead to cradle her face and deepen the kiss. He licked along the seam of her lips, and when she opened in surprise, his tongue swept in to taste her. Her taste was sweet and enticing, making his mind immediately wonder how sweet other parts of her would taste. She allowed his explorations for a moment, but then boldly thrust her own tongue to twine and dance with his.

Cam gave himself into the kiss, thrusting his tongue in a lewd approximation of what he longed to do with a different appendage. Thalia eagerly engaged with him, and Cam was very close to spreading her on this dented wooden table and giving them both what they wanted.

He felt a stab of conscience at that erotic image, though he had never been harder in his life. With deep regret, he forced himself to end the kiss.

He pressed his forehead to hers, still holding her face.

"It is late, Thalia," he said regretfully, his breath coming out in pants as he struggled for control. "You need to rest. I worry that you are overwrought."

Thalia's eyes flashed and he could see stormy anger brewing in their depths.

"I am an adult, Campbell," she managed through clenched teeth.

Thalia stood and came around the table to stand before him. She grabbed his lapels and pulled him to her again and kissed him hotly. Her tongue delved into his mouth, as though claiming

him. She stepped between his parted thighs and pressed her lush body against his.

Cam could no longer resist her and gave into her fierce explorations. Thalia's kisses made him wild.

"We must stop," he gasped, pulling back; his gaze intense upon hers.

Their panting breaths filled the silence of the night. Thalia looked so incredibly seductive, her red lips were swollen with the pulse of blood rushing to them, her glazed eyes unfocused. Like a freshly tumbled woman. Cam forced his hands off of her and shifted uncomfortably.

Thalia's cheeks flushed red and she busied her hands with smoothing her skirts. Though she averted his eyes, he could read the disappointment in them as she slipped away to fuss over gathering her things.

"Why did you come tonight?" she asked as she shoved various items into a basket and fumbled with her keys.

Cam forced his brain to focus as he scrambled to come up with an answer.

Finally he said, "I was thinking about you."

He scratched the back of his neck.

Thalia turned to him, and their eyes held, sharing an unspoken connection. Cam swallowed hard, the sound reverberating in his head.

He truly hadn't planned to come to the shop, but his feet had carried him here anyway. And just in time to save Thalia from a possible assault. Anger flared at that thought, and Cam had to force himself to calm down.

"Are you ready to close up for the night?" he asked, striving for an even tone.

Thalia raised her brows.

"Yes, are you offering me an escort?" she asked with a coy smile.

Cam's blood heated, pulsing through his veins in anticipation.

"I wouldn't be able to sleep tonight if I didn't know that you were safe," he said.

Her blue eyes melted, staring up at him like he had arrived on a white steed, ready to slay her foes. God, she shouldn't be looking at him like that. He would only disappoint her. Cam felt an intense stab of regret.

Cam followed Thalia out the front door, and watched her lock it, while keeping an eye on the street. Not a soul was out in the darkness, but the wind rustled softly through the nearby willow branches, and frogs were calling out for each other's company along the riverbank.

They walked side by side to the boarding house. Cam had not offered his arm, and Thalia hadn't moved to take it. The atmosphere was awkward, and Cam was kicking himself for being such an idiot. Why must he always muck things up?

After what felt like an eternity, they reached the boarding house. Every window was dark, save one, and a fat black cat lay boneless on the steps. Thalia stopped, and turned to Cam, her eyes full of doubt.

"Thank you," she said, conjuring up a half smile.

Cam took her hand, lifting it to press a kiss to the back. He inhaled her intoxicating sugary scent and blinked against the consuming need that suddenly gripped him. He let go of her hand and stepped back.

"Be safe," he said, cringing at the demanding tone of his words, and wished himself capable of sounding as smooth and charming as Garrett would undoubtedly be in the same position.

Thalia smiled softly. "Goodnight, Campbell," she said, before slipping inside and closing the door firmly behind her.

Cam stared at the door for a moment, the sound of Thalia's voice lingering in his ears. As he turned to leave a shudder of anger washed over his body. Thalia was certainly fierce, but how could she defend herself in this world from the likes of men like Marville?

The scoundrel would have to be dealt with.

n the first Tuesday of every month Campbell met the estate tenants at the largest pub in town, The Black Horse. The establishment's sign outside featured a large black stallion rearing up on his hind legs to paw at the sky with his golden hooves. The gaslight scattered golden stars across the ground as the sign blew in the wind. It wasn't Cam's usual night to drink with the tenants, but he would bet several men would be present.

Cam loosened his collar as he walked. The night air was still hot, despite the breeze. Hopefully the pub would be fractionally cooler inside, and the ale would be refreshing.

Cam ducked his head as he stepped through the door, which had sunk several inches into the ground over the eons it had endured. Campbell released a sigh of relief as he closed the door behind him; he felt the cooler air of the pub and was soothed by the familiar sounds of clinking glasses and murmuring voices.

His eyes took a moment to adjust to the dim light, but he instantly heard the welcoming calls of the tenants who were there. Once he could see better, Cam made his way over to them, and took a seat at the table.

"Good evening, everyone," he said amiably, and gratefully accepted the mug of ale that was slid his way. "I needed that," he said after taking a long swallow.

"It's been too hot of a summer," one of the farmers lamented.

The farmer's name was John Bolt, and he was one of the older tenants who had lived through several hard seasons before. Campbell considered him as he drank. John had so much experience that Cam viewed him as possibly the most valuable asset on the estate.

"How is the new drainage ditch working for your parcel, John?"

The man scratched his scruffy beard and shook his head slowly. "It's doing well in that there have been no big puddles in that back section. But I'm worried we don't have enough water up where we need it now. We haven't seen rain like we usually do this year, and the wheat is dry."

Campbell took this in, tapping the top of his hat as he thought. What could they do to bring water to the drier areas? They could attempt to pump it, but that would be labor and cost intensive. Shelling out a small fortune for more irrigation would certainly not make Garrett too happy.

"I'll do some research and see what we can do about the water issue, John. I'm not sure what the best method is just yet. But what I can do is promise to figure it out," Cam said.

He was glad to be able to help someone in some way, because he needed to do something other than track down Marville and beat him to a bloody pulp. Cam took a long swallow of his ale.

After an hour, Campbell figured that he had had enough to drink, and he needed to be able to get himself home. He paid his tab and shook hands with his drinking partners.

"Good evening lads, I'll see some of you sooner than others. Enjoy yourselves." he called, as he staggered to the door.

"Don't fall in the ditch on yer way home, Marlow!" someone called out, causing a roar of laughter.

Cam chuckled and forced himself out the door. He had to shake his head a few times and take a deep breath to get his mind right.

I can get myself home, he mentally assured himself.

He took a few steps and realized that he could in fact walk a fairly straight line. Perhaps he was just stiff from sitting for so long, and not actually drunk. As he walked along, he grew in confidence. He was doing fine, and quite possibly he could get back to the estate in time to get something for dinner.

His mouth started watering at the thought of the oversized dinners of several courses that Garrett dined on every night. Cam would gratefully settle for a hunk of the chef's excellent bread and some cheese, he was so hungry.

He paused outside the window of a shop, realizing that he might have gone the wrong way. The wind was still blowing, causing shop signs to swing and the flames of the gas lamps to flicker. Cam stared at the sign in front of him and realized that it was Thalia's shop.

His hand curled into a fist as he remembered seeing that repugnant gentry scum accosting her. The rage was building up inside him once again, and he wanted to find Marville and have a talk with him.

It was a bad idea, but Cam had a singular thought in his drunken brain, and it was to protect Thalia. He wanted to taste the blood of the man who would do her harm.

Cam didn't know if Marville would be at his office this late, but he was going to pay him a visit and see. And thanks to a bit of information gleaned at the pub, he now knew where Marville's office was.

* * *

Marville was seated behind his massive mahogany desk when the door to his study burst open. The door banged against the wall, causing him to startle at the sound, eyes on the wall as though concerned for the possible dent in the expensive paneling.

"Who would dare intrude upon my privacy in this way?" he demanded, rising from his seat, prepared to unleash his wrath upon the interloper. Then recognition appeared in his eyes when he saw Cam in the doorway. "You."

"Me."

It was very late in the evening, and Cam's eyes were likely rimmed with red from the way they ached. He moved with a drunkard's looseness as he stepped inside the room and shut the door.

Sir Marville sat back down with a bored sigh. He didn't ruffle easily. "It is rather late, but please do come in," he said, gesturing to the chair on the opposite side of the desk. "Was there something you forgot to say earlier?"

Cam stalked across the room to stand before the desk instead, battling a murderous instinct. He leaned forward, spreading his hands on the wood to keep them from touching the toff.

"I did not come for a pleasant chat over tea," Cam growled, baring his teeth.

Sir Marville sighed. "Well, that is disappointing. What have you come for then?"

"Stay the hell away from Miss Ward," Campbell spat out.

Sir Marville chuckled softly and shook his head. "One would almost think that you are involved with the woman. Is that so? Have you laid claim to her?"

Campbell glared back. A muscle in his jaw twitched.

"She does not seek your attention. Leave her be," he said.

Sir Marville tapped his long, manicured fingernails on the gleaming desk, looking thoughtful.

"She may not be seeking it, as you say. However, she will be most grateful to hear of my intentions towards her. Miss Ward is a very appealing young woman. Very sweet. She makes me long for a taste of her wares," Marville said, smiling tauntingly.

Marlow slammed one large fist down on the desk, his eyes burned with rage.

"You will leave her be, or I will see to it that you won't be able to sample anything again. Do you catch my meaning?" Marlow's lips twisted in a grim smile.

"I ask again, is she yours?" Marville asked.

"It doesn't matter who she is to me," Cam bit out. "The lady is not interested in your attention. If you come near her again, I will see to it that you cannot bother her, or any other woman, again."

Cam had recovered his composure and straightened, affecting a deceptively relaxed posture. He casually removed a folding knife from his trouser pocket and tapped it, still closed, on the table. Marville's eyes took in the implied threat, but merely raised an elegant brow, refusing to be cowed.

"I will geld you with my favorite knife, and hang your balls from my mantle," Cam said, his tone flat and serious.

Marville narrowed his eyes.

Cam smiled like a panther at his prey. Then he made a show of pressing the little button on the hilt of the knife, which caused the blade to swing out in an alarmingly quick fashion. Snap. It gleamed in the gaslight, its tip angled and incredibly sharp.

Marville swallowed hard. "You wouldn't dare gut me," he said.

"We shall find out."

"Well, I certainly wouldn't want that, Marlow," Sir Marville said evenly.. "Very well, I shall end my efforts toward Miss Ward. There are, after all, plenty of other women that would beg for the chance to have me."

"I hope for your sake you keep to that promise," Cam said, sliding the knife back into his pocket as he turned to leave.

Then, Sir Marville called out, "Marlow, I hope you will confide in me once you have bedded Miss Ward. Let me know how sweet her little pussy is. I am simply dying to know."

Marville grunted as Cam's fist collided with his face. His hands went up to protect himself, but it was already too late. Cam was too fast, hitting Marville again and again, even after the man had fallen to the floor.

"I told you to watch your fucking mouth," Cam said through his teeth, kneeling over the other man.

Marville emitted a mad laugh as Cam, finally exhausted, stood over him and wiped his hands on a handkerchief pulled from his jacket pocket.

Cam left Marville lying on the floor behind his desk, blood smeared all over the toff's fine clothes.

* * *

Back at the estate, Cam stalked across the library, heading for the nearest bottle of strong drink. He was rumpled, his coat torn, and he was smeared with blood.

"What's happened to you, Campbell?" Garrett asked with alarm. He jumped out of his chair, knocking over the glass of liquor he had been nursing.

Cam merely grunted in response. He picked up a bottle of brandy, a very good and very expensive one. He poured himself a large glass and downed it in two swallows.

Garrett sputtered in protest, "You cannot gulp that down as if it were water! That bottle cost a fortune!"

Cam turned his powerful stare on his friend and poured himself another glass.

"Tell me what happened," Garrett demanded.

Cam finished his second glass, and then threw himself into a chair, burying his face in his hands, knuckles raw from pummeling another man.

"I do not know," he mumbled.

Garrett sat again, filling a glass of his own. He leaned heavily to one side and sipped.

"Why are you covered in blood? Surely you know that much at least," he prompted, his voice muffled by the glass.

Cam sighed.

"I beat Sir Marville in his offices earlier," he muttered.

Even saying the man's name caused him to feel a surge of ferocious desire to punch things.

"Good God man, why did you do that?" Garrett asked, eyes wide over the rim of his glass.

"He deserved it."

"Many men deserve a sound thrashing, but that doesn't mean we can just go around dispelling justice, Cam," Garrett said, frowning.

Marville has been forcing his unwanted attentions on a certain woman in the village," Cam said evenly.

He stared down at his hands, avoiding Garrett's eyes.

Garrett considered his friend. Cam knew that he looked terrible and smelled of the pub. He willed Garrett to leave him alone.

"Which townswoman has he been after?" Garrett asked, raising a knowing brow.

"Miss Ward," Cam said. He met Garrett's eyes and sighed. "Look, I know what you are probably thinking right now."

"Oh, do you?" Garrett shot back.

"Yes, I do. But that's not what is going on," Cam said firmly, eyes daring Garrett to contradict him.

"Mhm."

"It's not! Look, I simply cannot abide any woman being assaulted in such a way. That is all." Cam knew he sounded defensive. He needed to shut up, but couldn't seem to stop explaining. "I do not feel sentimental about her."

Cam crossed his arms, and looked over at Garrett, who was looking quite skeptical.

"I might have laid a hand, or two, on a peer of the realm. I could hang."

"That only makes it more convincing that you fancy this Miss Ward, Cam," Garrett laughed. "Thankfully no one would dare bring charges against you for this. I'd say you are safe on that score. However, you now have quite a problem to deal with concerning this woman of yours."

"She is not my woman," Cam said, though he felt an intense spike of possessive pleasure at those words.

"Of course not. Miss Ward is just some woman you do not care about at all, even though you hunt down her adversaries for violent punishment in your free time. Makes perfect sense,"

Garrett rolled his eyes dramatically. "Don't allow Miss Ward to keep you from your goals, my dear friend. You are forcing me to plan a house party for you, during which you plan to select a blue-blooded bride. You need to focus, Campbell."

"I know. You are right," Cam groaned, rubbing his temples.

"I am not inviting a dozen women into my home just to have you lose interest in the idea," Garrett said firmly, pushing himself up to stand.

"I won't," Cam replied.

"Good. Now I am off to bed." Garrett offered a wobbly salute, and disappeared down the hall.

Cam sighed, and leaned back in his chair, closing his eyes. The brandy and ale were not sitting well in his stomach, and he was sore from his visit to Marville. He desperately needed to sleep, but his body refused to rise and find his bed. Here would have to do for now.

Cam shifted until he was comfortable, and laced his fingers over his stomach as his mind began to drift. Dreams of Thalia filled his sleep, unbidden. And he wondered if she was thinking of him.

Thalia wore a new straw hat, purchased on her way to the shop that very morning. It was decorated with a spray of purple and white cloth flowers. The purchase had been rather out of character, as Thalia was not one to buy a great many things for herself, but it made her feel a little more positive.

As she walked toward the river, Thalia felt her shoulders relax. The green smell of the river grew stronger as she approached.

She was looking forward to this picnic. After working past her usual lunch hour, she longed for a sandwich and cold lemonade. Not to mention the chance to stretch out her legs and rest.

As she ducked under the long fronds of a weeping willow tree, she was careful to hold her skirts, knowing how easy it was to trip over the willow's shallow roots. She had done so in the past. More than once.

Once she emerged from the cool privacy of the willow and into the sunshine again, she scanned the riverbank for her friends. They were not far off, sitting on a large blanket.

Mena, wearing a simple white cotton dress, sat on her heels, and was busy pulling paper wrapped sandwiches from the large woven basket. Lemonade had already been poured from a tall, corked bottle, into three tin cups.

Clem sat with her ankles crossed in front of her; her shoes had been removed and set off to the side. She wore her usual uniform, a white blouse and dark skirt. Waves of glossy ebony hair were piled up haphazardly on top of her head with the aid of what looked like two hundred hair pins.

"There you ladies are," Thalia called to her friends brightly.

Clem turned her head, eyes narrowed, looking Thalia over with her perceptive gaze.

"Here we are," Mena said, smiling. In the sun, her brown hair glinted with hints of gold and red.

"I heard that loathsome Sir Marville has been sniffing about the orphanage," Clem announced in lieu of a greeting. She leaned forward and took a sandwich from the selection laid out by Mena. She folded the paper down, and took a large bite, looking at Thalia as she chewed.

The mention of Sir Marville made Thalia feel nauseous. She was trying hard not to think of his unwanted advances, his coldness, and his complete disregard for her autonomy. Men who behaved in such a way were dangerous. He had seemed to enjoy making her uncomfortable.

Thalia focused on breathing deeply as she claimed a seat beside her friends, and slowly unwrapped the brown paper of her own sandwich. She was no longer looking forward to luncheon, but knew that she should eat. She looked under one of the slices of bread and saw ham and salad inside. Her stomach grumbled, apparently unconcerned with unscrupulous men.

"Yes, I saw him there the other day. Thankfully Mrs. Farningham is aware of his…behavior. She won't let him get too comfortable," Thalia replied, taking comfort in the knowledge she had support.

"I suspect that Sir Marville will take some convincing. It's quite pathetic," Mena said hotly. She bit fiercely into her sandwich and glared out at the water.

A perfect pair of swans chose that moment to glide by. Thalia released a breath and took in the lovely English scenery in front of her.

"I am not worried for my safety, and neither should you be," Thalia assured them, and herself.

If she could just fake confidence for a while, surely she would start to feel confident, she reasoned. She was used to that sort of thing, having been on her own since both her parents tragically passed away when Thalia was just seventeen.

"I am not worried," Clem argued. "In fact, neither of you seem to be aware that Mr. Marlow beat Sir Marville half to death in his own offices three days ago. That might have knocked some sense into the blighter."

Thalia gaped at her friend. Surely that wasn't true.

"Are you serious, Clem?" she demanded.

"Yes, of course. I wouldn't make this up," Clem said, clearly offended by the insinuation. She crossed her legs, sitting up straighter, and put her sandwich down on her lap. "It was the same night that you were accosted, Thalia. Marlow went right to the pub and then to deliver his message, so to speak."

She grinned at her friend's shocked expressions.

"I told you that human behavior can be studied like any animal's," Mena said.

"I'm not sure how to feel about this," Thalia admitted.

She chewed her lower lip and studied the sluggish river. The swans had moved on, leaving them with a muddy river and scores of dragonflies buzzing around.

"He really likes you," Clem offered, her face soft with sympathy.

Thalia considered that. Did Campbell have an infatuation with her? She wanted to believe it; her heart clenched at the thought. He certainly behaved as though he might. He kissed like he did. But Thalia had enough life experience to doubt the staying power of any flirtation.

The taste of bitterness on her tongue made her frown. Clem reached out, and grasped her hand, giving it a squeeze.

"I am simply trying to decide how I am going to protect you. Should I wait outside your door, like a security guard? Should I bring a hammer to defend you?" Clem asked.

Her lovely green cat eyes flashed wickedly, causing Thalia to laugh.

"I would love to see that, Clem. Do you have your own hammer, or should I put it on my shopping list?" she asked playfully.

"If only humans had tiger claws," Mena sighed, resulting in more laughter.

"I could sharpen my fingernails," Clem offered.

"Or we could just glue nails to our hands," Thalia shrugged, and finally bit into her own sandwich.

She decided to put this entire episode out of her mind. She and her friends would simply do what women all around the world did every single day: protect themselves and watch out for each other.

They all ate quietly for a while. She forced herself to relax and enjoy the warm sun.

"So tell us about your latest project, Clem," Mena prodded as she was gathering the used paper and unwrapping a box of biscuits.

Clem smiled mischievously.

"Oh, this one is going to be interesting," she said. "The old factory was finally sold to some business tycoon from London. Word is that he treats his employees terribly, especially the women. He fires anyone who makes even a squeak in complaint. Rules with an iron fist, it sounds like."

She shook her head, mouth set in disdain.

"How are you tackling this one then?" Mena asked.

Clem sighed and said "Well we didn't have any warning about the factory sale, unfortunately. So he's already ahead of us. I plan to begin a campaign warning about accepting employment from him. Then I shall have to lodge a formal complaint with the town council to try and oust the factory altogether."

She said all this with perfect calm. Thalia couldn't imagine going up against some powerful man like that. Clem wasn't afraid of anyone.

"I shall be happy to help in any way," Mena replied.

"Count me in as well," Thalia said. "How likely is it that the town will oust a 'job creator' though?"

Clem grimaced.

"Not very likely. The town council isn't one to turn away money," she said.

"What do you know about the man buying the factory?" Mena asked thoughtfully.

Clem squinted while she pondered the question.

"Well, he's not terribly old, I know. Apparently he's a rather big brute," she shrugged, as if that didn't matter.

"A brute?" Thalia asked pointedly. "Why, he sounds so harmless."

Clem laughed, "I am not afraid of some man." The last word was spat out with venom, as though cursing the entire gender.

"Yes well, just be careful," Mena began, and then hastily amended "As I know you always are!"

Clem sighed, letting her head hang back for a moment, exposing the long column of her throat.

"I would never do anything to put myself in danger. I will wage a war of organized protest against this interloper, and he will take his money elsewhere. That is all. We will behave like civilized modern people," she said firmly.

For some absurd reason, Thalia's mind flashed to a rather uncivilized image of her and Campbell lying together in bed, entwined in the throes of passion.

Her face heated, and she forced her attention back to Clem and her man problem.

"Men are not fully civilized. Nor are they at all modern in any sense," Mena commented dryly, eliciting laughter from her companions.

"That is definitely an accurate assessment," Thalia said when she caught her breath.

"Now, we said we would discuss the midsummer dance," Clem said, deftly changing the subject.

Mena looked down at her lap and took a deep breath before answering.

"Yes, I think it would be a good thing to attend. Much as I want to hide from such things...I need to start getting used to people again." She raised her soft brown eyes to look at her friends.

Thalia smiled warmly. She knew how hard it was for Mena, whose mother had been downright abusive in pursuit of feminine perfection. Mena had her meals restricted, her corset tightly laced, and was sent off to a horrendous boarding school. It had almost broken her gentle spirit. As a result, when her mother died, Mena had shut herself away from society altogether, except for her friendships with Clem and Thalia.

"I think it would be an excellent way to dip your toe into large gatherings again. We can stay for however long we wish and then go have dessert in private."

"Good, then it's settled. I was hoping you both would agree to attend. I feel a need to dance," Clem smiled happily.

Thalia needed the outlet too, and was grateful to have such friends to ease her worries.

Fifteen

As the summer was drawing to a close, the air began to carry a distinctly cooler edge. The bees no longer sluggishly buzzed about the flowers but moved with renewed purpose. Everyone was starting to sense the change and began preparing for winter.

The village was a flurry of activity, getting ready for the coming harvest season. Thalia had finished creating the new window display, using tulle to create the effect of frothy waves for her beach scene.

Today she was finishing the last set of treacle sweets for a garden party. She was glad to get the commissions for private events, since they added much needed revenue for her expansion plans to hire more women for her shop, providing an alternative to service or factory work.

Women didn't have many options for employment, and most women couldn't afford to be kept at home in a gilded cage. It was a particular focus of Clem's advocacy, who sought to emancipate women. If women could get the same education and employment opportunities as men, they would have more choice.

Thalia hummed to herself as she cranked the handle of the candy press. The ruby colored hard candies came out in a long ribbon of perfectly shaped strawberries that glinted in the light. Thalia's assistant, Abigail, stood at her elbow and took the rapidly cooling sheet and expertly massaged the little gems from the sheet, gathering them in a glass covered dish.

They had to work quickly to maintain the proper texture. Too hard, and they could break. Too soft and they wouldn't hold their shape. Abigail had been Thalia's shop assistant for going on nine months now, and they worked together beautifully, almost never making mistakes. Having grown up in the orphanage, Abigail was a perfect fit to be Thalia's apprentice when she came of age for employment, and Thalia had been pleased to offer her the position.

Abigail took the dish and stowed it beneath the counter, and then carried the press into the back room, while Thalia used a cloth to wipe the counter clean.

The bell chimed, and Thalia looked up to greet the customer.

It was Campbell.

Thalia's heart skipped a beat, and she couldn't quell the excitement stirring her blood. She had been feeling completely out of sorts, not knowing when she might see him again.

He was wearing his usual dark colors, in this case a very deep blue colored suit. Every inch of him was controlled and orderly. His close-cropped hair added to the severity of his style.

Campbell came in the door with confident strides and proceeded to stand guard at the end of the counter, his eyes singeing Thalia with their intensity.

Thalia smiled shyly and left the cloth she had been cleaning with on the counter as she approached him, drawn like a moth to flame. She self-consciously smoothed the stray wisps of hair from her face.

"I wasn't certain if I should expect to see you again," she commented lightly, coming to stand before him.

Cam nodded slightly, his expression serious, as usual. His knuckles still bore the telltale marks of a fight, and there was a scratch along the left side of his neck. So he really had fought for her honor.

The thought was incredibly arousing, in a most uncivilized way—surely she was not the sort of woman to become aroused by violence. Who was she becoming?

"I find myself unable to stay away," he replied, his deep voice sending hot shivers down her spine.

He reached out and tucked an errant curl behind her ear. Thalia bit her lip to keep from breaking out into an idiotic smile. Her knees threatened to turn to pudding.

"Well, I was thinking about you as well," she confessed softly, hoping her shop assistant couldn't hear them.

Campbell's mouth turned up in a lascivious smile.

"Is that so?" he asked, clearly pleased with the notion.

Thalia regarded him in mock rebuke, but she couldn't stop a bright smile from eventually slipping past her defenses.

"I wondered if you might escort me to the orphanage this afternoon. I mean to speak with the headmistress about the apprentice boy we discussed," he continued.

Thalia was moved by his request. Did he seek her approval? Or was it just her company? Whatever the reason, she wanted to do a little dance for joy but managed to control herself.

"That would be lovely," she replied. "I just need to speak with my assistant for a moment, and we can be off."

Thalia ducked behind the curtain to the backroom and caught the attention of her young shop assistant. "Abigail, I'm off to the orphanage for a visit. I intend to return in two hours."

"Yes, ma'am," Abigail called back in response.

She was tying red and orange ribbons of gossamer around several boxes that would be displayed in the front window. With the changing seasons, the window display would be revamped to a harvest theme, replacing the ocean scene currently on display. The design would be a traditional cornucopia of marzipan fruits and vegetables. It had been one of the most fun to design, and Thalia was looking forward to it. She loved creating the little tableaus in the front window—it was probably her favorite part of owning a shop.

She returned from the back room and came to Cam's side. Though she strove to act nonchalant, Thalia couldn't help a bubbling giddiness that overtook her. She felt like a schoolgirl with her first beau.

"Shall we?" she asked brightly.

They stepped out onto the street and were immediately assaulted by the sun's wrath. Thankfully the cool breeze helped alleviate the worst of the lingering summer heat. Thalia eyed Campbell's suit and sighed, thankful that she wasn't forced to wear a starched collar and jacket. Then her mind began creating images of his body stripped of said clothing, and she fought a fierce blush.

"How has your day been?" he asked, unaware of her naughty thoughts.

"Tedious," she replied, affecting a light tone. "We have been busy working on an order for a garden party. But I am happy to be done with that finally, and now I can turn my efforts to the new display for the front window."

"I like the one you have currently. The little seashells are very fitting for summer," he replied, surprising her with his observation.

"I thought so too. But summer is ending. Can't you feel it in the air?" she teased.

"I can. In fact, I've been busy myself with the tenants. All the end of season concerns," he said. "So it is for the common folk that you advertise expensive sweets?"

Thalia frowned, bristling for an argument that she had already had so many times with others who just weren't ready to understand what she was working hard to accomplish. She turned her chin up to deliver a set-down. But then she caught the twinkle in Cam's eyes and the smirk playing on his handsome lips.

"You almost had me ready to fight you, Campbell," she huffed, but started to smile despite herself. "I want everyone to be able to enjoy simple pleasures. Chocolates should not exist solely for the wealthy to enjoy. I'll let you in on a little secret of mine, if you will promise not to tell anyone."

Cam stopped walking, and pulled Thalia into a narrow alley between two shops. A merry pink flower arrangement hung down to hide them from view. He gathered her in his arms and pulled her against his hard body.

"Tell me your secret," he murmured before brushing his lips over hers, enticing her to open for him.

Thalia kissed him back, sliding her tongue along his in a sensual dance. She had missed this—missed him.

"I markup my wares for the wealthy," she whispered hotly.

Cam pulled back to meet her eyes, his own wide with surprise.

"You little minx," he praised.

Thalia smiled proudly. "I consider it my way of democratizing confections," she explained.

She grew serious then. Her eyes remained fixed on Cam's lapel. "Tell me what happened with Sir Marville after you left me the other night."

He regarded her with his inscrutable, dark eyes. "I had a few drinks, and thought it would be a good idea to have a little talk with him," Cam said with a shrug, though he was pulling away, shuttering himself.

Thalia raised a brow skeptically, and crossed her arms. "It appears to have been more than just words that were exchanged," she said dryly, nodding to his knuckles.

Cam grimaced, and glanced down at his hands. He flexed them, as if testing how they felt, with their scrapes and bruises. "Yes, it went a bit further than that," he allowed.

Thalia waited, but Cam didn't offer more. She huffed and said pointedly, "Yes, well I want to know the details. It concerns me, after all."

Cam's lips flattened in a line, but he finally met her eyes. "Alright," he said. "He continued to be offensive, so I hit him a few times."

He watched her expression intently, but his chin was set stubbornly. He had no need to be defensive.

Thalia uncrossed her arms, and reached out to grasp one of his hands in hers, running a thumb gently over the marred flesh of his knuckles. She pulled it to her chest, pressing it over her beating heart. "Were you trying to protect me, or yourself?" she asked softly, as she held his gaze.

Cam's brow furrowed. "It was about you, Thalia," he growled.

Thalia couldn't help the lurch of her heart at Cam's words. It felt terribly unevolved to feel such a strong surge of lust at the idea of two men fighting over her. It was a novel experience.

"Are you going to get arrested for striking him?" she asked, suddenly seized by terror at the notion.

He leaned towards her, a hungry gleam in his eyes. His free hand came up to tilt her head back, and his lips met hers and they melted together. Thalia was mortified to hear herself moan as his tongue explored her, tasting her, knowing her. She was exposed to him in a way she never had been with a man before.

Thalia knew that she was no great beauty, and that she would never achieve the fashionable wasp-waist that was all the rage. Men didn't yearn for her, or form attachments. This was madness. Delicious, delirious madness.

"You don't have to worry about me, Thalia," Cam said. "And he won't be bothering you again."

Thalia instinctually doubted that, but she didn't let on to Cam about her reservations. Nor would she bother scolding him for the presumptuous nature of his actions. In fact, she burned with desire for this man; wanted to let him claim her.

She tilted her chin up to consider him.

"Well thank you for looking out for me, Campbell," she said with a coy smile.

Cam kissed her again, a brief brush of his warm lips on hers, before linking hands with her, and pulled her back onto the street to continue their walk.

"I will not tell a soul about the duplicitous nature of your pricing, Sugar Queen, but I do expect you to pay me for my silence," he cast a suggestive look her way.

Thalia laughed in delight. She was happy to put any talk of Sir Marville behind them.

"Blackmail is unlawful, but I suppose I can think of a way to help you hold your tongue," she teased with a saucy smile.

"Careful now, or I will be forced to escort you somewhere other than the orphanage in haste," he chided.

"Very naughty," she said sternly, with her chin held high.

Cam's throaty chuckle sent little quivers of excitement shooting down her belly, and Thalia had to be very stern with herself to keep from dragging Cam off into the shadows like a cavewoman. Her attraction to this man made her feel positively feral with lust.

Thankfully they were now within sight of the orphanage's tall slate roof and iron gate. Without a word, they had both slowed their steps as they approached. Thalia squeezed Cam's fingers.

"Bartholomew will be very happy to see you," she said.

"Bartholomew?"

Thalia nodded as she led him inside.

Sixteen

Cam followed Thalia up the stairs to the headmistress's office. He regretted the loss of her hand, but Thalia had released her grip in order to precede him up the stairs. He did enjoy the view though, as her generous hips swung side to side with each step.

Cam forced his gaze away and tried to think of something decidedly non-sensual. Ducks! Housing for ducks, feed, egg prices, slaughter for Christmas…

He desperately thought of waterfowl.

Their footsteps echoed down the long empty hallway.

Finally they reached an office door with Mrs. Farningham's name painted on the glass. Thalia knocked, but twisted the knob only seconds later, and entered. Cam followed her in and shut the door behind him.

"Good afternoon, Mrs. Farningham," Thalia said brightly as she swept towards the massive desk that monopolized the room.

The headmistress sat behind the desk, which was covered with heaps of papers, books, pencils, and other bits and bobs. She looked him up and down with a critical eye, her mouth pursed in a sour frown.

"Good afternoon, Mrs. Farningham. It is a pleasure to meet you," Cam extended his hand, bowing politely.

The headmistress blinked at him, and finally reached out to shake the proffered hand. Something about her reminded him of a falcon, sharp eyed and alert. Though he was intimidated by her, Cam would never admit the fact.

"Good to meet you, Mr. Marlow," she replied, her voice a firm clip.

Cam looked to Thalia, who gestured for them to both sit in the chairs that stood before the desk. They were a mismatched pair of well-worn wood and were surprisingly comfortable.

Cam looked around the room, taking in the various random items and stacks of paper filling every available surface. Several pictures that had clearly been painted by children hung on the wall.

Mrs. Farningham cleared her throat, and Cam's attention returned to her. Her eyes narrowed at him.

"Well, let's get right to it. Please describe the living arrangements and work to be performed," she demanded, pen ready to write down every word he said.

"Um," was all Cam could manage, his mind suddenly blank.

The syllable, if one could call it that, hung there in the silence. Cam should have prepared to make some sort of case for himself, but he'd rather assumed they would just hand him a child since he had asked.

Thalia eyed him in confusion.

"I told you all about it already, Mrs. Farningham, and I saw the estate myself," she interjected, saving Cam from answering.

Mrs. Farningham raised a brow, but her lips were tugged up in amusement at the corners.

"I wanted to hear it from Mr. Marlow," she said, spearing him with her sharp gaze.

Cam swallowed.

"Well, um...the boy would be apprenticed to the estate, working in the stables. His Grace keeps a dozen of the best carriage horses. He does not breed them, or race them, so it has less risk than some other positions. Though I suppose that means he would not gain those valuable experiences," Cam faltered.

He tried to channel his usual calm, and continue. "The boy would sleep with the other grooms, but would have his own room. He would be taught to keep accounts, and care for the tack and gear, as well as tend to the animals. There is potential for more in the future, as he grows into the role." Cam hoped he sounded self-assured.

He felt distinctly uncomfortable under the collective watch of these two women. Usually, he was in command of the room, but these two women were very different from the sort he usually interacted with—the sort who wanted to please him in some way, and who mostly existed as decoration.

Mrs. Farningham considered his words, and finally nodded, satisfied.

"Well, I expect you to hold to your word on that. It will be in the contract, after all," she said, and threw him a look. "Given Miss Ward's support of you, I think it would be a fine arrangement. I shall fetch Bart and introduce you."

Mrs. Farningham rose from her chair and came around the desk. Cam was struck by how short the woman was. How could someone so formidable be so tiny? In her severe black dress and short stature, she more resembled a raven. Still a bird of prey.

"I really think that you and Bart will get along," Thalia said with excitement.

Cam turned to her and found her smiling at him. He felt a strange thump in his chest. He liked pleasing her. And suddenly he felt an intense need to kiss her smiling lips and drink in her happiness.

But Mrs. Farningham returned, announcing herself by banging the door against the wall. A small boy trailed in behind her. He looked decently well fed, but was very small, and he looked at Cam with dark, impassive eyes.

Mrs. Farningham stood behind the boy, her bony hands resting on his shoulders as though holding him still for the necessary introductions.

"Bartholomew, this is Mr. Marlow. He is to take you to the Duke of Bedford's estate where you will work with horses in the stables. It is a wonderful opportunity," she said, her voice full of warmth and empathy.

The boy squinted up at Cam in frank assessment. His eyes were aged beyond his years, though he was surely no older than seven years old. The boy stood still, but his little body was humming with unspent energy. No wonder this boy was selected as his apprentice; Cam was offering wide open spaces and physical labor, which this child so obviously needed.

"It's good to meet you, Bartholomew," Cam said in greeting, bending down to look the boy in the eye. "Do you like being called Bart?"

The boy scrunched up his face in confusion.

"My name is Bartholomew," he replied after a moment of consideration.

"Ah, alright. So no to Bart then?" Cam confirmed, amused.

"Hmm," the boy scratched his head, and looked about. "Yeah, just Bart is fine. When do I get to see the horses?" he blurted, his eyes lighting up.

"Soon enough," Cam replied, straightening.

He couldn't help but smile at the boy's excitement. Cam looked at Thalia and caught her watching him with a strange expression. Was it yearning? But she quickly shook herself and her expression became shuttered.

Cam needed to take his leave, as he had work to do at the estate. He promised to send for his new apprentice within the week. Bart stayed behind in Mrs. Farningham's office, so she could explain to him the terms of his apprenticeship, and ready the boy for this change in living situation.

Cam and Thalia left the office together, walking slowly, unconsciously putting off the moment when they would part ways. It was a new experience, having a woman simply want his company.

He was used to relationships that were entirely transactional. He guarded his private self, keeping others at a distance. Even Garrett was held at arm's length.

"Well, I will let you get back to your work," Thalia said, turning her face up toward his.

Cam wasn't sure what to say. He was out of excuses to see her. He reached down, capturing her hand in his, and raised it to his lips. He lingered over her warm skin, feeling the satiny slide of her softness.

Thalia's breath caught, and her eyelids drooped in desire. Cam's pulse throbbed, demanding that he kiss her and bury himself in her softness. But he resisted. He let her hand go and stepped back.

"Thank you for the assistance, Thalia. Have a lovely afternoon," he said, forcing a smile.

She sent him a searching look, but made no comment.

"Good afternoon, Campbell," she called as he walked through the door.

As he walked away, back to his horse, he felt a disturbing feeling developing in his gut. He reminded himself of what he stood to gain by walking away. But the steps grew no easier as he walked. Would he see Thalia again?

* * *

Thalia closed the door behind Campbell. He had had an odd sadness in his eyes when he'd left. Thalia wasn't sure what to make of that.

She had stayed behind at the orphanage, hoping to see Mena and Clem. They were found in the large dining room, helping to fix dinner for the children. Mena was slicing the freshly made bread, and Clem was stirring a huge cauldron of stew. Mena turned to greet Thalia, and wiped the perspiration that ran down her face on the hem of her apron.

"Hello," Thalia called out as she made her way past the rows of long tables and benches that ran the length of the room. Without children at them to help fill the space, she heard her voice echo as she walked toward the back where the open kitchen was located.

"I didn't know today was your day to come in," Clem said, raising one brow.

"I was assisting Mrs. Farningham with an apprenticeship interview," she said lightly.

Mena and Clem shared a look between them. Clem's full lips quirked up on one side.

"And who was the child being apprenticed to?" Clem asked pointedly.

Thalia rolled her eyes. "Mr. Marlow," she replied.

"I knew it," Clem said happily, and turned back to the stew she had been stirring.

Thalia looked at Mena, hoping for an ally, but Mena was studiously avoiding her gaze, and was fiddling with the arrangement of bread slices on the serving plates.

"We kissed again," Thalia offered, knowing that they would want to know the details.

Clem didn't even turn around.

"Yes, obviously," she said.

"What do you mean? I haven't told you about it yet!" Thalia exclaimed, feeling frustrated.

"Mr. Marlow has been coming around to see you quite a bit. It stands to reason that you would be...moving the relationship forward, so to speak," Mena said in her quiet voice.

Her pale cheeks were scorched red with blotches. Thalia knew Mena was not comfortable with these discussions, suspecting that inexperience was the cause. It took a lot of courage to push through the nerves and speak about such things, and Thalia was moved by her friend's desire to support her.

"So what's your next move?" Clem asked, waving the ladle around as she spoke, flinging bits of stew all over the place.

"Um," said Thalia as she played with an errant curl. "To be honest, I hadn't thought about it."

"Well, it depends on what you want to happen," Clem said. She had turned to face Thalia, one hand on her hip.

Thalia considered that. What did she want?

Marriage had never been a priority of hers, but she would enjoy having children and a family. An image popped into her head, of her and Cam taking their children to the park to run around. Perhaps they would have a dog. She had always liked Scottish terriers. The idea of a life like that with Campbell warmed her heart.

She shook herself, realizing that she was getting way ahead of the situation.

If she were being very honest, she would admit that she wanted to be with Cam physically. She would be happy and satisfied with her life if she could just run her business and have pleasure as well. Going to bed alone was a sad affair, especially in the cold winter months.

"I want to see where this goes," she said simply.

Clem nodded, understanding immediately. She wasn't big on long term plans herself, preferring to stay free. Mena, however, was considering her with her usual inscrutable expression.

"Guard your heart," Mena finally said.

Thalia coughed out a laugh. "I'm not falling in love with him," she protested.

"That is something you do not have control over," Mena replied calmly.

Thalia looked at Clem, who was frowning, looking troubled.

"I should hope that we do," Clem grumbled, and threw a handful of chopped herbs into the cauldron.

"Love seems to be a rare thing," Thalia commented thoughtfully. "Most people join together for other reasons. In my case, loneliness and lust."

She smiled wickedly, hoping to make Clem laugh. But Clem remained focused on her task.

"I'm just saying to be careful," Mena said.

Thalia reached out and gave Mena's hand a squeeze. Mena nursed a private wound in silence. Thalia wished that she would let her friends support her, but knew better than to push. Then she came around the long table and hugged Clem from behind.

"Are we still getting together on Sunday evening?" Thalia asked them as she prepared to leave.

"Yes, but we need to have a nightcap tomorrow. I have some news regarding that factory we talked about," Clem perked up, always ready to fight injustice.

"Ok, let's meet at the boarding house then? Or should we go to Mena's?" Thalia asked.

Mena shook her head. "No, the boarding house would be best."

"Alright, it's a plan," Clem said.

Thalia said her goodbyes and went out the kitchen door and around the stables to leave. She felt it necessary to vary her way of walking home and be less predictable. It was unwise to assume that Sir Marville would stay away for long.

Best to be careful.

Seventeen

Cam worked under the hot sun, sweat making his shirt stick to his back. He was digging and moving soil for the drainage trench alongside the tenants that could be spared, and some extra hired hands from the village. It was slow, difficult work, and the men eagerly gulped their rations of ale at every break without pausing for a single breath. Cam understood their thirst.

The handle of Cam's worn shovel was dry and cracked. The sharp splinters bit into the flesh of his hands as he worked, turning any remaining softness into hard calluses. He paused to wipe the sweat from his brow with his forearm and squinted up to determine the sun's position.

Time was moving along at a crawl. It could only be just past noon. Only an hour from the last break. His throat was already dry and he coughed.

Cam had hoped that throwing himself into physical labor would excise his fixation on Thalia, but so far it had done little but give his mind time to focus even more on her. He shoveled dirt and thought of escaping into the arms of a soft, warm, woman. God, he would give anything to be with her rather than suffering under the hot sun. This was mental torture.

Cam knew that he should stay away from her. He needed to focus. He had plans. Cam stabbed the earth with his shovel, channeling all his pent-up frustration into this labor.

Later that day, Cam arrived at the estate dining room, still dirty and sweaty from his labor. Garrett was already there tucking into a plate of cold ham and cheese with lovely crusty white bread and pickles. He raised his brows at the state of Cam's attire, but said nothing. Cam filled his plate from the sideboard, and sat across from his friend, studiously avoiding eye contact as he chewed.

"Well, it appears that you have given up on the plan to become a gentleman, then," Garrett finally remarked with a smirk.

Cam glared at his friend, and tried to focus on chewing. He disliked having Garrett so...involved in his private affairs. Cam was normally quite reclusive, and hated asking for help. But he did need Garrett's help if he wanted to gain a foothold into the upper rungs of society.

But did he still want that?

Cam shook himself. Of course it was what he wanted. His entire life had been focused on becoming so wealthy and powerful, he wouldn't need to fear the nightmares of his childhood any longer. He couldn't even imagine a future without achieving that goal.

He didn't know who he even was, other than the hard kernel of hate that he carried inside him.

Garrett casually slid a paper across the table, and went back to eating. It was a list of names. Ladies' names, to be exact.

Cam scanned the list, considering which ones to invite to the party. His mind quickly glazed over quickly from the tedium. He hardly cared about the details regarding his potential wife, beyond that she be decently attractive and in possession of property.

"I don't know any of these women," Cam said finally, setting aside the list.

Garrett shook his head in bemusement. "What do you need to know beyond what is written there?" he asked.

"Are they attractive?" Cam asked pointedly.

"Obviously they are, or I wouldn't have included their names. Honestly, Campbell," Garrett sighed in obvious disappointment.

"You might as well just invite whomever you think I should consider," Cam replied with a shrug, entirely disinterested in the process.

"So now I'm to play matchmaker, as well as host? You really are a selfish bastard," Garrett grumbled.

Cam felt a pang of guilt, but refused to let it affect him.

"Here, I'll do it," he said as he neatly tore the paper in two. He handed one half to Garrett. "Here's the list of women I want invited. Send my regards to your sister for me when you write to her," he said, voice calm.

Garrett made a show of taking the paper while affecting exhaustion. He practically collapsed on the table with the effort it took. Cam frowned, growing frustrated with Garrett's theatrics.

"Go on then. Indulge in the martyr routine. I'm off to take a bath," Cam said as he rose from the table, leaving behind his mostly unfinished plate.

Garret rolled his eyes and resumed eating. He waved a hand goodbye without turning around.

Cam stalked out the door, and headed out toward the footpath that led from the main house to his cottage. The little path was leafy and rich with little flowers and moss. It had a whimsical look. And once you reached the cottage, you understood the theme.

The cottage looked like a fairy house, complete with climbing ivy and intricate woodwork around the edge of the roof and around the windows and doors. Lush hedges of peonies and roses filled the space between the walls and the little white fence that went around the property.

It was an indulgence, built by a previous duke for his wife. This had been the duchess' private space, and what she had created was a feminine sugar puffed fantasy. Garrett hadn't wanted anything to do with it, and Cam had strangely rather liked it. It felt very safe and warm. And he didn't care to analyze that feeling further.

Inside, he was alone. There was no housekeeper or servants here. Cam had someone come out to clean once a week, and he took most of his meals at the main house.

Cam drew himself a bath in the newly installed modern bathroom and washed away the dust and grime of his day. He let his head fall back and closed his eyes. His aching muscles began to relax in the heat.

As he began to doze off, Thalia filled his dreams.

He wanted to savor every moment he could with her, before he was forced to walk away. He was a selfish bastard, but she was a woman who understood how the world operated. She would understand, and probably was thinking the same—of living for the moment.

It was dark outside when Cam went to the boarding house. He had convinced himself not to go several times, and yet here he was, standing in the moonlight below Thalia's window.

He picked up several small pebbles from the ground. Her window was still aglow with the light from her lamp. He threw a stone, tapping the window glass. Nothing stirred in the window above. But a moment later the curtains fluttered and were pulled aside.

Thalia's face appeared, illuminated in the bright moonlight. She fumbled with the window sash, finally getting it raised up partway, and thrust her head through.

"Campbell? What are you doing?" she whispered loudly down to him.

"I had to see you," Cam called up as softly as he could.

Thalia looked at him for a moment, before sliding the window shut and disappearing from view. Cam was rocked with a sharp feeling of loss. He went around to the front door, and hoped that perhaps she was coming down.

* * *

With her heart in her throat, and butterflies in her belly, Thalia descended the stairs to let her lover in.

Lover. What a scandalous word! But surely that was what she should call Campbell. In the night he came to her; what else could he want?

She refused to give voice to the fear that this was a good-bye, that she might not see him again after tonight.

Thalia smiled shyly at him and took his hand to lead him inside to her room. She shut the front door and slid the lock into place. Then she led Campbell up the stairs to her room, guiding him around the various squeaky and creaky spots. His weight lent an entirely different cadence to the sounds emanating from the ancient wood, but nothing too noticeable. Then they were safely in her room, with the door shut and locked behind them.

Thalia leaned back against the door, trying to calm her erratic breathing. Campbell stood in her room and looked around at her things. Her private place, no man had ever entered before.

His bulk and heat seemed to fill the small space, adding to her flustered state.

"I'm glad you came," was all she managed, before he pulled her against him.

He held her close with one hand spanning her lower back, and he used the other to cup the back of her head, tilting her face for him as he proceeded to kiss her.

Oh yes, this was perfect. Thalia's toes curled in her ragged slippers. She was all too aware of her threadbare nightgown and wrapper, both leftover remnants of her former life as a cherished daughter. She hoped Campbell wouldn't notice or comment. If he just kept kissing her, everything would be alright.

They lay side by side on her small bed, which creaked with every slight movement they made, even a slight shift in position. Campbell and Thalia shared a conspiratorial look, both knowing that it would be difficult to be as quiet as they must.

"Let me show you pleasure, love," he begged Thalia, his lips wandering down the long smooth column of her neck to the edge of her nightgown.

"Yes!" was her eager response, and she began tearing at his shirt buttons.

He let out a surprised huff of laughter, but he allowed her to expose his chest for her attentions. Once she finished the buttons, Thalia roughly pulled the sides of his shirt apart, and feasted her eyes upon his naked flesh.

Campbell quickly slid her wrapper down the length of her arms. He set shaking hands to the ribbon at the base of her throat that secured her nightgown, and removed it as well. He then reached for her with great care, and caressed her breasts with bare hands, the sensation electric. Thalia threw back her head and moaned, her pink nipples tightening under his rough hands. He leaned forward and tugged at one with his teeth, causing Thalia to clench his hair in her little fists, crying out his name as he nibbled and suckled her flesh.

"I want to watch you come for me, love," Campbell whispered to her.

She smiled like a wanton temptress and reached for his straining cock, delighted by the surprised look on his face. Clearly, from the way he stiffened in her grasp, the fact that she hadn't been scandalized by his admission had shocked him to his core.

Campbell grabbed Thalia's wrist and stopped her further administrations. "No, love, I meant to focus on your pleasure alone."

He slowly lifted the nightgown over her head, tossing it aside, then turned to assess her reaction. Thalia smiled up at him, completely trusting. Her legs were open to him, and Campbell reached for her, drifting over her flesh with maddening lightness. At once Thalia became a tigress. She grabbed his hand and pulled it to her core.

"Here," she growled, rocking her hips against his rough skin.

She felt his body tremble and felt another wave of excitement rush through her own body. It only heightened her own feelings of pleasure to know that he was turned on by a woman who knew what she wanted, and how to get it.

Her cleft was slick with desire, plump lips begging for his attentions. Campbell slid his thumb down the seam, eliciting a moan of expectant pleasure from her throat. He practically fell to his knees before her. Thalia met his eyes, a look of triumph upon her face. He eased his thumb inside her sheath, and marveled at how hot and wet she was for him.

"My god," he breathed in reverence. "You are so wet for me."

"Please," Thalia begged, her breath catching on a sob. Campbell could no longer hold himself back, and he roughly pressed her knees as wide as she could take, baring her private blonde curls to his ravenous gaze.

"Perfection," he growled before leaning forward to suckle at her.

Thalia's body convulsed in pleasure, and she cried out his name, gripping him by the hair. Campbell worked her body ruthlessly, drawing moans and cries from her as she rocked against his mouth. At last Thalia felt herself shatter into a million golden sparks as she reached the crest of her pleasure. He continued to lathe her as she returned to Earth, and then he slid one long thick finger into her. Thalia was boneless, limp with spent pleasure, but she felt the stirrings of passion again as Campbell thrust his finger inside her.

"Cam, I don't know if I can…" she begged, unsure if she wanted him to stop or continue.

He seemed to know what she needed.

"So tight, my love. Such a tight little pussy," he growled.

His words of appreciation heightened Thalia's building pleasure, and she knew then that she would come again for this man.

"Cam, oh God, yes!" she cried as he slid a second finger inside, stretching her swollen flesh.

His thumb circled her straining bud, and Thalia screamed his name as she came apart again. Campbell came up quickly, covering her cries with his mouth. Thalia could taste her own musk on his lips, and she felt only a little ashamed as she rode his thrusting fingers until her pleasure subsided again. When she was done and limp in his arms, her shallow breathing slowly returning to normal, Thalia held his face in her hands and kissed him again and again.

"You are an unbelievable woman," Campbell said softly, resting his forehead against hers.

Thalia smiled. "You are quite something yourself, sir," she replied.

He pulled away from her embrace and began setting himself to rights. Thalia slid down to the floor, shaking out her skirts, and fixing her bodice back into place. She smoothed her hair and pressed her hands to her flushed cheeks.

Faced with Campbell's broad back, she wasn't sure what to say, or where they would go from here. When she was finished, she cleared her throat and smiled shyly at Cam as he turned to her. She felt a strange tightening in her chest as their eyes met.

"We mustn't do this again," he said, cutting off her thoughts. He rubbed the back of his neck awkwardly.

Thalia felt her stomach plummet down to the floor, but she strove to appear nonchalant. What she wanted to ask was why? But instead she said, "Alright."

She laced her fingers together in front of her and made her face as blank as she could under the circumstances.

He scanned her face, as if looking for signs as to her true feelings. But he would find nothing. Thalia would not trap him for the sake of a few moments of passion. He was a good man and did not deserve any underhanded machinations.

"Of course, I want it to happen again," Cam said, smiling ruefully at himself. "But I do not think it is wise."

"I will not force myself upon you, Campbell," Thalia laughed. "I do hope that we are friends, though."

* * *

Cam stared at this incredible woman before him. One moment she was coming apart under him, and the next she was letting him go without any fuss and asking to be friends. It took all of his resolve not to throw her over his shoulder and haul her off to his lair for a lifetime of pleasure. A lifetime, where had that thought come from?

Cam was not one to visit the same woman's bed twice, nor did he want a lifetime of pleasure. He wanted only the elite standing that an advantageous marriage could bring, and he needed to remember that, especially when he was near this temptress. For her part, Thalia was better off without him mucking things up for her. He would only bring her pain in the end.

Cam came closer and brushed a gentle caress down Thalia's cheek.

"I do not know if I can in truth call you simply a friend, but I remain an ally. If you need anything, know that I will come to your aid in an instant. You are safe."

After kissing Thalia goodbye, and sneaking back out of the boarding house, Cam slipped through the shadows towards home. It was a miracle they hadn't been caught – it had been a huge risk to be together when the house rules clearly stated "no men". But it had been worth every stolen moment.

Now, how would Cam go back to a life without Thalia in his arms?

Eighteen

The next day proved to be a blistering hot one. People went about their usual business at a much slower pace, and women could be seen furtively blotting their faces with their handkerchiefs at every opportunity. The men who worked without jackets had visible sweat stains before the sun had risen above the tree line.

Thalia wore her lightest summer dress – a simple white muslin design with short, capped sleeves. Still, it felt stifling to be wearing so many layers. Corsets were a horrid ordeal during the hottest months of the year. Though, if she were being charitable, Thalia would have to acknowledge that men were similarly forced to don uncomfortable attire in this heat—the worst part being their starched collars.

She made the short walk from the boarding house to her shop and unlocked the front door. After she turned the sign in the window to declare the store 'open', she placed a brick beside the door to hold it open. Hopefully it would encourage some fresh air to take up residence inside.

The glass jars gracing the wall and countertop looked inviting, but she hadn't dared make any chocolates this week, for fear of all her hard work coming to naught when they melted into puddles on the floor in this heat.

She continued on to the back room, where she unlocked the back door and propped that open as well. Perhaps if she tied back the curtain there would be something of a cross-breeze. Thalia moved to pull back the heavy linen fabric. Suddenly a face appeared in the doorway, startling her. It was only Abigail, her assistant.

"Good morning," Abigail said brightly as she entered. She wore a lovely cotton dress decorated with tiny brown flowers. She set her lunch pail down on the worktable and grabbed her apron from its peg.

"Good morning, Abigail," Thalia replied, pressing a hand to her chest. Beneath it her heart raced. "I wish the weather would turn. It is too hot for working over a stove."

"Aye, I am not looking forward to it at all," Abigail agreed pleasantly. She was a good girl, and a hard worker. Thalia was grateful to have her in her employ.

"I had been planning to make several batches of candied peel today," she said, "But honestly it might be a waste of time making anything today. Perhaps we could finally give ices a try?"

Abigail shrugged. "It would be popular on a day such as this." She was a pretty young woman, and energetic despite the perspiration gathering on her brow.

Thalia tapped her chin. She had no way of getting ice delivered today, and would have to seek out the ice merchant, Charles DeWitt. At least she had plenty of citrus fruits, having had them delivered yesterday afternoon directly from the train.

There was a knock at the back door. "Delivery."

Abigail went at once to answer. She turned back to face Thalia with her arms full. It looked like an oddly shaped bucket with a crank at the top. Abigail set it down on the table and pulled out the card to read.

"Thompson's iced cream maker," she read, her brow crinkled in confusion. "What is iced cream?"

"I believe it is a new cold dessert that has become rather popular in Bath and Dorset recently. People enjoying the summer by the seaside are having iced cream as a refreshing treat. I heard that it is much more satisfying than a lemon or cherry ice."

Abigail shrugged, unconvinced. "Did you order this?" she asked, cocking her head to the side to consider the machine.

"No," Thalia replied. "Was there another card? Anything to point to the gift-giver?"

The card was signed simply, C.

Thalia smiled to herself, and felt a blush warming her cheeks. Abigail eyed her with interest, but decided against comment.

Surely this meant...well, something. Didn't it? Hope bloomed in her chest. Thalia couldn't suppress her smile.

* * *

Later in the day, Thalia came out from the back room to see a well-dressed figure scrutinizing the bonbons she had artfully arranged near the entrance. It was the duke. Perhaps he was here to check on his order.

"Good day, your grace," Thalia called out as she came towards him. "It is wonderful to see you again, and in my shop no less. What can I assist you with?"

The duke straightened immediately, and turned his perfect features her way. He smiled smoothly, flashing his dazzling teeth, and tucked his hands into his pockets. His golden hair was carefully arranged to look permanently tousled.

"I came to see for myself what the fuss is all about, Miss Ward. You are becoming quite famous," he said, with a honeyed tone that probably melted every female heart within the vicinity.

Thalia laughed, charmed, despite herself, and crossed her arms over her chest.

"Oh come now, I'm certain that is hyperbole. I have been seeing quite an increase in business since the charity ball, but no one is beating down the door to get at my sweets," she laughed.

He raised an elegant brow at that.

"That is not what I've heard, Miss Ward," he said tauntingly.

Thalia didn't know what he was implying, but she began to feel uneasy. What exactly did the duke want? She narrowed her eyes and cleared her throat meaningfully.

"What can I help you with today, your grace?" she asked again, affecting a serious tone.

Bedford sighed and came closer. He rested his hands on the counter and leveled a steady gaze her way. Thalia was suddenly grateful that the shop was empty at the moment. She had a sinking feeling that the duke was about to get personal.

"I know that Mr. Marlow has been paying you some particular attention of late," he said carefully.

Thalia struggled to contain the bright flare of anger she experienced at those words. Her business was hers alone, and certainly not the duke's.

"Is that so, your grace?" she asked blankly.

She refused to show her emotions and held the duke's gaze steadily. He seemed to be searching for a break in her armor, but after a moment he dropped his eyes.

"I have known Campbell Marlow for a long time," he said, keeping his voice low. "I have never seen him so…distracted."

Thalia wasn't quite sure how to take that statement. Certainly, she was pleased to hear that she affected him so, but the way the duke described it made it sound bad. This was a rather thorny conversation.

"I find Mr. Marlow distracting as well," she admitted carefully.

Bedford looked at her again, his eyes flaring in panic. Which was an odd reaction, surely. Was this a warning off?

"It seemed to me that you are growing close, and I felt compelled to speak with you," he choked out.

Thalia breathed slowly and evenly, controlling her emotions. It was difficult to fathom that some practical stranger was here before her, wanting to discuss her private life. It was galling.

"I appreciate your concern, your grace, though I hardly think that it's your business," she said evenly, one eyebrow cocked in challenge, daring the duke to pursue this line of discussion.

Bedford sighed, and looked apologetic as he spoke. "He was born into a less than comfortable life, you see."

Thalia considered him, entirely confused.

"Campbell has always wanted to prove others wrong. He wants wealth and power, but what he desires most is the acceptance of the beau monde. He is relentless in this pursuit," the duke said, emphasizing the last bit for good measure.

"So he is after a blue-blooded bride," Thalia stated flatly.

Now she understood what the duke was getting at. He was warning her off. Well, she had known, hadn't she? Campbell was not the marrying kind. He was rather above her station, frankly. And it was hardly surprising that he would have ambitions.

But still, this news hurt. It knocked the wind out of her, but Thalia maintained her stoicism, refusing to crumble before the duke.

"I do not share his notion that joining the aristocracy is worth all the effort, but he has never listened to my advice. He believes it will bring him satisfaction, as well as more connections," he continued. "The party you are assisting us with…it is for Campbell to find a suitable bride. That is how he plans to accomplish his feat."

Bedford's expression was grim, his eyes held sufficient sympathy to make Thalia believe he was being truthful.

"Well then," she said, releasing a breath she hadn't realized she had been holding. "Thank you for the concern you've shown me, your grace. You will be pleased to know that I have formed no attachment to your friend, nor did I think that he was pursuing me for marriage. Now, what else can I help you with today?"

She attempted to laugh lightly but knew she had failed when the duke's eyes filled with pity. Thalia swallowed the lump forming in her throat and took a shaky breath.

Good lord, why was she growing emotional all of a sudden? It wasn't as if Campbell had made any promises, or given even the slightest hint of sentiment. No, Thalia was just deeply disappointed, that was all. She had really liked Campbell. She had liked him as a person, and also enjoyed their mutual attraction. It was lovely to have a beau, that's all. The heavy feeling settling down on her chest had nothing to do with heartbreak. She had begun to hope, it's true, but no matter. She had friends after all, and work that was very fulfilling. Romance just wasn't in the cards for her at the moment, but she would be fine.

"I'm so sorry, Thalia," the duke murmured.

His discomfort with the situation was obvious. He clearly took no pleasure in his task.

Thalia just needed him gone, and smiled as brightly as she could manage.

"If there is nothing else I can assist you with, then I must return to my work, your grace. I thank you again for your concern and kindness," she managed, then turned and all but fled the scene.

She disappeared into the backroom again, and hid there until the duke left. Once the door had shut behind him, Thalia came back out and began to hunt for small tasks to occupy herself. She always felt soothed by the rhythm of work, which freed her mind to turn over and explore her feelings. She found several items on the shelves that didn't need rearranging but moved them around anyway.

Truly it was no surprise that Campbell Marlow was not interested in marrying a local shop owner, and Thalia had been clear that she was not looking for a marriage. So then why did she feel such an ache at hearing the duke's words? She bit her lip until it hurt, keeping the tears from falling.

The duke had come to deliver some difficult and embarrassing information, when he could have simply ignored his close friend's dalliance with her. He had been very courteous to look out for her, and warn her not to become attached. So, she wouldn't. Simple as that, Thalia reaffirmed to herself, though a small corner of her conscious mind rolled its eyes at that idea. It was already too late.

Thalia knew she wasn't the sort of woman who inspired men to fall in love, but it still hurt to know she was once again being tossed aside. She had so badly wanted to hope for a different outcome, that this time was different. That Campbell was the one who would truly see her, and want to stay by her side. She wanted to be loved, as pathetic as that felt to admit.

All she wanted to do was curl into a ball and weep, but she held herself together with the remaining threads of her strength. Later she could indulge in self-pity, let loose the devastation from her heart, and mourn the death of her hopes. Then she would once again pick herself up and continue on, as she always had before.

* * *

That night, Thalia took refuge in the company of her friends. Though she was loath to bring it up, and look over the entire situation with a magnifying glass, she did as soon as her foot was over the threshold. Mena was stoic per usual, but her eyes were full of empathy and concern. Clem was filled with righteous fury.

"How dare he dally with your feelings?" Clem demanded of no one in particular, one fist punching the air with her words.

"It's not like that," Thalia protested tiredly.

She was ensconced in a large wingback chair in Mena's library. The feeling of being hugged by a chair was quite soothing.

"Well, he certainly didn't say, 'Hello, good day. I would like to kiss you, love, but first you must know that I have a fiancé.'" Clem replied sardonically.

"He doesn't have a fiancé. Yet," Thalia grumbled.

"Do you want to marry him?" Mena asked, her voice soft and serious.

Thalia looked over at her and smiled sadly.

"I hadn't really thought about it. But I really like him, and he's an excellent kisser," she grinned. "I wanted to see where it went, and perhaps someday...who knows?" She finished with a shrug.

"He isn't married or engaged yet. You still haven't seen where this goes," Mena commented sagely.

Clem frowned. She wanted vengeance, not civility. "He's a cad," she insisted; arms crossed and chin lifted in defiance.

"He's not!" Thalia protested. "He's wonderful, really. Campbell helped my business, took in an orphan, and defended my honor. I do not think that he was trying to lead me on."

"And yet he did exactly that," Clem contended.

Thalia found she couldn't argue with that. It would have been better to know from the start that Campbell was not going to be around for long. But then, would she have made a different choice? Would she change anything, given the chance?

No. Thalia wanted to soak up every moment she could with Campbell. Store up delicious memories to savor later, when she was inevitably and utterly alone.

"I wanted to be with him too, Clem. It's not as though he forced me," she said.

Clem's mouth set in a thin line, but she didn't argue.

"Animal attraction," Mena said, breaking the tense silence that had descended.

Thalia burst into surprised laughter, with Clem and Mena joining in swiftly. They laughed until tears streamed down their cheeks, and their stomachs hurt. It was an emotional release that Thalia had greatly needed, and she was so grateful for her friends.

But she could not protect her heart, which was busy making a home for Campbell Marlow, regardless of her intention. Thalia was certain that she would rather have the time with him now, than be left with regret in his absence.

Despite knowing better, her silly heart had fallen in love with a man she couldn't have.

Nineteen

The following day, Bart was delivered to the estate stables. The boy was bright eyed with excitement as he exited the rickety pony cart sent from the orphanage. He was a tiny bundle of energy who seemed to zip around the yard. Campbell already felt dizzy watching him run.

"Does he ever...sit?" Cam asked the old man driving the cart.

The old man barked a laugh.

"Naw, children are like puppies. They'll run 'til they peter out and just fall down where they stand. Good luck!" he said with a crooked smile.

He snapped the reins and began to drive away. Cam could hear his laughter all the way down the drive.

Cam turned, hands in his pockets, and considered the small boy, who was still running in circles around the yard trying to catch a chicken.

"Good lord," he sighed, rubbing his chin. "Come over here boy," he called, and thankfully the child came right over.

"Yes, sir?" Bart asked, the picture of perfect manners.

But Cam could see the energy humming through his thin body. The boy was trying so hard to be good. Cam couldn't help but see a smaller version of himself in this small boy. He had once been given a big opportunity, and had been intent on being the model of good behavior, to use the moment to rise up from the gutter of his birth. It was a lot to ask from a child. A tenderness began to seep through him, subtly taking root in his heart.

The fortress he had erected around the vital muscle had first been breached by Thalia, who snuck past his defenses. And now this child was working his way in too. Perhaps this was a chance for Cam to heal, to move past the sins of his father. The idea was less frightening in this moment than it might have been before these new relationships had sprouted up, tenaciously growing through the cracks in his walls.

"Now, Bart, let us go on an adventure. I want to show you the estate grounds today, so you can get an idea of where we are and what goes on here," Cam said with a smile.

The boy nodded fervently and bounced on his toes. At least he wore good, sturdy clothing and shoes. He wasn't malnourished and was clean. The boy had potential.

Bart trotted along after Cam as they walked around the stables to the pen behind, where several horses grazed lazily in the sun. A small white and brown speckled pony came over immediately, hoping for a treat. Bart broke into a huge smile as the pony nuzzled his outstretched hand with her velvety nose. He had seen horses before, but the orphanage didn't have its own carriage, and the children rarely ventured beyond the walls of their home.

The boy could talk – that much became evident as Bart asked endless questions about the horses. Cam felt pleased, like he had in fact done a good thing for someone, and he patiently answered the boy's questions. It was clear how eager the boy was to learn, and how quick he was as he took in and processed all of this new information. This child could make something of himself, given the right tutelage. How many countless other children could do the same if given the opportunity, Cam wondered.

Bart soon forgot all about decorum and ran to the fence that separated the horse pen from the pasture. There, a small herd of Swiss brown cows grazed alongside several sheep. The occasional fat chicken pecked its way along the stone wall, frequently pausing to scratch the ground. Bart laughed with delight when a particularly large hen flew up to stand on the stone wall, and cocked her head to consider him.

"Woah, look at the size of 'im!" Bart hollered, clearly impressed with the bird.

Cam turned, hands in his pockets, and considered the small boy, who was still running in circles around the yard trying to catch a chicken. What had he gotten himself into? He certainly had no experience with children but the boy's smile made Cam want to do all he could to give him a better future.

Then the boy's eyes shifted to the side and widened in amazement. Confused, Cam turned around and saw the stallion trotting around behind the fence. It was alone in its pen, not yet fully broken.

"He is a big beast," Cam said with a frown.

"Can I give 'im a pat?" Bart asked, breathless with awe.

The stallion snorted and tossed his mane. The sun gleamed off his smooth hide, which was reddish brown. With a darker brown mane and tail, the horse was a truly beautiful specimen. Garrett had never bought a racehorse before, but he had recently decided that he needed a new hobby. And here was the result.

Already the menace had chased off two trainers and appeared set on refusing to ever let a saddle sit upon his back. Not that Cam could blame him. But ultimately this horse was proving to be both a waste of money and dangerous. Cam wanted him gone, and was working out a ploy to convince Garrett to gamble off the horse at one of his London clubs.

Looking at the beast, Cam was suddenly transported back in time, to the small broken body lying on the grimy cobblestones in Spitalfields with the sound of horse hooves disappearing into the distance. The sight of so much blood had frozen his heart, and Cam sucked in a breath. He shook himself to clear away the memory, refusing to let it haunt him. The past was dead and buried.

* * *

Mentally running through the items to include in her update to Mrs. Farningham regarding the musicale, Thalia walked to the orphanage. She took her time, enjoying the way the long afternoon light filtered through the lush, trailing leaves of the willows that lined the small park in the center of the village square. There was a gentle breeze blowing in from the river, refreshing the hot summer air. This was the most glorious time of year.

Thalia hummed to herself and swung her basket as she walked along, focusing on the lovely nature all around rather than her heavy heart. Everything was coming together, and that was worth feeling satisfied about. Even if love was not a part of the equation.

As she neared the orphanage, there was a commotion involving a rather stately and expensive-looking carriage. Mrs.

Farningham and Mena were standing on the front steps, motioning to the other people. Even from a distance, she could see the panic in their eyes. Thalia picked up her skirts, and started running.

"What is it?" she called out once she was within earshot.

Mena saw her and held up a hand in greeting.

"Thalia! I'm so glad you're here. There was an accident. Bart is injured and needs the doctor," Mena said, her voice steady enough, but Thalia could see that she was almost frantic with worry.

"Oh my god!" Thalia gasped, a hand flying up to cover her mouth. "What happened? What can I do?"

She looked to the carriage, and saw a small child being carefully removed, carried by the coachman, who wore familiar livery. Of course, Bart had been sent just this morning to the duke's estate to work for Campbell. Thalia's heart seized in her chest. What if Campbell had been injured as well? Her knees almost gave out, and she grabbed Mena for balance. Mena peered into her face with concern, and gripped Thalia's shoulders.

"The doctor has already been sent for. Hopefully it is just a broken bone or two, but we don't know for sure yet. Go down to the kitchens and have a tray made up. We will bring Bart to the dormitory to rest and wait for the doctor," she said firmly.

Mena was even calm in a crisis.

Thalia nodded, her heart in her throat, and ran inside to fetch the tray. Her mind worked in overdrive as her footsteps echoed in the hall. Would Bart live? Where was Campbell? What had happened?

Two volunteers ran past into the kitchen and began to stoke the fire and fill a large pot with water to boil. Another volunteer arrived with an armload of linens, which she dumped onto the table and began tearing into strips.

Thalia focused on her task and tried not to think the worst. She found a tray and stacked several items that she grabbed blindly from the larder. She filled a teapot with shaking hands, and then made her way up to the boy's dormitory.

Doctor Blakely had come straight away, bag in hand, his whiskered face serious. Clem had come in with him, and she deftly assisted her father with his ministrations. After a careful inspection of Bart's wounds, it was determined to be a broken arm and some deep lacerations that required several stitches.

Bart was blessedly awake, but his young eyes were lined with exhaustion. He did his best to tell the doctor about what had happened, his voice weak. A horse had broken loose. Bart was lucky to have such minor wounds, compared to what could have occurred.

Thalia sagged with relief, knowing that the boy would most likely mend well and regain full use of his arm. She took Mena's hand, giving it a squeeze in relief. Mena smiled reassuringly.

Bart was tired, but he was adamant that he not miss out on his apprenticeship, and vowed to not make the same mistake twice. His fervor on insisting that he wanted to return to the estate almost broke Thalia's heart. She hoped his injuries healed quickly. It was going to be torture for such an energetic boy to be confined to a bed for several weeks.

Once Bart was settled, and being tended by Mena, who attempted to slowly spoon broth into him, Thalia pulled Mrs. Faringham aside for a word.

"I need to go to the estate and speak with Mr. Marlow," Thalia said, keeping her voice low.

Mrs. Faringham's eyes darted back to Bart, but she nodded.

"Yes, we need to hear the whole story from an adult who witnessed it," she agreed with a nod.

Then she turned back to spear Thalia with a look.

"Bart cannot lose this apprenticeship. He will not get another opportunity like this again. The poor boy could be resigned to begging—or worse—when he is older, especially if he loses the arm."

Mrs. Farningham's mouth twisted in a grimace as she worked to stifle her emotion. She shook her head. Thalia pulled the older woman into an embrace and held her tight.

"We won't let that happen," Thalia assured her. "I'll be back tomorrow first thing."

Then she left, hurrying out the door, on her way to the estate. She had a lot of walking to do before dark.

* * *

The last of the dying light winked through the trees as Thalia came around the bend and saw the estate entrance. Of course, the estate had a ridiculously long drive, so her walk was hardly finished. Thalia sighed and stretched her neck, rolling her shoulders as she did so.

Then she spied a different road, more of a path really, leading into the overgrown brush to the left of the stone archway that defined the estate's drive. She ventured toward it, drawn by curiosity. She peered down the path, seeing no end.

Following some strange impulse, she started down the path. It felt like stepping off the well-trod forest path in a fairytale and traveling into the undiscovered heart of the forest. Birds sung in the lush canopy above her.

Finally, she saw light ahead, and slowed her pace. The path ended in a clearing, and Thalia could smell the earthy aroma of the river nearby. A small house that looked like a fairy cottage sat in the dying afternoon light, dappled with flecks of gold and twining pink roses. Thalia almost expected a fairy godmother to emerge from the charming cottage. She wasn't sure what she had expected, though this certainly wasn't it.

There was a small porch along the front, and Campbell sat in shadow, leaning back against the post. He hadn't seen her yet, and Thalia watched him for a moment, trying to discern his mood. He looked uninjured, which gave her great relief.

Campbell reached down and picked up a bottle that sloshed with a dark liquid around the bottom of the glass. Had he drunk all of that just now? Thalia began walking briskly toward him once again, worried that he was about to collapse in a drunken heap on the ground.

She stood before him, hands on her hips, for several moments before his eyes slid over and took notice of her. A flash of such utter sadness crossed his features, and it stole her breath away, before his features shuttered again, and he took another long swallow from the bottle.

"What are you doing here?" he asked, his words slightly slurred.

A lock of his dark hair had fallen across his forehead. There was a terrible vulnerability to him that threatened to break Thalia's heart.

"I came to see how you were. I happened to be at the orphanage when Bart was brought in," Thalia replied softly, twisting her fingers together in front of her.

Hearing Bart's name caused Campbell to wince and curse softly.

"How is the boy?" he asked, his glazed eyes sliding over to meet hers.

Thalia sat down on the step beside him and folded her hands together on her knees. She considered Campbell, feeling so sad for him.

"Bart is going to be fine," she said, with more confidence than she truly felt. "His injuries were not as severe as they looked at first. His arm is broken, but cleanly and the doctor is confident that it will set well. There were also some deep cuts that will scar."

Campbell hung his head, his hands hanging loosely between his knees.

"It was my fault the boy was injured," his voice was so soft that Thalia had to lean in to hear him.

"Accidents happen all the time," she protested. "You cannot prevent every terrible event."

"I should not have let the boy get so close to the horses. He was so taken by them, and I indulged him." Cam coughed out a humorless chuckle. "It was a new horse Garrett had just bought, and a great mean bastard too. Any idiot would know not to let a child get close to that."

"Did he climb into the pen?" she asked.

"No!" Campbell said firmly. "The horse tried to jump the fence and made it out. Though he broke the top two rails when he did. One of the boards struck the boy."

"So it was an accident then," Thalia said, laying a hand on Campbell's knee and gently squeezing.

She wanted to comfort him, to ease his anguish, but knew all she could do was bear witness and provide company. It was important he not be alone.

Campbell looked down at her hand, his expression inscrutable but his eyes churned with intensity.

"I shouldn't have considered myself capable of looking after a child," he bit out through clenched teeth, a muscle twitching in his jaw.

Thalia listened in silence. The way Campbell blamed himself...perhaps there was something deeper to this.

"Campbell, we are friends, yes?" she asked.

He looked sideways at her, one brow raised.

"Is that what we are?" he asked softly, apparently unable to keep the seductive tone from his lips.

"Yes, I think so," Thalia said, her heartbeat tripping in anticipation. Would he deny it?

Campbell nodded slowly.

"We are friends," he confirmed.

Thalia nodded once, firmly, setting aside the stinging disappointment those words carried with them. "Then I will tell you how I view this. It was a mistake. You were not being negligent. No one would have known the horse would jump, or the fence break. I just hope that this doesn't cause you to want to end the apprenticeship. It would be the worst possible outcome for Bart," she said.

Campbell absorbed this in silence as he gazed out into the darkening forest. After a moment he placed the bottle down on the ground, and, sighing, turned to face Thalia.

"You're right. I don't want to make things even worse for him," he said. "He is welcome back when he is able. But I will put him under the supervision of someone else. I cannot...I just can't."

A muscle in his jaw twitched. Campbell took a deep breath, and looked at Thalia with a steady gaze.

"The accident today, it reminded me...there was a similar incident when I was young. My brother..." his voice cracked, and he stopped speaking.

He swallowed.

"My brother was killed by a runaway horse," he finished.

Thalia sucked in an audible breath. "Oh my God," Thalia whispered. "How old were you?"

"Ten. My brother was six. I was supposed to be taking care of him. My father never forgave me," Campbell said matter-of-factly.

* * *

Cam forced himself to focus on his breathing. Thalia's un-expected presence at his cottage, after the way he ended things, paired with her tenderness and the alcohol he had drunk, nearly undid him. The day's shocking events were making him soft, shattering his resolve.

Breathe. In and out, in and out, in and out.

This focus was what had kept him going all these years. The desire to crawl into a bottle could be kept in check only by his focus and control.

He pushed aside the memory of his mother, broken by grief, sobbing on the floor of their cramped, filthy apartment. She had energy only to cry and scream. His father had pushed all of his emotions down, condensed into a tiny ball of pure hate that fueled him for the rest of his miserable life. That hate had, more often than not, been expressed with his belt; indiscriminately raining blows upon his remaining family members whenever the impulse struck.

"I'm glad that you found a way to move forward, despite such a terrible event. That is no small feat. It means that you are strong—a survivor," Thalia said, her voice soft but firm; just like her. She slipped her hand into his.

Cam held onto her hand as if it were his lifeline in a stormy sea. Haunted, that was the word that came to mind. He was haunted by his past, and now the past had met the present, and he was hurting so badly inside. Thalia wanted to soothe him, but perhaps she had come to lean on him for her own reasons.

"Would you show me your home?" she asked shyly.

Despite the innocence of her request and the aching in his heart, her nearness stirred his lust and he relented. A better man would have sent her away, but Cam was weak and craved her closeness.

"Yes," he replied, voice low and rough, and pulled her to her feet and led her to the door.

am led Thalia by the hand through the front door, which opened into a large room with low ceilings in the classic Tudor style. An enormous painting of a swan hanging on the far wall next to the staircase served as a nod to the original owner while the thick red oriental rug that covered the expanse of the room created a warm, cozy ambience.

"This was one of Garrett's ancestor's silly constructions," Cam explained, feeling a little defensive of the dollhouse he called home. "Garrett allows me to live here without interruption."

Thalia nodded as she looked around, taking it in with wide eyes.

"It is a lovely little house," she said softly. "The roof is made of thatch? How does that hold up in the rain?"

Cam's lips quirked up in a smile. Thalia couldn't suppress her natural curiosity in any environment.

"Quite well actually," he replied. "Come see for yourself."

He gave her hand a squeeze, and tugged her toward the stairwell. The wall was covered with several small paintings, mostly landscapes of the river, and a few photographs as well. Lots of swans.

"Those were all done by Garrett's aunt, Lady Winnifred," Cam supplied as Thalia paused to squint at the signature scrawled in the corner of a small painting.

"She was quite an accomplished painter it seems," she murmured.

"According to legend, she had little else to occupy her time as she never married nor had any interest in high society," Cam supplied, not sure why he was blathering on so.

Was he nervous? How ridiculous.

Thalia slid a conspiratorial smile towards him, her blue eyes twinkling. Cm's breath caught.

"I can't say that I blame her, though I wouldn't stay sane for long with only painting to occupy my time," she said coyly.

Cam reached for her, cupping her face in his hands. Thalia's eyes widened in surprise, and then fluttered closed as she anticipated his kiss. He claimed her soft lips, moved by an urgency that surprised him.

He drank deeply from her, licking along her lips and tongue. The tiny moans and gasps she elicited were driving him wild. Cam rocked against her, letting her feel the hard length of his cock. Thalia threw back her head and moaned, her hips grinding against him. She gripped his shoulders, as though she couldn't stand on her own.

Finally he pulled himself away from her and continued to draw her up the stairs. His heart pounded in his chest, and he felt more youthful than he possibly ever had. They went down the short hall, and stopped at Cam's bedroom door. Thalia held his eyes boldly, her lush mouth curved in a sinful smile. What little blood he had left in his body rushed to his groin, and he let out a low, guttural sound as he pulled her to him while pushing through the door.

They kissed feverishly, tearing at each other's clothing as they reached the bed. Cam threw off his waistcoat, and neckcloth, his shirt already half unbuttoned. Thalia had far too many items keeping her body from his view, and Cam was in no mood to wait. He gave up on the tiny row of hooks along the side of her dress, and tore the fabric with his large hands. Thalia gasped, her eyes bright with excitement. Her dress was pulled down over her hips and discarded.

Cam motioned for Thalia to sit on the bed, and then knelt down on the floor, quickly divesting her of her boots and unrolling her stockings. She was left sitting there in her undergarments and corset, hair still up in a simple chignon, her cheeks pink, lips swollen from his kisses. She looked so sweet and sensual, Cam felt a stab of lust so intense he was left shaken.

"Come here, Mr. Marlow," Thalia teased, crooking a finger at him.

She laughed in delight as Cam loomed over her, helping her lay back on the bed, leaving her legs dangling over the edge. Cam kissed along her throat and collar bone, inhaling her scent – sugar, soap, and warm woman. He pressed his hips between her thighs, reveling in her reaction, her moans and cries of pleasure.

He covered her mouth with his in a fierce kiss that threatened to consume them both. Her fingers scraped through Cam's hair, as her tongue tangled with his. He tried to persuade his brain to work logically again. This woman would be the death of him. He needed to make sure they were on the same page, though all he wanted to do was rip off the rest of their clothes and bury himself in her heat.

"Do you want me to fuck you?" Cam growled, trying to ask for consent, but barely maintaining control.

Thalia's blue eyes widened in shock, but he sensed how his crudeness had excited her. Cam clenched his teeth.

"Tell me," he said, barely able to keep his voice steady.

Thalia held his gaze.

"I want you," she breathed.

Her berry-colored lips were parted, and her little tongue darted out to wet them. Campbell instantly had several ideas for that tongue but forced himself to focus.

"Tell me what you want me to do," he demanded.

He wove his fingers into her coiffure, pulling slightly on the locks to test her reaction. Thalia nearly closed her eyes, and sagged into him; a soft sob of pleasure escaped her.

"I want…you to…pleasure me," she whimpered.

"You want me to fuck you," he clarified, as he rolled his hips to rub against her cleft.

"Yes. Please Cam," Thalia begged, with her clever fingers working to rid him of his shirt.

Cam growled again, and pulled his shirt over his head, tossing it across the room, and quickly divested himself of his trousers. As he straightened, he saw Thalia looking him over appreciatively. Cam felt his cock pulse as Thalia licked her lips, her eyes locked on the throbbing length of him.

"God love, when you look at me like that…" he trailed off.

"I like what I see," she said simply, her blue eyes glassy with desire.

She purred her approval, and reached for him, moaning as he lowered himself atop her. Cam slid one hand up her thigh, lifting the edge of her chemise to expose her drawers. Thalia moaned in excitement and opened her mouth to his explorations.

"You are the most beautiful woman I've ever seen," he breathed.

Thalia didn't look convinced, and Cam was seized with the need to make her feel beautiful.

Her lush, soft curves cradled his hard body. She opened herself to him completely and gasped at the sensation of his hot length resting at the entrance to her body. Their tongues tangled and stroked as their hands roamed over each other's bodies. Her long legs wrapped around his hips, holding him against her.

"I need you," she murmured against his lips.

"Me too," he whispered in between kisses.

Cam reached down between them and caressed her hot slick folds. She was so wet, and ready for him. His heart thundered in his chest, a ballooning feeling of triumph and rightness as he settled between her thighs and began to slide inside.

"God, you're so tight, love," he gasped.

"You're so big," Thalia whimpered, and Cam burned with primal appreciation.

He entered her as slow and gentle as he could, but her slick heat drew him in, greedy for the sensation he provided. Thalia lifted her hips encouragingly, whispering that it felt good, to give her more of him. Cam thrust into the hilt, giving her every inch of himself, and froze, his face contorted in exquisite pain. God, he could come right now, like a green youth.

"Campbell, are you alright?" she asked with concern.

Cam opened his eyes, spearing her with a look of intense yet inscrutable emotion. Then he smoothed his features, and kissed her again, proceeding to thrust within her. Sensation built up until

Thalia thought she couldn't take it anymore. There was so much feeling, it was almost overwhelming.

"Please, Cam!" she cried out, her heels digging into his back as she urged him on.

Campbell understood what she needed and reached down to stroke the little bud at the opening of her sex. Thalia was over-taken by a wave of incredible bliss, crying out his name again and again. She clung to Campbell as he somehow grew thicker within her, and lost control. He thrust harder and faster, holding Thalia's hips steady with his large hands, spreading her legs wider.

His breathing took on a ragged edge, and he grunted with the effort. Thalia was weak from her own release, and opened her eyes to watch Cam. He held her gaze, thrusting faster and fast-er until he abruptly withdrew, and found his own release, head thrown back.

***

He pressed kisses along Thalia's shoulder and neck and the tops of her breasts. And finally, he kissed her lips with a gentle sweetness that made Thalia suddenly want to cry. She was losing her heart to this man.

Campbell crossed the room and left through a different door. The sound of a tap turning and running water came from within, and he soon returned holding a wet cloth. He proceeded to gently clean her body of the evidence of their shared pleasure. Thalia lay on her back, allowing his ministrations. She felt sore but relaxed, her body utterly spent.

Then Campbell climbed in to lay in the bed beside her, pulling her back against him in a protective cuddle. Thalia felt completely enveloped in his warmth and smell, letting herself sink into the welcome relaxation he provided her. She had never been held thus, and she was now realizing how much she had missed out on before meeting Campbell Marlow. He was upending her life in many ways.

"That was very good," she whispered.

They lay together on the bed, their breathing slowly returning to normal. Campbell kissed her shoulder, brushing his lips over her skin in a possessive gesture. And just like that, Thalia was reminded that this would not last. She would need to gather herself up, and leave this warm embrace, and face the world alone once again. She tried to sort out her tumultuous emotions.

Thalia tried to convince herself to be happy for what she had been able to share with him, and make a good exit. She could practically hear Campbell's mind working to come up with something to say, and she had to head him off. She needed to be the one to walk away. Her confidence depended on it.

She rolled over and met his eyes.

"That was spectacular, but I want you to know that you don't owe me anything, Campbell," she said evenly.

His expression was steady and inscrutable.

Thalia soldiered on regardless, "Though perhaps you would like to do this again sometime?"

Thalia sat up, scooted to the edge of the bed, and set about putting herself together, which was admittedly quite difficult when your clothing had been ripped apart. She raised a brow at Campbell over her shoulder, admonishing him for his feral behavior. He merely watched her with his fathomless eyes, but a smile played at his lips.

How was she to walk home with her dress ripped apart? It was too warm for a cloak, but that was her only respectable option. She did her best to dress, and then took a step toward the bed, ready to make her goodbyes.

Campbell stood and came to her, completely and unashamedly nude. He framed her face in his large hands, and kissed her deeply, his mouth and tongue saying things his voice could not. Thalia held onto his wrists for support, and sagged when he pulled back. Her legs felt weak, but she forced herself to stand straight regardless.

"Why don't you stay?" he asked as he laid his forehead against hers.

Thalia's heart skipped a beat, daring to indulge in hope again. Was it possible he loved her too?

"I cannot," she said with regret, and she pulled away. It was better to leave now, and cling to the possibility of a future together, than to stay and have her hopes dashed once again. She wanted to hold onto her dreams for a little while longer, even if that made her a coward.

"Well then I insist on escorting you home, madam," Campbell said firmly.

He began gathering up his clothing. Thalia was sorry to see him dressed again. She wanted to tear his shirt off all over again.

Campbell walked with her back downstairs and out the front door, his hand on her lower back, burning through the fabric of her dress. To Thalia's surprise, he led her along a different path, which led to where the stables could be seen in the dim evening light. Thalia shivered, despite the summer heat, knowing that this was where the accident had happened.

Campbell gave her a searching look and bid her to wait in the shadows of the tree line while he went into the stables to ready his horse. Thalia had expected him to bring out a carriage, but he returned, leading a lone mare by the reins, saddled and ready to go.

"Are we riding together?" she asked, keeping her voice low.

Campbell nodded, flashing a boyish smile. Then he lifted her easily and set her up on the horse before swinging up behind her. Thalia found her bottom tucked into the cradle of his strong thighs and couldn't keep her thoughts from taking a naughty turn.

Though her quim was pleasantly sore from their love making, Thalia felt lust building within herself again. Campbell held her close, keeping a hand splayed low on her belly as they rode. Thalia was tempted to ask him to turn around and return them to his bed.

The moon shone bright in the gathering darkness. An owl hooted distantly in the trees. Thalia was glad to have the escort.

"Thank you, Cam," she said, and let herself relax back against the strong wall of his chest.

He kissed the side of her head. Thalia closed her eyes, imagining, just for a moment, that Campbell would change his path now. After what they had shared, how good it was, maybe he would stay.

Before long they were back in the village and walking up to the boardinghouse. Not a soul was in sight, which was good. Thalia didn't worry over her reputation, but neither did she wish to be known as the town strumpet.

Campbell dismounted, and then reached for her, setting her down gently on the firm ground. He didn't immediately release her, but held her waist in his grip, looking at her with an intensity that stole her breath.

"Good night, Cam," Thalia whispered, and stood on her toes to press a kiss to his mouth.

He kissed her back, lingering over her lips. But finally he released her, and Thalia made herself walk away.

"Good night, Sugar Queen" he called, his voice a low rumble.

Thalia did not look back and opened the front door to the boarding house as silently as possible. She eased the door shut behind her, blocking off her view of her lover as he stood illuminated in the moonlight. It was too much. She wanted to throw herself at him, against all better judgment. She had wanted to stay the night with him in his large bed.

But no, she had left. Because it was for the best, Thalia reminded herself sternly. Though she didn't feel comforted by that, and after removing her boots, she curled up on her bed, arms wrapped around herself. It didn't feel nearly as warm and safe as Campbell's embrace had been.

Twenty-One

The sun was just barely peeking over the tree line when Thalia's eyes opened. The neighborhood rooster started up his morning calls, a little late, but he was getting on eight years old now. Somewhere below a door slammed shut, sending a quake up through the wall.

Her sleep had been deep and dreamless, or at least she didn't remember any dreams. Thalia stretched and forced herself up and out of bed. She dressed methodically and poured herself some water from an old tin pitcher and washed her face and neck with a worn cloth. She scrubbed her teeth, and then arranged her hair in the usual, efficient way. Long ago she had given up on learning to braid or try anything remotely fancy. Once she was presentable, she sat on the bed and pulled on her boots.

Thalia sighed. She was relying on habit to avoid thinking again. She decided to give in to indulgence and let herself think of Cam and what they had shared. It had been so different from her other experiences. So beautiful. Surely it meant something. She felt connected to Campbell in a new, deeper way. Maybe he thought so too. Thalia hated waiting, but she wanted to be patient, to let him come to her. These felt like silly, childish games, when all she wanted to do was see him again.

This morning she would go back to the orphanage to check on Bart. A sinking feeling of worry settled in her stomach, but Thalia told herself to think positively. Dr. Blakely had been sure that the arm would heal well, and the cuts were not as deep as they had appeared due to the amount of blood. Barring infection, the boy would be alright.

Thalia walked first to her shop and told Abigail that she was out for the morning. Then she continued on to the orphanage. Every footstep brought her closer to having to face the injured boy again. Her stomach roiled with anxiety.

When she finally arrived at his room, Thalia peered in the doorway, steeling herself for the sight of the injured child. Bart lay in his bed, a shell of his usual self. His face was pale, but he rested peacefully. Seeing a fellow volunteer sitting on a chair keeping watch, Thalia smiled and came forward.

"How was he last night?" Thalia asked, keeping her voice hushed.

Bart didn't stir. His cracked lips were parted, his eyes moving rapidly behind his closed eyes.

The volunteer, Sally, met Thalia's eyes.

"It was difficult," she replied, mouth pinched. "The shock has worn off, but he was exhausted and in pain. Dr. Blakeley doesn't like prescribing addictive narcotics, but he left a bottle of laudanum, mostly to help the boy rest."

Thalia felt the sting of unspent tears pressing behind her eyes. She rested her forehead against the wall and closed her eyes for a moment. Bart would be alright. He would be running around soon enough, full of energy. But seeing him so fragile and weak, knowing that he suffered, was hard to bear.

Mrs. Farningham swept into the room, a tray in her hands.

"Good morning, dear," she said, acknowledging Thalia, and set the tray down on the side table.

"Morning," Thalia said, wiping the corner of her eye and straightening up.

"Bartholomew needs to eat," Mrs. Farningham tutted, shaking her head.

"He will wake soon, do not fear, ma'am," Sally soothed, and patted Bart's feet through the blanket.

"Rest is just as important for him," Thalia reminded her.

The older woman nodded with a sigh. Then she turned to Thalia, rubbing her hands together. All business.

"How was Mr. Marlow?" she asked.

Thalia jerked her gaze up to meet the older woman's eyes, startled. Did Mrs. Farningham somehow know about Thalia's irresponsibility? Her misdeeds? Her indiscretion?

None of those words were right. They didn't capture the essence of what had occurred.

"You went to his house last night?" the older woman prompted, clearly confused by Thalia's silence.

"Yes, I did pay him a visit, and he was not injured, thank God," Thalia said nervously.

"Good, good," Mrs. Farningham replied, nodding. "And is he going to terminate the apprenticeship?"

Her voice was apprehensive, though she remained her usual calm self. She worried over each and every child under her roof.

"He plans to honor his obligation to Bart," Thalia said firmly, knowing in her very soul that Campbell was a good man and would honor his commitments.

A light knock on the doorframe caused Thalia to jump. The two women turned to see who had arrived, Thalia expecting Dr. Blakely. But no, it was Campbell, looking rumpled from sleep in an entirely adorable way. How dreadful. Thalia's pulse increased, though she was torn between anxiety and lust.

His dark eyes held hers with an almost palpable intensity. Then his gaze dropped, and lingered over her body, spreading warmth wherever he touched her with his eyes. Thalia swallowed, and tore her attention away. Mrs. Farningham raised a questioning brow, but said nothing.

"Good morning, Mr. Marlow," the older woman said. "Bart is sleeping soundly, and the doctor has assured us that he will heal well."

Campbell's eyes flicked over the boy, but he quickly looked away again. Fine lines around his mouth were emphasized by the hardness of his expression. He fought so hard to maintain his stoic mask, Thalia realized. Her heart squeezed for this man.

"Good morning, ladies," Campbell said with his hands in his pockets as he shifted uncomfortably. "I'm glad to hear of the boy's condition. I was...worried."

Thalia wanted to reach out and hold his hand but resisted the absurd impulse. She had no claim on him, and therefore didn't have the right to publicly console him.

"Bart will be fine," Mrs. Farningham assured him, smiling sadly. "Don't you worry. We will take good care of him, and then he will be ready to rejoin you at the duke's estate."

Mrs. Farningham had thrown a gauntlet into the middle of the room and stood with her chin raised. Her eyes were sharp and penetrating, daring Campbell to defy her pronouncement.

Campbell looked to Bart again, then back to meet the older woman's eyes. He nodded, expression grave.

"Bart is welcome back whenever he is healed. But I don't want to risk further injury by rushing the process. Mending bones can take a while," he said. "I want you to know that...I am sorry for the boy's injury. He will be better protected in the future. And I will, of course, pay all medical expenses."

Mrs. Farningham fairly glowed from his words, her smile beaming.

"You are a good man, Mr. Marlow," she said, and gave his arm a squeeze. "Now, I must ask you both to leave Bart to rest. He must eat as soon as he awakens, and I do not expect him to be ready for company today."

She gently guided Thalia and Campbell from the room, and firmly shut the door in their faces, closing off the sounds of children laughing and talking in the hall.

Thalia looked up at him, feeling awkward. She twisted her fingers together in front of her. "Well, it was really good of you to come see Bart," Thalia said with a small smile, trying to sound upbeat, despite her hammering heart and fluttering stomach.

Campbell gave her a long, searching look. "I'm glad that he is doing well. I will check on him again soon," he said.

Thalia nodded slowly. "I should get back to the shop," she said finally.

"Of course," Campbell replied.

Thalia smiled politely and turned to walk down the hall. Campbell's heavy footsteps followed her, keeping pace.

"It was good to see you again," he murmured.

Thalia felt a blush creep over her cheeks, and she ducked her head. They really shouldn't discuss anything personal here at the orphanage.

"I feel the same," she replied softly, and cast a shy look his way.

Campbell's gaze was fixed firmly ahead, but a tiny smile played at the corner of his mouth. They continued along, making their way out of the building. The street noise enveloped them, an assault to the senses after the cool, quiet of the orphanage. Thalia felt Campbell's presence looming behind her as she walked.

Suddenly, he grabbed her arm, and pulled her into an alley. Their mouths met with an urgency that threatened to incinerate her. Campbell's hands speared into her hair, loosening her chignon, as his mouth ravaged hers, making love to her with his tongue. Thalia moaned, and surrendered completely to his plundering. It felt so right to be with him, to comfort each other, and worship each other with their bodies.

Campbell kissed her for a moment longer, and finally pulled away. His breaths came in sharp pants, and he held her face, calloused thumbs resting against her soft skin.

"Very good to see you again," he murmured, and brushed her lips softly with his before releasing her and stepping back.

His eyes raked over her body lasciviously, before he looked away and visibly shook himself. Thalia ran her damp hands over her skirts, smoothing the rumpled fabric. How was she going to go to work, now that she was all titillated and mussed? She wanted to stomp her foot in frustration, but then laughed at herself. Campbell gave her a bemused look.

"I'm going to have a hard time being productive today, I fear," she said, her voice filled with laughter. "That was very distracting, sir."

"I am quite distracted myself," Campbell replied, mouth quirked up in a rare smile.

"Well, we had best part ways now," Thalia said, feeling the loss of his company already. "I cannot walk with you the whole way. It would look...well, you know," she gestured vaguely.

"Have a good afternoon, Thalia," he said.

The way her name rolled off his tongue sent hot shivers down her spine.

"Good afternoon, Campbell," she returned, somehow knowing that this was not goodbye.

She forced herself to exit the alley and walk away. It was difficult indeed, but she did not look back.

* * *

It was almost dark out when a knock came at Cam's front door. He rose from his seat on a settee and went to see who it could be. The door opened to reveal Thalia. She stood there, smiling shyly in her prim striped dress. Her hair was starting to come free of its pins, and she had a smudge of chocolate on her chin. Cam wanted to lick that from her skin, and revel in her soft curves.

He let his dark eyes travel over Thalia's lush body, taking his time. The flare of lust that swept through him was powerful. He leaned one forearm against the top of the doorframe and considered his visitor.

Women were rarely so bold as to pursue a man and show up at his home in this manner, but Thalia took what she wanted from life. And she brought Cam a box of butterscotch candies, as an excuse to visit. Heat bloomed in his chest as he looked at her, his mouth dry.

"Well, aren't you going to invite me in?" she asked sweetly, lifting the box of butterscotches with a broad smile.

Guilt warred with desire as he thought of the looming house party, where he still planned to select a bride. A bride who was not the woman waiting on his doorstep. A crushing sensation in his chest stole away his breath for a moment. He was going to lose her, and there was nothing to be done about it. This could be their last moment together.

Cam knew he was not a good man. He was not strong enough to turn Thalia away. He was selfish, needing one last night with her to sustain him for the coming days, when he would be offering someone else forever. Some part of him knew he would never have this connection with another woman, and that he was bargaining away this relationship for status. It made him queasy, the realization of the enormity hitting him at last. Violently shoving those thoughts aside, Cam made his decision.

Thalia's tentative smile turned lascivious when he silently reached out and pulled her to him, pressing against her softness. Cam thrust a hand into her hair, and kissed her deeply, passionately, as though they had not just parted hours ago. His tongue claimed her mouth with hot strokes, as one of his large hands smoothed down her back to grip her derriere, pulling her hips tighter against his own.

Thalia brought her hands up to his chest, marveling over the ripple of his muscles. She couldn't help squirming against him, enjoying the sensation of his body, so unlike her own. He was hard where she was soft, and the sensations drove her wild.

Cam kissed along her jaw, and down her neck, pressing his tongue to the place where her pulse throbbed at the base of her throat. Thalia moaned, her eyes closed as she focused on every sensation. Cam moved back up to nibble her earlobe, eliciting a little yelp of surprise.

"Come inside," he whispered hotly in her ear.

"Yes," she answered, and tried to capture his lips again.

He pulled away, denying her, but kept one arm locked around Thalia's waist. Cam led her up to his bedchamber and closed the door with a firm click behind them. He gently pushed Thalia down to sit on the edge of the bed.

"I want to try something different tonight," he said, brushing his fingers down the long tendrils of her hair, sending her pins flying off toward the floor.

Thalia could only nod in response, her breathing coming in fast huffs, and she blinked lazily against the soothing feeling of his fingers on her scalp.

"You must tell me to stop if you do not like it," his voice firm.

Thalia nodded again, her tongue darted out to lick her lips, and Cam's eyes flared as they tracked her movement. He nodded to himself, and then bid Thalia to turn around so that he could undress her. He stripped off every article of clothing this time, wanting to see all of her.

"I want you to get onto your knees," he directed.

Thalia's eyes widened in surprise, but she did as she was told, turning around and climbing onto the bed. Thalia looked back over her shoulder, and felt her breath catch as she locked eyes with Cam, who stood naked and erect behind her. She licked her lips in anticipation.

"I am going to ride you hard, Thalia," he growled, his fingers gripping her hips. He waited for a beat. "Do you want it hard?" he asked, waiting.

"Yes," she replied, her voice sounding more like a whimper.

Cam growled in response, his cock nudging at her entrance.

"So wet for me," Cam said, pushing inside with excruciating slowness.

Thalia moaned and buried her face into the bed. Cam was all sensation, existing only for this feeling, this moment.

"That's it, love. You take that cock so well, like a good girl," he moaned.

His large strong hands gripped her, and spread her wider, enjoying the view of his cock plunging in and out, as his breathing turned into pants.

He knew her release was close, and she lifted her head to beg, "Please, Cam, please!"

Cam only grunted in response, and instead slowed his pace. He gave her his cock in rough, deep strokes. He was playing with her, prolonging her release, tormenting her. She whimpered in frustration, so perilously close to that moment of ecstasy she sought.

But she had her own solution. She brought one hand down to rub herself just above where her body was joined with his. She moaned as her fingers stroked over her most sensitive peak. Cam stilled as he noticed her activity. It was the most erotic thing he had ever seen.

"Yes, that's it, love. Take what you need," he coaxed, resuming his movements in furious strokes.

Thalia cried out, falling over the cliff into her pleasure. At the same moment, Cam found his release, groaning with animal abandon as he pulled free from her body and spent his seed in great spurts. He bent forward, breathing hard. Thalia turned her face away from the bed and sighed in contentment.

"I am utterly spent," she breathed, a drunken and joyful smile spreading across her face.

"I'm glad you enjoyed it," Cam said, feeling a warmth grow within him from her praise. "I'll admit that I wasn't sure if you would appreciate being handled so roughly."

* * *

Thalia rolled over and considered Campbell. He stood beside the bed, cleaning away the evidence of their union from his body, before finding his trousers from among the discarded clothing on the floor. He looked relaxed and happy, she decided, which pleased her.

Suddenly, Thalia's heart felt full to bursting, and she struggled to breathe through the intensity of her emotion. Despite her attempts to keep her heart protected, and despite what she knew of his aspirations to marry an aristocrat, she had come to care deeply for this man. Campbell Marlow had burrowed beneath her defenses, and into her very soul. She doubted that he would declare the same emotions and didn't want to frighten him off by proclaiming her own.

Campbell was watching her closely, and he climbed up on the bed to stretch out beside her. He must have noticed her troubled expression, and Thalia forced herself to smile.

"Are you planning to feed me dinner, sir?" she asked, her tone playful as she reached to lift a lock of hair from his forehead.

The last thing she wanted was to make things complicated. She should simply enjoy every moment, and not worry about the future. This was all she was going to get in life, and should be happy for the taste of happiness. But she wanted forever.

Campbell laughed. "I am ravenous too after all that activity," he said, and kissed her lightly. "Shall I bring something up to you, or would you prefer to come down?"

Thalia considered this.

"I should like to come down, but I shall have to get my dress back on first," she laughed.

Campbell helped her dress, and they descended the stairs together. Thalia was led to the sitting area arranged near the charming stone fireplace in the main room. There was no fire set today, and the large windows along the far wall were opened to the inviting summer breeze. The window overlooked the river, but along the house grew several rose bushes. The fragrance filtered in with the breeze and filled the room with a lovely scent.

Thalia breathed deeply and relaxed in her chair. She was very much looking forward to a bite to eat and a cup of tea. Before long, Campbell returned with a tray weighted with a tea service and several plates of offerings. He sat in a chair across from Thalia and served her like an attentive beau.

Thalia dared to hope that Campbell might be coming around to the idea that they could be together in a lasting relationship. She sipped her tea, watching him over the rim of her cup. She could tell that he was pretending not to notice her staring, but the slight curl of the corner of his mouth told her that he was aware. Then he leaned forward and offered her a bite of a tart that he held in his bare fingers. This rather mundane activity, taking tea together, was becoming incredibly flirtatious.

She would have to convince him that she would make him happy. Happier than a rich and well-connected wife could. Thalia frowned into her cup. How on earth was she to accomplish that? She could change his mind, and convince him that they could find love and contentment together. But that path was a frightening one, with the potential to break her heart.

To be rejected, after offering her heart to him, would destroy her. What if he walked away? It was better to enjoy the moment for what it was, and hope for nothing and risk nothing. But it was difficult to hide her feelings and affect a happy state she did not really exist within. She was filled with turmoil and uncertainty, her heart anxious and sad. Along with a touch of anger.

It was not without risk, their secret trysts. If they were found out, Thalia risked losing the good will of the villagers which could see her business shuttered. She could even lose her room at the boardinghouse. The injustice rankled, as a man would never face such retaliation for indulging in an affair, but a woman could be utterly destroyed by even the appearance of impropriety.

* * *

Cam watched Thalia's expression become troubled, with little lines forming between her brow. He wondered what was bothering her, but wasn't sure that he wanted to ask. He had made it clear that this relationship could not last. Perhaps she was working up the courage to break things off.

He had been trying to convince himself that he should stick to the plan and marry an aristocratic bride, to continue on his path, but he found no excitement in the idea of hunting down a bride. None of his future plans filled him with energy and focus anymore. Every one of his dreams were filled with her. If he didn't know himself better, Cam would think that he was falling in love with Thalia.

Alarmed by that thought, Cam shifted in his seat. He needed to stop this, now, before he fell in deeper and became trapped. Thalia deserved better than a man who was distracted by courting his intended bride. And soon enough he would be courting some nameless, faceless aristocrat. And he would lose the company of this vibrant, amazing woman. His stomach clenched at that.

Cam set down his cup, and leaned forward, resting his forearms on his knees. His heart hammered sickly in his chest. Hesitation paralyzed him. He took a deep breath and forced himself to speak.

"Thalia, we need to talk," he said, voice gruff with emotion.

Thalia's expression immediately shuttered, but not before Cam caught the spasm of pain that contorted her features. Her gaze shifted away from his, pretending extreme interest in the walls. That look struck Cam right in his heart and stole his breath. He cared so much for her. Too much, in fact. And he had never wanted to hurt her.

But he couldn't make her happy. He would only hurt and disappoint her in the end. She might fancy that she could love him, but Cam knew the truth—he was unlovable. He was too hard, too cruel, too base. Thalia would tire of him eventually, and it was better that she not get attached to him. She should be free to live her life, run her business, and in time to find a solid bland man who could give her children if she desired. She did not want to get involved in Cam's black swamp of a soul.

"Campbell, you don't need to explain. I understand. You made it clear from the beginning that this wasn't going to last," she said carefully, clearly putting in effort to keep her voice steady and not betray her emotions.

Cam longed to smooth her furrowed brow, but he willed himself to harden his heart.

"I enjoy spending time with you, and what we have shared has been good," he began, hoping to convey his sincerity.

She cut him off with a sharp swipe of her hand. "No, I understand what this is. Don't trouble yourself," she said.

Cam's gut twisted. This was going badly. "There is no future for us, Thalia. Soon enough you would have seen that for yourself," he said flatly.

Thalia flinched as if struck. She swallowed and took a steadying breath. "I care for you, Campbell," she said softly, her cheeks flushing a fierce shade of crimson.

She briefly met Cam's eyes before looking toward the door as though calculating the distance between her and freedom. She chewed her lower lip, drawing his attention to her lush mouth.

"I never made any promises to you," Cam said, suppressing the desire to reverse course and make this torture end.

"You are right," she agreed. "I let myself hope for more. That is my own fault. My apologies for making this awkward."

Thalia bent down and put on her boots. Working quickly to lace them, she was soon done and looking about for anything she might be in danger of leaving behind. Then she stood and walked with an iron spine to the door. Cam shot to his feet, but resisted the urge to follow her.

"Thalia, I am sorry I can't give you more," he said lamely.

At the door, Thalia laid her forehead against the wood for a moment. Then she turned with a sad smile and said, "You can Campbell, you just won't."

And with that she was out the door and gone. Cam let her go. He sat back down heavily in his chair. He stared at the table before him, at Thalia's tea cup and the crumbs of her post-coital French pastry.

It took all his effort not to chase after her and beg for forgiveness. He wanted to feel Thalia holding him tightly as he gave her pleasure one last time. But he forced himself to stay seated. He let out the breath he had been holding.

It was done. Over with. Now he could focus on the weekend party and selecting a bride. Sadly, that didn't bring him the usual feeling of focus and determination that it once had. Instead, he was filled with a desolation that threatened to bring him to his knees. The sensation of loss was blinding.

* * *

Thalia walked with as much dignity as she could muster down the lane, but once Cam's house was out of sight she began to run. She ran as the tears began to pour out of her in great sobs. She tried to convince herself that she was best rid of him. Walking along in the gathering darkness hardened her feelings into an angry, bitter kernel. The cad hadn't even insisted on walking her home. He was dishonorable in the extreme, and she would not mourn his loss. She stomped her way home, head held high, even as her heart was shattering.

Twenty-Two

For the past three days, Thalia had successfully kept Cam from her thoughts. It had been difficult, but the nights were certainly the worst of it. During the day she could focus on her work and had the comfort of Abigail's company. But at night she lay awake in her small bed alone, ruminating on what her future might now hold.

Would she be alone for the rest of her days? Surely her friends would someday marry, and while they would insist that she visit them, it wouldn't be enough. She wanted something of her own; someone to come home to after a long day of work, and possibly children of her own. She needed more out of life than work and friendship. She wanted companionship, romance, closeness.

She wanted to curl into a ball and sleep. To ignore everything until nothing could hurt anymore. The idea of bridging the gap between them rankled on principle, and was exhausting to contemplate. Why should she be the one to make that effort? How could anything be resolved if she did not?

She was not wealthy or titled. She was not fashionably slim and elegant. She worked for a living. But she loved her life. Why couldn't Cam be satisfied to share that life with her? Instead of ruthlessly and callously chasing power and riches.

A sharp knock at the door interrupted her melancholy. Thalia rolled over to face the door.

"What?" she croaked out.

The door opened, and Mena and Clem came into the room, just in time for their usual evening chat. Both of them looked concerned. Clem came to sit at the foot of the bed, her green eyes flashing with outrage. Mena bid Thalia to sit up a bit, and slid to sit with Thalia's head on her lap.

She patted Thalia's hair soothingly, and Thalia was at once struck with a feeling of annoyance and raw need to be held. She wanted to be alone, and yet needed her friends. It was an emotional turmoil she had never experienced with such intensity before.

"Forget that bastard," Mena demanded imperiously. "The dance is tomorrow night, and we are going to get dressed up and enjoy ourselves as single ladies can. Men are terrible, and we are best free of them." She sat with her arms crossed, thin shoulders hunched forward.

Clem looked fit to fight a boxing match with someone. It eased the tension Thalia felt, knowing that this warrior was on her side. Thalia's eyes, swollen from her tears, squeezed shut against the sharp stab of pain that ripped through her. These friends meant so much, but they weren't Campbell. Her connection with him was different. And now it had been severed so suddenly. She felt like a drowning sailor desperately clinging to a piece of wood to protect herself from a stormy sea.

"What will we wear to the dance?" she forced herself to say; her voice but a whisper.

Mena smoothed her hand over Thalia's hair, murmuring soothing sounds to comfort her.

"We will wear our best gowns, and look fabulous. We will flirt, and dance, and drink, and thoroughly enjoy ourselves," Clem said firmly.

Thalia sighed and pushed herself to sit up.

"I don't know if I can...but it sounds wonderful," she said.

She tucked her legs under her and picked at the hem of her striped work dress. Beside her, Mena shifted to lean back against the headboard. Her usual smooth countenance was marred by her furrowed brow and pinched mouth. For Mena this was practically screaming and throwing items across the room.

"You are your own woman, Thalia," she said firmly, with a slight growl to her tone. "We will leave whenever you wish, but I agree with Clem that a night out dancing is just the thing."

Thalia was shocked. Mena never advocated for going out; she was practically a hermit.

"It's quite pathetic, is what it is," Mena declared. "What a coward."

She glared at the far wall, her arms crossed over her thin chest. Thalia wanted to curl into a ball and disappear into the floor. Logically, she knew what her friends were saying was probably true. And yet she also fiercely wanted to defend Campbell. What a confusing emotional turmoil this was.

"Are you worried about running into him?" Clem asked.

Thalia barely considered the idea.

"No, I am not worried about that at all. Why on earth would he attend such a low-class event?" she scoffed, feeling quite bitter. "Surely he will be busy preparing for his perfect aristocratic bride."

"All the more reason to enjoy ourselves. We are free women and can do as we please, thank you very much," Clem said calmly, her lush lips curled into a wicked smile.

Thalia snorted, rejecting the idea, yet part of her wanted to set down the heavy weight she carried and lose herself. At least for a little while. "I don't think so, Clem."

"Come on," Clem wheedled, "What else are we going to do? It's the end of summer, it's hot, let's go and have some refreshments and we can always come back straight away if it's too much for you both."

"It would be lovely to dance with you both," Mena added.

Thalia sighed, willing herself to get energized for the outing. "Suppose we go for a couple of dances—" Thalia began, but was swiftly cut off.

'Excellent!" Clem said, clapping her hands together.

Thalia's mind turned to Campbell, and breathed through the sharp pain that resulted. She had to find a way to move on from him, even though she knew in her heart she would never forget their time together. When she was old and wrinkled, lying in her bed alone, she would think of the incredible pleasure he had given her. In his arms, she had felt beautiful and special. Perhaps that was worth the heartache.

* * *

Cam paced around his tiny fairy house, threatening to wear a trail into the thick carpeting. An intense restlessness had settled inside him, and he couldn't seem to get rid of the jittering energy within. He couldn't spend every day drinking, sadly, because he had work to do. He had gone to help dig the canals for the past two days, and that had been an enormous help. But once he arrived home, he was alone with nothing to do but think.

He could not allow himself to dwell on the situation with Thalia. He had made a choice, and needed to honor that decision. Garrett's sister, Lady Claire, was finalizing menus and schedules for the weekend party, and it was barely a month away now. If all went well, Cam would be married by the end of the year. But the thought of that wasn't satisfying, like it used to be. Instead, he felt such loss, it nearly brought him to his knees.

Cam checked the time on his pocket watch. Only six o'clock, which left a long, lonely Friday evening ahead. It was incredibly depressing. As much as he wished to avoid Garrett's questions and possible lectures, he decided to head to the main house for dinner.

The sun sat low on the horizon, but there was still plenty of light at this time of the year. Somewhere in the wildflowers, bees droned lazily in the late heat of the day. The beauty of it made Cam feel bitter. He didn't want to be reminded of beautiful things at the moment.

Thrusting his hands into his pockets, he marched down the path, across the drive, and up the front steps. He barged into the house, catching the butler off guard. The older man rushed forward, trying to salvage his position, but Cam didn't slow down. He rounded the corner and burst into the dining room. Garrett paused with his hands aloft, holding his cutlery.

"Good to see you. It's been a few days," Garrett said, and began to cut his meat. "You look like shit."

Cam sat and waited for the footman to come and serve him. He fought to keep his expression bland.

"I've been helping with the trenches, and deserve a good meal," he said, wincing at the defensiveness evident in his tone.

"By all means, eat from my table at your leisure," Garrett said, voice dripping in sarcasm.

Cam heard the bite in his friend's voice but ignored it, finding comfort in the familiar lopsided smile that curved at the edges of Garrett's mouth. Slowly, he began to relax in the company of his friend. The footman returned with a second servant close behind. The footman set out Cam's dinnerware with expert precision, and then pivoted with a dancer's grace to serve wine from the tray carried by the other servant.

In the center of the table was some kind of meat cooked in a brown sauce, a whitish substance in a bowl, and a large platter of vegetables. Whatever it was, the food was always excellent here. He didn't particularly care what it was. Cam served himself from the selection, and tucked in. He hadn't realized how hungry he was, and soon he was polishing off the last bite of food. Garrett chewed slowly and watched Cam with a bemused expression.

"How have you been, Cam?" he asked as he set down his cutlery and sat back in his chair.

Oh Christ, Cam thought. Here it came. The lecture.

"I'm fine," he said. A muscle in his jaw twitched. "I'm looking forward to the arrival of Lady Claire."

Garrett considered him for a moment, but finally nodded and picked up his glass.

"Yes, me too," he said insincerely, and drained his wine. "And alas, she will be here very soon. We must endeavor to enjoy ourselves before then. Savor the moment, and all that." He waved a hand dismissively.

"Tragically this part of the country is not known for its many diversions," Cam replied sardonically.

Garrett snorted.

"Too true. Surely, we can find some entertainment though, even if it's at the pub. Charles, is there anywhere we can go for some fun tonight," Garett called over to the footman who was standing in the corner.

The young man came forward at once.

"There is the late summer dance in town, your grace," he answered to the wall, looking past the table rather than at either man seated there.

The man was immune to making eye contact. A well trained servant, indeed.

"A country dance?" Cam asked skeptically, and finished his wine.

Charles immediately moved to refill their glasses. He stepped back and wiped the mouth of the bottle with a white cloth he kept draped over his left arm. His precise movements would have impressed even the most exacting military general.

"If I may say so, your grace, this dance is the best one of the year. The ladies will be in need of dance partners, and it is warm outside which encourages walks in the moonlight," the young man said, and had the audacity to wink, though he directed it to the wall.

Garrett's grin widened, and he turned to spear Cam with a look.

"I'm not interested," Cam said firmly, and took a drink of wine, barely tasting it.

"Come on, Campbell. It will be amusing, and our drinking will appear social rather than merely depressing," Garrett wheedled.

Cam's jaw clenched. A country dance sounded awful, and a terrible idea. What if Thalia was there? Or one of her friends? He shuddered at the thought of having to face her fiery friend, the dark-haired one. Even he found the woman formidable.

But he did want to drink and he didn't want to be alone. To please Garrett, Cam would go to this idiotic dance, and perhaps he would be lucky enough to catch a glimpse of the woman who continued to haunt his dreams. He returned Garrett's gaze and nodded once. The duke's eyes lit up, and he clapped one hand on the table.

"Yes! Tonight will be fun. Excellent suggestion, Charles. Many thanks," Garrett said, his voice already reaching levels that could best be described as boisterous.

Cam already regretted agreeing to this outing. But it was too late now. He grabbed a crust of bread to soak up the sauce left on his plate, knowing that he had a long night of drinking ahead of him.

"I'm going to go change, "Garrett announced with enthusiasm, and he rose from the table. He turned back and raked a critical eye over Cam's attire. "You should probably change as well, and take a bath."

Cam rolled his eyes. Great, now he was expected to get gussied up, when all he wanted to do was hide.

"When are we leaving?" he asked.

"We should go to the pub first, so let's say an hour from now," Garrett answered as he swept out the door, not waiting for a confirmation.

Well, there was no going back now. Cam smiled slightly to himself, even as his stomach roiled with dread. Leave it to Garrett to find a way to make even a broken-hearted man smile.

With a sigh, Cam pushed back from the table and stood, ready to try his damnedest to find something clean to wear. For Garrett's sake. He could do this, it just required a bit of fortitude and control, which he had a lifetime of experience cultivating. Surely it wouldn't be too terrible.

Twenty-Three

The annual late summer dance was traditionally held at the largest inn in the village, as it had the most spacious ballroom. Almost the whole of the village would be in attendance as there were not many opportunities for all levels of society to mingle and cavort together. Last year the weather had been dreadful, with never-ending downpours that turned the roads to slop. So the excitement in town was palpable this year, with days of clear blue skies and gentle breezes. People were in the mood for celebrating.

Thalia did not really feel up to it, but she put on her finest dress, a pearl gray cotton affair with small puffed sleeves, and went, regardless. She had taken the time to carefully twist her hair into a more elegant coiffure than usual and had pinned on her mother's green glass carbobe. She held her shoulders back, affecting the confidence that she didn't really feel.

As she approached the inn, Thalia slowed her steps and searched for her friends in the crowd. She couldn't stop the flare of hope that Campbell might attend the dance too, and see her looking so beautiful that he would come to her and profess his undying love. She snorted at that pathetic dream, and sternly smothered such romantic impulses. She was going to spend time with her friends, and hopefully have a bit of fun. And that was it.

She reminded herself that she could hardly have been holding out hope that Campbell would stick around forever. A man like him had aspirations. Like most men, he sought wealth and power. The duke had tried to warn her. Thalia was not the kind of woman Campbell should hitch his wagon to. She was a country nobody, and tied to the small brick shop she had made her own. She couldn't go away to London for months at a stretch, and no one would welcome her there. No, Thalia was content to stay in this small village for the rest of her days, rather than be isolated and an outcast in the big city.

Thalia imagined herself stuffed into a fancy ensemble and forced to sit in various parlors discussing the weather and drinking tea. The image made her chuckle, the sound echoing cold and hollow in her ears. And that was if she was very, very lucky to have invitations at all. It would be fun to play lady on occasion, but Thalia was born with far too much energy to stay cooped up in a gilded cage. It was too bad Campbell desired a woman like that, but Thalia wouldn't stand in his way. She would have to let him go, and cease dwelling on him.

"Thalia! Over here!" a familiar voice called over.

Thalia turned and spotted Mena and Clem. She made her way over.

"Good evening, ladies!" Thalia said with an overly bright tone, her smile far too wide.

Clem's eyes instantly narrowed.

"You promised not to think about that idiot," she scolded.

"I'm not!" Thalia protested, but she felt her cheeks burning. She should have known better than to try to fool her friends. They knew her too well to not see past the false cheer.

"We are here to enjoy ourselves as free and single women. We do not need men," Clem said staunchly.

Mena coughed out a laugh, but she didn't argue. They made their way inside the ballroom by way of the open terrace doors. A crush of people filled the small garden area, and Thalia and her friends had to force their way through. Raucous music came from inside, and the stomp of the dancer's feet could be felt by vibrations from the floor. They finally arrived at the edge of the dance floor, and paused to admire the group laughing their way through an energetic Scottish reel. A servant passed by with a tray of glasses. Clem shot her hands out and grabbed two. The small man was moving quickly, and after handing off the drinks to her companions, Clem had to almost chase one down for herself.

She returned, a little out of breath but radiating beauty in an almost annoying way. Rather like some kind of angel gracing the lowly humans with her presence. Thalia shook herself. Feeling bitter and jealous of a friend wasn't like her. She sniffed her glass, trying to deduce what was inside.

Mena and Clem took partners for the next dance, and were immediately pulled into the smiling throng of dancers on the floor. Thalia laughed, though her face hurt from effort.

"Why aren't you dancing?" Campbell's deep voice came from over her shoulder, startling her.

Thalia spun around, a hand pressed to her chest, eyes wide.

"What are you doing here?" she sputtered, feeling unsteady.

Campbell looked at her uncertainly. He seemed unsure of himself in a novel way.

"I wanted to check on you," he replied cautiously.

Hot anger filled her. How dare he?

"As the source of my sadness, you have no right to badger me to smile more," she said through her teeth, chin lifted.

"I did not tell you to smile," he protested.

Surely his furrowed brow and thunderous eyes would have intimidated anyone else, but Thalia was uncowed. She crossed her arms and stared him down in defiance. Campbell's eyes narrowed, but he leaned back against the wall to affect a relaxed pose.

"I heard some news. From your friend, the duke," she said then, wanting to unsettle him, to take away his precious control.

She immediately noticed a cloud cross his visage as he tried, but failed, to conceal his apprehension.

"And what news would that be?" he asked warily.

With a little scoff, Thalia narrowed her eyes. Was he not going to be truthful with her? It was galling to be treated this way. She had trusted him. She had fallen for him. Bloody hell, what a ninny she had been.

"That you are hunting a blue-blooded bride. In fact, I am to help in this endeavor with my confections," she said, her cheeks burning with hot anger.

"Garrett told you this." His voice was flat and emotionless, but his eyes were deep shimmering pools of regret and sadness.

Thalia refused to let it sway her. Why should she leap to soothe him, when he had behaved so callously? His regret wasn't strong enough to change his mind.

"I've known for some time, but hoped it wasn't true. Or at least, I hoped you might change your mind. But I now see how silly that was. I am not about to start attaching strings to you, Campbell. You are a free man. We made each other no promises." She was proud of her ability to keep the tone of her voice even, but failed at preventing the single tear that escaped and trailed down her cheek.

Thalia ferociously wiped it away and raised her large blue eyes to meet Cam's. He held himself very still as he listened.

She shook her head sadly. "I told myself that I wasn't going to hope," she whispered, her expression tortured, heart twisting in her chest.

Taking a shaky breath, Thalia tore her gaze away. She couldn't stand another moment here, where she wasn't wanted. It hurt too much, and she lacked the strength to face him any longer.

Suddenly a raucous group exited the dance floor near them and interrupted their discussion. Thalia straightened her shoulders and pasted a stoic mask upon her face. A wash of relief swept over her as she spied her friends in the crowd.

"Thalia," Cam called out as the crowd separated them.

Thalia did not respond, and forced herself to walk away.

She practically ran to Clem and Mena. She touched a hand to her face, checking for errant tears. Then she pasted a bright smile on her face as she approached them. Blessedly, they were standing beside the refreshment table. Thalia took a lemonade, focusing on the sweet tartness on her tongue as she sipped from the glass.

Mena reached over to take Thalia's free hand, giving it a squeeze, acknowledging her heartache in silence. Thalia blinked back a fresh rush of tears at the tender gesture. What would she do without her friends?

"I brought Russian vodka," Clem said brightly, pulling a silver flask from her reticule. She poured a generous measure in each of their cups. "Unfortunately, I forgot a spoon to stir with." She grimaced apologetically, and bravely took a gulp of the concoction. "Blech! The alcohol has a terrible tendency to sit at the top."

"I've never understood the appeal of a cocktail," Mena demurred, but sipped hers regardless.

"Don't judge the entire category on this swill," Clem replied irreverently.

Thalia wanted so much to forget about Campbell and enjoy the evening, but her chest still felt tight. It was impossible to ignore the aching grief within. She took a large swallow of her drink, willing the concoction to ease away her anguish. It certainly warmed her throat as it went down, which was pleasant enough.

"What is it?" Clem asked, her voice sharp with concern.

Thalia sighed. "I bumped into Mr. Marlow," she confessed, keeping her eyes downcast to avoid seeing their reactions.

"The man who is hunting a wife who is not you," Clem stated flatly, her disgust apparent.

"Indeed," Thalia confirmed.

She took a second deep gulp of her drink and felt a small comfort from the sting of the vodka on her tongue. She needed to just not feel…so much. At least for a little while.

"Bastard," Mena said softly beneath her breath, brows furrowed.

She was usually quite sympathetic to most people and their struggles, but once her mind was set against someone, it would be difficult to change her mind. Mena was often overlooked as a soft, simple woman, but she was made of steel.

"I never liked him," Clem declared with a toss of her head, and glared in the direction she assumed the man had slunk off.

Thalia nearly choked on her drink, eyes growing wide as she looked at her friend in surprise.

"Is that true?" Mena asked, her usual stoic expression giving nothing away.

Clem shrugged and took a sip of her lemonade. "He's boring for one thing," she replied.

A surprised laugh escaped Thalia before she protested, "He is not boring!" She really should be feeling so defensive. He deserved the scorn of her friends.

"He's also a snob," Clem insisted, unrelenting in her quest to tear him down.

"He is rather a social climber. Obviously," Mena concurred.

Thalia couldn't argue with that really. It was only too true. She didn't believe Campbell to be a snob, but he did have his sights set on joining the aristocracy. He would do almost anything to achieve that goal. Even cast her aside. Thalia took a shuddering breath and felt her fingernails bite into the soft flesh of her palm as she clenched her fist. She was not going to cry over a man. Anymore.

"Well, it hardly matters anyway," Thalia forced a brightness she didn't feel into her voice.

Clem raised one elegant brow. Thalia pulled a face and shrugged, forcing herself not to care about her broken heart. Nothing in her life had changed really, just another experience of a man setting her aside after determining she wasn't good enough for him.

"I'm not looking for a husband, and he hardly wants to marry someone in my position. We were simply having fun for a little while, nothing more," she said, affecting a nonchalant tone.

"Why wouldn't he want to marry you?" Mena demanded, outraged by the very idea.

"I am well aware that I am quite a catch," Thalia replied, and winked playfully, as though her heart wasn't a smoldering pile of broken bits in the crater of her chest. "But Campbell Marlow has aspirations. Ones that would never include a sweet shop owner with no reputation. Or a dowry, for that matter."

Thalia looked out at the dancers spinning by. Bleakness settled over her shoulders like a mantle. Her determination not to care didn't seem to be working very well just now, but she had no choice but to soldier on.

"And it's a good thing too. We don't need a man to shepherd us through our own lives," Clem said firmly, her voice leaving no room for dispute. "Men are a bother generally. They are like a weight tied around your neck."

Thalia laughed mirthlessly. "I don't have such strong feelings, but I agree they create more work for us," she allowed.

"I should like to marry," Mena said thoughtfully, eyeing the dancers with cautious interest.

Thalia looked at her friend, surprised. Mena was a private woman, and so when she shared a part of herself, it really meant something. She stood with her spine ramrod straight. The tiny furrow between her brows betrayed her emotions, and her high cheekbones were splashed with pink.

"There is nothing wrong with wanting to marry. I'm not opposed to the institution. As long as it's the right man," Thalia said softly.

Clem snorted. Her lips were twisted in a cynical smile. "Good luck finding that." Then her eyes caught Mena's, and she softened instantly. "I just want to see you happy, love," she said, lifting one shoulder apologetically.

Mena smiled, shaking her head slowly. "I know. Don't get all weepy on me," she teased.

Once again, two men approached and whisked Clem and Mena off to dance for the next set. Thalia felt a stab of resentment that no one was asking her but refused to give in to such pettiness. She was happy for her friends and would find a way to enjoy herself somehow. It felt good to be among happy people. Perhaps some of their joy would rub off on her. The alcohol she had consumed was beginning to work its way through her veins, loosening her limbs and relaxing her tight shoulders, clearing away some of her misery.

Thalia decided to try and get some air, and motioned to Clem that she was leaving the room. She hoped Clem saw the gesture, anyway. Making her way through the crowd, she escaped into the open air of the garden where she could breathe more freely. Torches burned brightly, illuminating the space. Thalia felt safe enough, and wandered farther out, toward the river where the crowd was thinner.

She stood admiring the slow-moving water in the flickering light and was rewarded with a lovely swan pair gliding by. Their white feathers glowed in the moonlight. Swans mate for life, she remembered then, resulting in a fresh spurt of misery seeping through her chest. *Bloody hell.*

She stayed there, watching the river, until the dance ended. The absence of music created an emptiness, making Thalia realize how alone and vulnerable she was. But there were so many people about, it didn't immediately alarm her.

As she turned to return to the ballroom, the thick stand of bushes nearby rustled, sending an icy stab of fear pumping through her veins. Realizing how far she had strayed from the door, she hastened her pace to reach the safety of the crowd when, suddenly, a hand shot out of the shadows by the door, pulling her off her feet.

Thalia gasped in surprise as she lost her balance and struggled to regain the breath to call out. The hand gripping her was punishingly strong, fingers biting into her skin, surely causing bruising. Thalia knew that this was not a friend. A hand clamped over her mouth, and she was hauled further into the shadows.

She was unceremoniously pushed into an awaiting rowboat. It was too dark out here, beyond the torches, for her to make anything out. Fear gripped her heart, but she forced herself to breathe.

An enormous man climbed into the boat, causing it to rock violently in the water. His knee brushed hers and Thalia cringed away, holding herself tightly at the far end of the small vessel.

"What is going on?" she gasped, the clarity of her new reality hitting her with force.

The man only grunted in reply as he shoved the boat away from the shore with a long handled paddle.

Holy hell, she was being kidnapped. But by who? Her mind immediately flew to Sir Marville, as he had promised to return, and clearly did not believe in a woman's consent, but then who was this man?

Thalia gripped the edges of the wooden plank she sat on and tried to come up with a plan. If this was indeed orchestrated by Marville, she needed to act fast and escape, before he had her in his clutches. No one would know where she was either. *Fuck.*

"You are being escorted to your wedding, Miss Ward," the man finally said, his voice thick with humor chilling her to the bone.

With each second that passed, the dread filling her stomach only deepened. "What wedding?" she demanded, determined not to let her abductor hear the fear in her voice.

The man laughed. It was a cold, wheezing sound that made Thalia's skin crawl.

"Don't you know your own fiancé?" he asked.

Thalia's stomach clenched. Could she survive flinging herself into the river? Her dress would weigh her down. That and her shoes. Damn.

"Sir Marville," she said.

The man continued to laugh in the darkness, but didn't answer. He didn't have to. He simply continued to row steadily down the river, bringing Thalia ever closer to her doom.

Twenty-Four

When the rowboat finally bumped against the sandy shore, having reached its destination, Thalia was almost thrown out into the water. The man who had abducted her grabbed her arm roughly to steady her, his punishing grip would surely leave bruises. Once he was certain she wouldn't fall, he jumped out onto the banked and pulled the boat up to rest on the ground. He'd done it so easily, it was a testament to the man's incredible strength. Then he grabbed Thalia again, yanking her from the boat.

Her feet tripped on the slippery grass, legs tangling in her skirts, and the man was forced to drag her along. Ahead in the shadows was a carriage waiting, its lamplight beckoning to them. As they grew close, Thalia tried to make out any identifying features of the carriage and team, but it was all just black. The door was thrown open, and she was unceremoniously tossed inside.

As the door shut behind her, Thalia straightened on the seat and raised her eyes to see Sir Marville sitting opposite her. His cold eyes looked almost black in the meager lamplight.

"Good evening, my dear," he crooned with an immensely satisfied smile.

"What are you doing?" she asked, keeping her voice even, though her harsh breaths filled the carriage, revealing her panic.

Marville tilted his head, eyes cruelly raking over her body. "We are getting married, my dear. I never gave up hope for us, and I sensed an opportunity to step in," he replied, then bared his teeth in a sinister smile.

Listing a gold-topped cane, he tapped on the carriage roof, and the vehicle set to motion with a lurch. Thalia was almost thrown into his lap but retained her seat by the strength of her fingernails sunken into the velvet upholstery. She refused to let the man touch any part of her.

"I will not be marrying you, *sir*," she said acidly, chin held high, though she was trembling.

Lord Marville lifted a hand, as though to point out her lack of options. Then he relaxed back against the velvet upholstery, stretched his long legs across the carriage and crossed his ankles. His elegant hands were folded over his stomach. He watched her, looking amused, as if these were perfectly normal circumstances.

Thalia shivered and looked around, trying to find a way out. She wasn't restrained, thank God, and there were windows on either side of the carriage. But she couldn't move quickly enough to get past Lord Marville. He was like a snake, able to strike without warning. She needed to think, and quickly.

Thalia forced herself to breathe slowly and evenly, keeping the rising hysteria at bay. A bead of sweat rolled down the side of her face, disappearing into the high neck of her gown. Her eyes carefully tracked Sir Marville's every movement, however slight, ever fearful of an attack.

How was she going to escape him?

* * *

Cam stalked the edge of the ballroom, searching for Thalia in the crowd. After she left him, he had kept an eye on her and her friends. She had yet to dance, which was bloody mystifying. The woman was a goddess, all lush curves and rosebud lips. Cam wanted to throttle all the men in attendance for not appreciating her, even as his fingers itched to do violence if they did. What a bloody mess. He rubbed a hand over his face, weariness settling into his bones.

Garrett was enjoying flashing his titles around and was getting all the attention he could have asked for. He was being passed around as a dance partner by an endless supply of ladies. No surprise there.

Cam rolled his eyes and growled in frustration. He had lost sight of Thalia, and noticed her friends seemed to also be looking about the room for her in puzzlement. A cold sense of dread began building inside him. His search for her in the crowd became more focused. Where was she?

He made his way across the ballroom, directly through the swath of dancers, and he didn't slow his pace until he reached Thalia's two friends. The fierce dark-haired one glared at him, as though she wished he would burst into flames on the spot. The rather plain one peered up at him in surprise.

"Have you seen Thalia?" she asked him.

He blinked at her, then shook his head. "I was about to ask you the same thing," Cam replied, with rising alarm.

"She wouldn't just leave without telling us," the plain one explained, wringing her hands in worry.

"When did you last see her?" the fierce one demanded.

She stood with her arms crossed, staring him down with narrowed eyes. Cam jammed a hand into his hair in frustration, feeling far too exposed to these women.

"I'd say it's been about a quarter hour since I saw her. She was over there," he gestured to a corner of the ballroom.

The two women shared a knowing look. Cam shifted, uncomfortable but too concerned about Thalia to be run off by her friends.

"We were dancing and she wasn't waiting for us when the song finished," the plain one said, biting her lower lip, dark eyes wide and shimmering with gathering tears.

Cam blew out a breath as his heart slammed against the cage of his ribs. "Alright, let's not panic," he said firmly. "You both will search inside, and I will search the garden."

"Good plan," the plain one said, nodding.

The fierce one continued to glare at him for a moment, but then she nodded too.

"Well, we know that she is not here in the ballroom, so let's start in the ladies retiring room," she said to her friend.

They turned and together began heading toward the doors to the left of the room. Their dark heads were bent together as they went. Cam watched them for a moment, and then turned to search the garden.

He pushed his way through the crowd, only to find the garden just as teeming with smiling people as the ballroom had been. People of all incomes milled about together, admiring the roses and sipping drinks. Cam scanned the crowd but didn't see Thalia. Exasperated, he clenched his hands into fists until the nails bit into the flesh of his palms. He was growing a bit frantic as the minutes ticked past. Where was she?

Suddenly Cam stilled. When was the last time he had thought of Marville? That slippery bastard hadn't shown his face in the village in days. He could very well have gone to London on business, but instinct told Cam that Marville was still local. He turned back to the ballroom, determined to find Garrett and elicit his help.

Cam found his friend chatting with some of the local gentry and wealthy capitalists. Garrett laughed along with their jokes and exuded everything ducal. He turned as Cam approached, and immediately his posture changed, perhaps sensing the alarm bells bringing in his friend's head. He stood straighter, growing serious.

"You all must excuse me. Enjoy your evening," Garrett said to the group, nodding to the ladies as he turned to follow Cam away.

Once they were out of earshot, he asked, "what's wrong?"

"Thalia is missing. I am concerned that Marville might be involved," Cam replied, trying to stay calm as the terrifying reality was voiced aloud.

Holy fuck, what if she was hurt? He swallowed down the panic rising up in his throat. Panicking wouldn't bring her back safely.

Garrett's face scrunched up in confusion. "Why do you think that? Surely she has just gone home, or back to her shop."

Cam shook his head.

"No. She wouldn't just walk away from her friends. They haven't seen her either. They're looking in the retiring room."

Garrett nodded grimly.

"Alright. I'll check the front, including carriages. You locate her friends and see if they have found anything yet. Then we will meet back up at the entrance, and decide next steps," he said.

"Thank you," Cam said, blowing out a harsh breath as he rubbed at the center of his chest, where his heart continued to fight for escape.

Garrett held his gaze for a moment.

"We will find her, Campbell," he said firmly, then set off to search.

Cam's muscles tensed; he wanted to howl at the moon in agony. This was all his fault. If he hadn't treated her so poorly, and thrown away her love, Thalia would be safe now. Safe from him, as well.

With a grim shake of his head, clearing away those troubled thoughts, Cam turned and set off in the direction Thalia's friends had gone earlier, which unfortunately appeared to lead to the ladies' retiring room. It was located at the far end of the hall leading off the ballroom, and currently crowded with women of all sorts standing about, talking, fanning themselves, and adjusting their clothing.

Cam was trapped in some kind of nightmare scenario, pushing his way down the densely packed corridor, but he had to find Thalia's friends. Then he finally spied the dark-haired one muscling her way down the hall toward him. Praising a God he had never believed in, Cam worked to meet her, eager for an update on what she had discovered. *Lord, please let it be that Thalia was here the whole time.*

"She isn't anywhere," the dark-haired woman said upon reaching him, her face strained with worry.

"Do you think she would have gone home or to the shop?" he asked, desperate for a crumb of hope Thalia wasn't truly missing.

But the woman was shaking her head emphatically before he'd finished speaking.

"No, she wouldn't just leave us. Even if she were upset," she said with a judging glare, as if the very idea was besmirching her friend's good name.

A wave of fear and guilt gripped Cam, almost forcing him to his knees. But he fought back the panic. *This was all his fault.*

"His Grace is checking the front. I will expand my search along the river. Why don't you ladies go to the boarding house and wait for her there, in case she returns."

"Do you suspect foul play?" the plain woman asked as she peered from behind the fierce one's shoulder.

"I think we should be open to all possibilities at the moment." Cam tried to keep his voice even, hoping he sounded calm and confident, though his voice cracked and betrayed his fears.

The plain one's expression softened a fraction, and she stepped closer to grab his arm.

"Thalia is strong, and we will find her," she said firmly.

Cam nodded, but couldn't speak. The fierce one gave his shoulder an awkward pat, and then they were gone. Cam turned to resume his search of the garden, but Garrett called out from the ballroom end of the corridor.

"Campbell!" His ducal voice reverberated through the crowd, turning the heads of dozens of women in an instant.

Cam pushed back down the hall, seized with hope for good news. "Did you find her?" he asked, desperately.

Garrett shook his head, panting from the run across the house to find Cam. Cam's hopes fell to the ground; it felt like a physical blow to the gut.

"No, but I ran into a mutual acquaintance of Marville. He was seen lurking about with his carriage up the road, by the river," Garrett said, offering confirmation of Cam's worst fears.

His heart slammed to a stop in his chest, narrowing his vision. No, he would not let the panic overpower him. He needed to rescue Thalia.

"The bastard kidnapped her," Cam growled.

Garrett's eyes widened, and he took Cam by the shoulder, steering him out the front door of the crowded inn and away from the very public scene. He didn't release Cam until they were out of earshot of the inn, and crossing the dirt expanse between the various buildings occupying the square.

Heading to the stables where the ducal carriage waited, Garret looked askance at Cam and said, "We don't know what happened for certain, Campbell. But we will follow Marville's trail, just in case he does have her."

Cam flexed his fingers in agitation, itching for something to punch.

He took a deep breath, then slowly released it while counting to five. He needed to remain calm. He needed to hunt down this man and squeeze the life out of him with his bare hands. But first, he needed to think.

"Alright. Good," Cam said through clenched teeth. Control was his greatest asset right now. "So Marville was seen by the river. Let's head in that direction. Get the carriage. I'm going to look for some more witnesses."

He stalked off toward the stables without waiting for Garrett's reply. He glared into the shadows as he walked, searching for anyone who might have seen something. Finally he found an elderly man sitting on the front steps of a slanted brick building constructed beside the stables.

The man was drinking from a clear glass bottle, taking a long swig every couple of minutes as he stared without blinking at the inn across the way. Laughter floated over on the wind, and the faintest strains of music could also be heard. Cam stopped before the man, and asked, "Have you seen an expensive carriage recently?"

The old man jumped in surprise at the sound of Cam's voice, almost dropping his bottle.

"What?" the man asked, alcohol-induced confusion clouding his eyes.

"A carriage. The sort a toff would own. Seen any?" Cam asked again, gritting his teeth in frustration.

The man scratched his head, causing his low brimmed cap to fall off. As he reached down to retrieve it, he suddenly swayed violently to one side, almost falling to the dirt himself. Cam quickly moved to steady him, easing the elderly man back upright on his perch. He squinted up at Cam with suspicion as he settled back and took another swig off his bottle.

"I did see a carriage. Almost knocked me down," he said finally.

"How long ago?" Cam asked.

"Well now. Maybe an hour ago," the old man said uncertainly.

Cam's stomach dropped. An hour was far too much time gone. He would never catch up to them. He wouldn't be there to protect Thalia. Nausea gripped him at the thought of her being afraid and in danger.

"Are you certain?" he asked weakly.

The old man just looked at him and drank from his bottle again.

"I dunno," he finally said with a shrug.

Cam wanted to throttle the old man, but held back.

"Do you know how long you've been sitting here?" he asked, forcing patience into his tone.

"Was about sundown," the old man replied.

"Alright, and you've been sitting here since then? Did you get up at all, for a piss or something?"

"I did, as a matter of fact," the old man grinned. "Right before you came up."

"And how long before that do you think you saw the carriage?" Cam asked in a clipped tone.

The old man rubbed his chin in thought.

"It wasn't long. Perhaps a quarter hour?" he said.

"Good, thank you," Cam responded as Garrett's barouche came rolling out from the stables.

Once the carriage stopped beside Cam, he nodded to the old man before jumped up to sit beside the duke behind the pair of stunning white mares purchased to compliment the gig they pulled. Any other time, Cam wouldn't miss the chance to prod Garrett about his ridiculous and ill-advised use of money, but all he cared about at the moment was speed. This was the duke's time to prove the cost of the team was worth it.

"Marville might have been headed this way. Not much of a reliable witness there," Cam bit out, focused on the road ahead.

Garrett eyed him with sympathy as he drove the barouche into the inky black night. The tension was unbearable.

"Do you think they're headed to Gretna Greene?" the duke asked cautiously.

"I hadn't considered that, actually," Cam replied, ice in his veins at the mention of the popular destination for runaway couples in need of a swift and easy wedding. "I wasn't thinking of…that."

"But Marville most likely is. What else would he do with a kidnapped woman who is well known and will be missed? He wouldn't be able to come back here, where he lives," Garrett said.

This made too much sense. Cam wasn't sure whether to feel relieved or even more scared. If Marville was after marriage,

he probably would be on better behavior than if he were just after…" He stopped, swallowing down the bile rising in his throat.
"But Gretna Greene was a ways away, which meant he had time to
save Thalia.

"We should check in at the train station," Cam said.

"You think Marville would attempt to take a kidnapped
woman on a train?" Garret asked in surprise.

"It's too far to travel by carriage, and Marville would want
to be quick about it. I don't know how he plans to pull it off, but
he is likely going to the train station," Cam said grimly.

He would have gladly traded anything he owned in that
moment, if it would secure Thalia's instant release. Anything. Cam
found himself repeating the same words in his mind as the barouche raced down the road, unable to see much ahead even with
the moon out.

They needed to go faster. Thalia was in danger.

His fingernails dug into the leather seat, wishing the fabric
belonged to a different sort of animal, one who deserved the kind
of pain coming his way.

* * *

Thalia's foot tapped on the floor of the carriage as she
considered her options. Well, option. It was the only plan she was
able to pull off. It was a pretty bad plan, but it was all she had.
First, she would try to distract Marville, and then she would make
a break for it using the door.

Sir Marville lay back, looking relaxed and confident. But
his eyes were focused, watchful. No doubt he could hear the tapping of Thalia's foot and had examined her movements to guess
her thoughts. It was utterly unnerving to be scrutinized with the
man's penetrating gaze.

It was too dark outside to see much of anything, but she was fairly sure they were traveling north along the fields, given the position of the river, which she could smell in the air rushing by. If she were lucky, Thalia would land in the grass after leaping out. If she were unlucky, she would break her neck. But best not to dwell on that prospect. Thalia gathered her confidence, heart hammering in her chest.

"My lord, would you give me some modicum of respect and tell me where we are headed?" Thalia asked, trying to inject some sweetness into her tone.

Sir Marville's lips curled into a sinister smile that shot an icy lance of fear down her spine. Thalia suppressed a shiver, refusing to quake in this man's presence.

Marville remained relaxed, but his eyes were alert on her now. "Don't you enjoy surprises?" he teased.

Thalia smiled tightly. "Please?" she asked, throwing in a painful smile for good measure.

Suddenly, Marville moved, leaning towards Thalia, invading her space. His fingers brushed her thigh, just over her knee. Thalia recoiled, terrified he was about to pounce on her right there in the carriage.

"How can I resist when you beg me, my dear?" his voice rasped.

Thalia pressed back against the carriage seat. She steeled herself for his touch again, but the feel of Marville's hand lifting hers to press a kiss to the back of it caused a wave of nausea and fear that threatened to swamp her. His dry lips lingered over her skin, before he finally released her and sat back again. Thalia forced herself to breathe.

She stared at Marville, afraid to blink in case he pounced. Several minutes passed, counted out by the fervent beating of

Thalia's heart. Marville made no move to continue speaking, obviously enjoying the power he was wielding.

"Well?" she said, unable to keep the impatience out of her tone.

Marville sighed. "Very well. We are headed to the train station, and from there we are off to Scotland like so many romantic couples before us, eager for the altar."

Thalia's blood froze in her veins, her vision going black. She blinked furiously, struggling to maintain her composure. Scotland was the perfect place to bring an unwilling bride. There would be no escape. No one would give a fig about her reluctance, especially when intervening meant earning a wealthy man's ire. Sir Marville could simply accuse her of playing coy, and force her hand anyway.

She would not faint and leave herself more vulnerable to him. She took a deep breath, and another. She needed to keep it together.

"The train station is not this far from the inn," Thalia commented softly.

Marville looked genuinely impressed.

"This is why I like you so much, my dear. You are a smart and beautiful woman. And you are correct. We are not going to the village station, but one farther on. Just in case anyone is looking for us," he said with a wink.

Blast. So she would have to jump after all.

* * *

Cam and Garrett checked the local station, but Marville was not there, and no one had seen him.

"Perhaps the bastard thought to leave from a different station," Garret suggested.

Cam nodded, feeling bleak. They went on to the next station, but nothing again. Losing hope, they pressed on to the next station, traveling at the fastest speed they could.

Suddenly, there was a carriage lumbering up ahead, turning into the next bend in the road. As it completed the turn, the insignia decorating the door was illuminated by the barouche's lamps. Cam almost laughed at the absurdity. Marville couldn't possibly be such an idiot as to use his own carriage, marked for all to see, as he kidnapped a woman.

"We should pull up alongside and try to run them off the road," Garrett suggested as they gained on the other vehicle.

"No, I won't put Thalia in further danger," Cam said. "I'll try and jump onto the carriage as we pass by. Then you get in front and slow them down."

But as Cam leaned out the window to gauge the jump, he saw the other carriage door burst open, then a blur of flapping fabric as someone jumped out. He turned to look back, and saw Thalia rolling along the side of the road into the tall weeds. His heart stopped, and he jumped out of the carriage without thinking. His only thought was getting to her. As he hit the ground all the wind was knocked from him, face scraping along the dirt. He lay dazed for a moment, confused by his inability to rise.

"Campbell?" Thalia moaned as she crawled over to him.

The sound of her voice sent relief coursing through him, giving him the strength to roll over and find her with his eyes, to see if she was hurt. Thalia's eyes were wide in fear and shock, and her lower lip trembled, though she was clearly trying hard to hold herself together as she crouched beside the road. The sound of the two carriages had faded into the distance.

"Is anything broken?" he asked, wincing in pain as he pushed up to his knees.

Thalia shook her head. "You?"

"I don't think so," he replied, pressing a hand to his left side where it hurt to breathe. Thalia didn't need to be worrying over a broken rib or two, not when they had yet to ensure her safety from Marville. "If you can walk, we should head to the train station back up the road. It isn't far."

"Alright," she said, gingerly rising to stand. She took a cautious step forward, testing the strength of her legs. "I should be fine," she concluded, sweeping a doubtful eye over Cam from his position on the ground.

Gritting his teeth, Cam struggled to his feet, and began leading the way down the road. He wouldn't stop fighting to keep Thalia safe, not even if it killed him in the process. And his ribs were threatening to push him back to the ground with each throbbing step that felt like the slash of a knife.

"Are you certain you can make it, Campbell? You don't look good," she said, concerned enough to set a hand on his arm, as though she didn't hate him for pushing her away.

"Don't worry about me. I've been through far worse than that," he replied, striving for a light tone, but his sudden grimace of pain likely ruined the effect.

They walked along in silence, heading for the dim lights of the train station, where they would be able to find help. The duke would take care of Marville, Cam had no doubt. His only concern now was the woman beside him, who appeared determined to keep distance between them. Her arms were wrapped about herself, shoulders drawn forward as she strode along.

The silence grew awkward the longer it went on, but Cam was at a loss for how to end it. He dared to hope she might forgive him someday, and understand his reasons for ending things between them. He saw now how the only thing keeping them apart–keeping them from happiness–were his aspirations.

But the moment Thalia had been placed in danger, she had been Cam's whole focus. How could he want anyone other than this woman? She was a bloody goddess. But how could he simply set aside everything he had worked for? It wasn't that simple.

Cam burned to tell her how he felt, but couldn't find the words. It was too mixed up in his mind, too overwhelming. Besides, Thalia needed rest, and time to heal from this traumatic evening. He was determined to see her safely home, and ensure Marville was dealt with. Anything else would have to wait.

Twenty-Five

Thalia went to the orphanage the next day, seeking the comfort of the familiar halls and the laughter of the children there. Would she ever have her own children? Likely not, given her inability to find a husband.

Good lord, she was feeling gloomy.

Without fully realizing her destination, she found herself standing before Mrs. Farningham's office door, and rapping softly on the glass.

"Come in," the headmistress called from within.

Thalia entered, instantly soothed by the sight of the older woman behind her desk, furiously scribbling notes, surrounded by the usual piles of papers. Closing the door behind her, Thalia sat down in one of the chairs by the desk.

"Good morning, ma'am," she said, striving for a cheerful tone, but the effort of maintaining the facade made her face ache.

"What is it, my dear?" the older woman asked bluntly, eyeing Thalia with concern.

Thalia looked at her hands in her lap and swallowed, torn between confiding in Mrs. Farningham and hiding her pain, as though embarrassed by the depth of her feelings for a man who didn't want her. What she needed in this moment was a mother figure, as she felt about to burst with despair.

"Thalia, you look miserable. Please let me help you, come here," Mrs. Farningham said soothingly as she moved closer to sit on the edge of her wide desk and took Thalia's hands in her warm, soft ones. "I remember when you first came to St. James'. You are so young. Far too young to be so alone in the world. From that very first day, you have been like a daughter to me. Let me be there for you again, my dear, because I can see the pain in your eyes. So similar to that day, so long ago now."

Thalia felt her lower lip tremble, and the burn of angry tears began before she could mask them. Suddenly she was enveloped in a bosomy hug, and she collapsed into the devastation she had been struggling to conceal. Thalia sobbed until the pain had been wrung out of her body, then she sat back in her chair, wiping her face clean with a handkerchief pressed into her hand by Mrs. Faringham. The older woman patted Thalia's back, giving her the space to feel and not be alone.

"Feel better now?" she asked Thalia, who nodded. "Good. Now, let's get you a nice cup of tea and we'll have a chat."

Mrs. Farningham stood and poured a cup from the brass samovar that sat in the corner of the office. The brew was kept heated via a small tube of burning charcoal that slid inside the pot.

It was a bit ostentatious for the typically frugal headmistress, but a lot of tea was consumed in this room.

"Here you are, my dear," she said with a gentle smile.

The older woman's attention was entirely on Thalia again, waiting for her to lay bare her thoughts and feelings about such a private situation…it was unnerving.

"He all but abandoned Bart," Thalia accused, feeling churlish; needing some other reason to build a defense for her wounded heart.

She wanted to hate Campbell Marlow, to be immune to him.

Mrs. Farningham raised her brows in surprise and frowned. "Mr. Marlow? No he hasn't, my dear. Bart returned to the duke's estate just this morning. Picked up by Mr. Marlow himself, and in a nice carriage too."

Thalia sat there, absorbing this. *Damn.* Campbell was so kind, and wonderful. And she loved him. And that hurt most of all.

"He doesn't want me," she whispered, her composure slipping.

Mrs. Farningham scoffed, and squeezed her hand. "That man is madly in love with you, Thalia. He'll come around, don't you worry."

Thalia was surprised by the older woman' words, since she thought she had kept their relationship hidden so well. She hated the hope that flared with the older woman's words, and ruthlessly rejected that emotion. It was over; their time together was done. She would not wait around for a man who would marry someone else and reject her love.

"I appreciate the sentiment, Mrs. Farningham," she managed with a watery smile.

Her head was beginning to ache from all of the crying and high emotions of the afternoon. A bath and a nap were required. She stood up and gave Mrs. Farningham a quick hug.

"Thank you for allowing me the moment here," she said awkwardly.

"You may come to me anytime you need a shoulder, my dear. Everyone needs a good cry now and then."

Thalia's head throbbed and she pressed a hand to her temple.

"Go and have a lie down, my dear. And drink some water," the older woman said, mothering her.

It felt good to be taken care of and fussed over. The world was just a little bit less in freefall at the moment.

"I will. Good afternoon," Thalia said as she turned to leave.

The walk back to the boarding house was unhappy, to say the least. The cloudy sky had finally released the rain that had been held back for weeks. It was a deluge, and Thalia fairly ran through the forming puddles, leaving her skirts soaked. She reached the safety of the boarding house and stood inside dripping on the frayed carpet in the foyer. Being soaked through felt poetic given her current mood.

Thalia stalked up the stairs, her skirts sticking to her legs, tripping her up.

"Just what I need, to break my neck," she muttered, wiping a slick tendril of hair from her brow.

Once she reached her door, Thalia locked it behind her and began stripping off her wet garments. She threw her shirtwaist on the floor, watching as it landed in a heap with a squelch. Then came her heavy cotton skirts and petticoats, leaving her standing in her boots and underclothes. She turned in a circle looking for something to dry off on, when she stopped short.

Someone had slipped a copy of the local newspaper beneath her door. She bent down and opened it, letting a slip of paper fall out. Frowning, she picked it up, and her heart skipped a beat at the message.

You need never worry about this again. Your name was not used. – C.

She released a long breath she hadn't realized she was holding, closing her eyes for a beat. Then she turned her attention to the newspaper. The front page featured a large rendering of Sir Marville, his handsome sneering face perfectly captured by the artist. Thalia almost dropped the paper, but managed to hang onto it with shaking hands.

Buckinghamshire Squire To Be Transported, Stripped of Title and Property.

Thalia read the headline twice before tossing the newspaper and note into the fireplace, which was less dramatic than it might have been had there actually been a fire. A shiver wracked her, and she wrapped her arms around herself for comfort.

Campbell might think she could put this behind her now, but she would still have to worry over her business and reputation. What if someone found out? What if someone else decided to try his luck? And here she was, all alone to face it.

But she wasn't, in fact, alone. There was a knock at the door, and the voices chattering behind it alerted Thalia to who was visiting. She crossed the small room and opened the door, tears already streaming down her face at the sight of her friends.

"Oh Thalia, it's alright," Mena gasped, pulling her friend into a warm embrace.

Clem closed the door and set down the basket she was carrying on the small table by the fireplace. She joined the embrace, adding the warmth of her support.

"Tell us. We are here for you," Clem demanded.

Thalia sighed. How could she put the entire confusing mess of her feelings into words?

"I am so disappointed. I guess I just expected a little too much from someone so...wounded. I feel completely worthless and rejected. I see him so clearly, but he can't see me." Thalia sobbed into the warm comfort of her friend's arms.

She felt like she would never feel happy again—which frightened her. She hadn't expected this kind of pain, and its raw power was overwhelming.

"It will be ok, dearest," Mena promised, her voice firm and sincere. "The sun will rise again, and you will get up one day and carry on as if this pathetic man does not even exist."

"That's right. He is a wastrel and you are well rid of him," Clem declared. "You are an amazing, loving, beautiful woman who has absolutely no need for any man, let alone such a low down scoundrel as he-who's-name-shall-never-be-mentioned-again."

"He is not a wastrel!" Thalia sat up, wiping her eyes. "Campbell is a good, kind, gentle man. I love him."

Her friends regarded her with sympathetic eyes, and neither were surprised by her declaration. Thalia blew out a frustrated breath. She didn't want to defend Campbell. He had broken her heart.

"This grief will pass," Clem said with her usual confidence.

"I know that in my mind, but my heart...it's just so painful."

Mena went to the basket Clem had brought and pulled out a bottle of brandy and three tin cups.

"We brought sustenance. You are not alone," she said firmly.

Thalia took the offered cup and sipped from it, relishing the warmth that spread through her chest as she swallowed. It was like a hug from within, and it helped settle her frayed nerves.

"I was so scared," she whispered.

Clem rubbed her upper arm soothingly.

"We were too. But we would never have rested without finding you, Thalia."

"And you would do the same for us," Mena added.

Thalia nodded. Thank God for friends.

"What's this?" Clem asked as she bent over to retrieve the balled-up newspaper from the fireplace.

"The morning's paper. The front page was notable," Thalia said dryly.

Clem flattened the pages so she could read. Her brows raised as she scanned the words.

"Well, that must have taken some doing. I thought the last convict ship sent to Australia was decades ago."

Thalia frowned.

"Is that so?"

"I suppose the duke must have had his hands in this. It's the only explanation. Who else could wake a magistrate up in the night and get this result so quickly? And he must have alerted the newspapers," Clem mused.

Mena gasped. "The duke was there last night?" she asked, eyes rounded.

Clem nodded absently, still reading. "Yes, he was with Mr. Marlow when all the excitement was happening."

Mena was silent, her face impassive. But Thalia suspected she was surprised that a duke would attend a public dance, let alone involve himself in a common woman's affairs. Thalia certainly was. The man had been nothing but kind to her, but he was still a duke.

"Campbell is very close to the duke," Thalia commented.

Clem nodded. "That explains it. Mr. Marlow is passionately in love with you, and the duke, as his close friend, threw his title
around to assist. Well, I am quite glad for his help."

Thalia was too. Without the duke she would be enduring
some horrendous treatment at the hands of that vile Sir Marville.
Perhaps even legally bound to the man forever. She shuddered at
the thought.

"You must get some rest," Mena said gently. "Finish your
drink and get into your nightgown. We will stay to watch over you."

"Oh, I hadn't even noticed what you were wearing!" Clem
exclaimed with a laugh. "Yes, let's get you warm and comfortable.
Are you hungry?"

Thalia shook her head; she couldn't fathom the thought of
eating right now when her stomach felt upside down. She allowed
Mena and Clem to help her out of her corset and underclothes,
and into a warm nightgown. Mena found a shawl and wrapped it
around Thalia's shoulders. Then they insisted she drink every drop
of brandy and lie down.

"Perhaps I shall get a cat," Thalia said with a yawn, once
the trembling had subsided.

Mena laughed softly.

"Cats are lovely. I can bring you one of mine if you like,"
she offered.

"They are much better than men, I can attest," Clem stated
with confidence, settling back in a chair to sit vigil by the bedside
of her friend.

Thalia smiled, ensconced in the warmth of friendship, She
felt safe. Maybe she could get through this. Tomorrow she would
rise, put on a fresh dress, and go to her shop. She would do it again
the day after, and the day after that. And perhaps one day the pain
wouldn't be so great, her heart having healed. But until then, Thalia
would have her friends, and a cat or two.

Twenty-Six

"You're a right sodding idiot, old friend," pronounced the duke, who sprawled comfortably in a chair before a roaring fire in his library, a glass of excellent whiskey in hand.

"I know that," Cam snapped back, and downed his glass in one gulp.

The cut crystal vessel would be so satisfying to smash against the wall. His fingertips pressed into the hard grooves carved into its surface, as he considered the idea. It would be exceedingly poor behavior; evidence of his ill-breeding. Cam eased his grip, and chose to refill the glass instead.

"Why don't you go to her and beg her to marry you, if you are so unhappy without the chit." The duke was sensible, but of course he could afford to act with nothing but sense. This was not a sensible situation at all.

Campbell had been working toward a singular goal for as long as he could remember. All he had ever wanted was to be a member of the elite aristocracy, and marrying a mere shopkeeper would never gain him that status he craved. Had craved. Did he even still want that? Cam wasn't sure anymore. All of his waking thoughts were of Thalia, and she haunted his dreams as well.

"For one, I am not sure she would have me," he began, causing Garrett to snort into his glass. As the duke erupted into a coughing fit, Cam threw him a glare and continued. "And secondly, I need a wife of consequence. All I have ever wanted and worked for is to marry up. Thalia, though beautiful and admirable, cannot bring me the status I require. I'm so close, Garrett. After all these years, its right fucking there within my reach."

The duke pondered this, his gaze locked on the golden liquid in his glass. Finally he asked quietly, "Are you certain that what you still truly desire is status?"

Cam was about to laugh and retort that of course it was what he desired, but suddenly he truly wasn't sure anymore. The silence was drawn out as Cam tossed the whiskey back in haste.

"It seems to me, old friend, that this woman has you mixed up. In all the time we've known each other, I have never seen you behave this way over a woman."

"What does that mean?" Cam's heart was thumping erratically, as every fiber of his being was focused on Garrett now.

"You love her." The duke said simply, and took a long draw of his whiskey.

Cam sat back in shock, looking dumbly at his friend, who causally regarded him back. There was no response that readily came to mind; quite the opposite in fact—Cam's entire being wanted to scream YES! Of course he loved Thalia, why hadn't he realized it before? It was so bloody clear.

What a mess he had made of things. With a groan, he leaned forward and massaged his temples with both hands. What could he do to fix it?

* * *

Thalia was gently brushing a tray of hand painted candy rocks into a wide mouthed glass jar for display when the bell chimed to signal a customer. She didn't bother to look up, and hoped that Abigail was welcoming them in. Thalia tried to focus on her task, letting the gentle sound of the small candies raining down soothe and relax her. She visualized the seaside, imagining the waves lapping at the sand.

She felt the weight of someone's gaze upon her, and looked up. There he was, looming in the doorway like a thief considering what to steal first. Thalia felt her heart seize in her chest, ever ready to hope. What a pathetic organ.

Campbell came nearer, moving slowly, as one would when approaching an easily startled animal. Thalia stiffened, standing tall; refusing to cower or flee.

"What are you doing here?" she asked, her voice sounded strained, and she had to swallow against the dryness in her throat.

"I came to invite you on a walk along the river," he replied.

His face was impassable as ever, his posture rigid. But his eyes were earnest and hopeful. She considered sending him away, but couldn't suppress an absurd jolt of joy. Ridiculous.

"Very well, but I can only give you a half hour," she replied, already hastening to untie her apron. "Abigail, I need to go out for a bit. Please continue working on the display, and I will return shortly," she called out.

Cam extended his elbow, but Thalia ignored him and swept out the door, leaving him to follow. They walked toward the village green in silence. Thalia refused to be the one to break the awkwardness between them, and tried to focus on keeping calm, imagining herself as a bird flying free without a care.

"This way," Cam said, finally breaking the silence.

Thalia looked at him, wondering where he wanted to take her. Her curiosity fought with her anger and desire to make the man suffer a bit. But she allowed Cam to lead the way across the grass to a stately brick house with a tidy little yard in front, behind a low iron fence. He stopped in front of the gate, his attention entirely on Thalia, who crossed her arms over her chest protectively. What was he doing?

"Well?" she demanded. "What did you want to say?"

Cam held her gaze intently, and then slowly sank to one knee before her right there on the street. Thalia's heart slammed to a stop, and she looked around in wild confusion. What was the man doing?

He continued to gaze at her with solemn reverence.

"Thalia, I love you with every inch of myself, heart, mind, and soul. I can never forgive myself for not appreciating what was growing between us sooner. Perhaps I didn't want to acknowledge this feeling. If I lose any chance of a future with you, then I have only myself to blame. And I deserve it. But if there is any chance that you could forgive me, please give me an opportunity to show you the depth of my feelings."

As he finished, Cam reached into his coat pocket and withdrew a red velvet box. A ring sized box. Thalia's heart felt like it would burst from the rush of emotions filling her. She pressed both hands to her cheeks.

"Thalia, please be my wife," Cam asked, flipping open the box to reveal a lovely ring set with a blue stone that shone in the sunlight.

Her mouth dropped open as she blinked at the offering. It was stunning. The man was asking for her hand. In marriage.

It felt like a dream, and Thalia didn't want to wake up.

"Yes!" she cried, and threw her arms around Campbell's neck.

He stood up, pulling her to him for a fierce embrace.

"Wait," Thalia suddenly pulled back to look in his eyes. "I won't give up my business, Campbell. Don't expect me to change just because we are married."

His lips lifted in a soft smile.

"I wouldn't ask it of you, love," he replied softly.

Thalia nodded, a brilliant smile spreading across her face, despite the tears gathering in her eyes.

"And what of you? Will you stay with the duke?"

Cam looked up at the sky, his smile uncertain.

"For now, but I think I shall find a new path for myself soon. Garrett doesn't need me anymore, though he doesn't trust himself yet. It's time for both of us to move on," he said, capturing her gaze once more with an arresting smile.

Thalia smiled back, feeling lighter than air. She had been prepared for a life alone, but suddenly she had everything she'd wanted here in her arms. Not wanting to waste another moment, she lifted up on her toes and claimed his mouth. Campbell kissed her back, pulling her body against his, holding her tight. She had missed this.

"Let's get married today," Thalia whispered as she kissed along his jaw. They had so much lost time to make up for.

"Are you sure? You don't want a fancy celebration with all your friends?" he asked.

Thalia smiled against the warm skin of his cheek, then moved to nip at his earlobe. Cam sucked in a breath with a hiss, and kissed her mouth with an urgency they both felt. Suddenly he broke the kiss and scooped her up in his arms.

"Wh— what are you doing?" Thalia shrieked, and clung to his neck as Cam entered the front gate of the brick house and continued up the little path to the door.

"I'm bringing you somewhere more private," he said, a dark promise in his words.

After a moment of juggling, Cam got the front door opened and carried Thalia over the threshold and into the house. It smelled clean and fresh inside, like lemon oil, and light spilled in from the numerous large windows.

"But whose house is this?" Thalia asked.

Cam smiled down at her.

"It's ours," he said. "I bought it, hoping that you would have me for your husband. If you had said no, I don't know what I would have done," he finished with a laugh.

Thalia was speechless. This man, who had been so cold and closed off, had bought a house for them, hoping that she would marry him. She was filled with tenderness for him.

"I hope you like it," Cam said with a sheepish grin as he set Thalia down on her feet once more.

Thalia turned in slow a circle, taking in all she could see of the house from the foyer. When she was facing Cam again, she threw herself at him, grinning as she twined her arms around his neck.

"I love it, and I love you," she said and kissed him. She kissed him long and hard until finally, when their lips were swollen and hungry to explore each other's bodies further, she pulled away. Taking Cam by the hand, she led him toward the stairs. "Does this house have any furnishings?" she asked with a coy smile.

Cam's eyes dark with desire.

"No," he said, clearly disappointed he hadn't thought to install a bed yet.

Thalia laughed, and continued to lead him.

"That's alright, we shall make do. Besides, I wouldn't want to be too comfortable," she said.

"And why is that?" Cam asked, letting her pull him up the narrow staircase.

"Because we are off to Scotland shortly, of course," Thalia said happily.

And they were.

Epilogue

Three weeks later, Thalia stood in the kitchen in their new house, using a wooden mold to turn out a batch of butter-scotches. The tidy kitchen boasted two large windows overlooking the back garden, and today they framed the early autumn scene complete with soft golden light. This was heaven, she had decided after settling into their new home.

Arms encircled her waist, pulling her back against a hard form. Thalia melted, arching like a cat into Campbell's heat. How delicious to call this man her husband. She still felt giddy by the idea.

"I thought you were asleep," she said with a laugh.

"I woke up lonely and came to find you." Cam kissed her neck, causing Thalia to catch her breath.

"Careful now, I'm almost done. Here." She reached up for Cam to take the sweet she offered. He leaned forward to lick it from her fingers. Thalia's blood heated.

"You are insatiable, my Sugar Queen," he said, angling his head to meet her lips in a searing kiss.

"You are quite the distraction," Thalia said with a laugh and pulled away to finish her work.

Cam let her go, and leaned against the sink, arms crossed and watching her. "How do you think Garrett is managing?"

Thalia smothered a laugh, feeling guilty. Poor Garrett. "The man is a saint. He should have canceled the whole affair, but instead he's refused to douse the dreams of all those ladies."

"That is until he declines to marry any of them. It's a waste of their time," Cam pointed out. "I imagine they will be plenty doused."

"True, although he might meet someone he fancies. You never know!" Thalia said, scowling at Cam's snort of derision at the idea of Garrett ever settling down.

"He's going to be eaten alive, is what," Cam said, shaking his head with a chuckle.

Thalia leveled a stern look at him. "It is your fault he is throwing this weekend party in the first place. The least you could do is not laugh at his misery."

"My love, you are correct. Perhaps this party is exactly what Garrett needs. It will do him good to be out mingling with polite society, and he would be lucky to catch a lovely bride."

"Perhaps indeed. I do have a person on the inside, so to speak."

"An informant?" Cam perked up, his eyes glittering with interest.

Thalia smiled like a sly fox. "Mena is attending the weekend party at the estate. She promised to relay all of the gossip."

"Mena doesn't seem the sort to enjoy large gatherings, especially of society folk."

"Oh, don't worry over Mena. She can handle herself. Though she despises society events, she will enjoy a stay at an enormous and obscenely wealthy estate with a duke for a host. I'm sure she will manage to enjoy herself."

Thalia waved a dismissive hand, and began to clean up.

Cam was silent for a moment, lost in thought. Suddenly a suspicious look crossed his face. "Are you up to something?"

"What, me?" Thalia turned to him, batting her eyes innocently but unable to hide her mischievous smile. "Whatever do you mean?"

"Why do you seem so sneaky, then?"

"Sneaky? That's ridiculous. I am merely eager for two people that I know and like to meet and enjoy each other's company."

"In other words, you are aspiring to a match between Garrett and Mena? Of all the pairs in the world, that seems very unlikely to pan out."

"We shall see, won't we?" Thalia replied nonchalantly. "Besides, they were bound to meet at the musicale at the end of the month anyway."

"Ah yes, and are the children looking forward to the grand event?" Cam asked.

"Apparently they are thrilled, according to Mrs. Farningham's letter. She has been so wonderful, taking over the preparations while we took some time away."

Her blood heated at the reminder of the days spent closed up in their room by the sea, where they had scarcely bothered to dress between bouts of lovemaking. And still she couldn't keep her hands off her husband.

A slow smile spread across Campbell's face, as if reading her mind.

"How did I get so lucky?" he wondered aloud.

Thalia arched a brow.

"Luck had nothing to do with it. It was fate," she declared.

Campbell's smile deepened. "I supposed that's what it was. At any rate, I love you."

"Of course you are," Thalia replied cheekily.

Campbell burst out laughing. "That is not a proper response," he said, reaching for her.

But Thalia danced away, keeping just out of reach.

"You shall have to think of a way to teach me a lesson, then," she taunted, already heading for the door, knowing Campbell would give chase.

They were both laughing as they raced up to their bedroom, leaving the cleaning up for another time.

About the Author

Rebeccah Wilson is a life-long lover of romance, having picked up the habit in middle school and never looked back. When she isn't writing, Rebeccah can be found in the garden or walking the numerous nature trails near her house. She lives in Massachusetts with her husband, three children, an ill-behaved dog, a bearded dragon, and far too many chickens.

Made in United States
North Haven, CT
24 December 2023

46507294R00157